PRAISE FOR CAROLINE MITCHELL

'If you like early Stephen King you'll love *The Midnight Man*' - **Robert Dugoni**, *New York Times* bestseller

'Caroline Mitchell at her dark and twisty best' - **Teresa Driscoll,** author of *I Am Watching You*

'Will keep you on the edge of your seat' - **Alice Hunter**, author of *The Serial Killer's Wife*

'A spine tingling, creepy book' - **John Marrs**, author of *The One*

'Creepy and intense' - **Mel Sherratt**, author of *Ten Days*

'A tense and deliciously creepy read' - **D.S. Butler**, author of *On Cold Ground*

'Twisty, tense and creepy as hell... I loved it!' - **K.L. Slater**, author of *The Widow*

'A spooky, twisty mystery with a spine-chillingly ending' - **Susi Holliday,** author of *The Last Resort*

D11195011

DON'T TURN AROUND

CAROLINE MITCHELL

ALSO BY CAROLINE MITCHELL

The DC Jennifer Knight Series

Don't Turn Around

Time To Die

The Silent Twin

The Slayton Series

The Midnight Man

The Night Whispers

The DI Amy Winter Series

Truth And Lies

The Secret Child

Left For Dead

Flesh And Blood

The DS Ruby Preston Series

Death Note

Sleep Tight

Murder Game

Individual Works

Paranormal Intruder

Witness

Silent Victim

The Perfect Mother

The Village

ACKNOWLEDGMENTS

I am hugely grateful to all of the people who have helped bring this book to fruition.

To Bookouture for originally signing this book. Thanks also to Angie, Lindsay, Renita and my fellow Bookouture authors whom I am lucky enough to know.

Tom Sanderson, who created this terrific cover and to Shelly Tegan and Holly Kammier for your encouragement along the way.

My sisters Ann, Louise, Bridie, my brother Robbie and of course Freddie and Dad, mum's loss has been hard to bear but I'm sure you'll agree with the dedication.

My children; you are growing up and finding your own way in the world. Thank you for being mine. My husband Neil, this tiny space is not enough to thank you for being such a huge part of my life. Without your encouragement, I would never have written this book.

To my readers, suspend your beliefs and open your mind as you prepare for the journey. My gratitude to you is never-ending.

To my mother, Bridie; I haven't really lost you because you're always in my heart.

PROLOGUE

Jennifer Knight would not have walked home alone had she
known the eyes of a serial killer were upon her. He retreated
into the side alley as she strode down the moonlit path. His
gloved fingers tightly wound around the handle of the jagged
hunting knife as she approached. He could almost hear her
heartbeat accelerate as the weight of his stare bore down.
The smell of her perfume reached his senses and he inhaled
her fragrance, his lips parting to accommodate his heavy
breath. *Turn around pretty, come see what I have for you,* he
thought, intoxicated by her presence. She was just like her
mother, Elizabeth. The same high cheekbones. The same
dark hair. The same intense commitment to her job. He
watched from the shadows as she paused to fiddle in her bag.
It brought forth the jangle of keys and she quickened her
pace.

Immeasurable boundaries were crossed to find her, to
make good the sweet promise he had made. The others were
irrelevant and served only to whet his appetite for what lay
ahead. His lips drew back in a sneer. Soon he would be able to

touch her, to feel the warmth of her blood. And when the time came, no one would stop him.

CHAPTER ONE

The concept of a paperless office was lost on Haven CID. Each desk carried the burden of dusty box files, frayed spiral notepads and reams of open cases demanding attention. All except DC Jennifer Knight's, whose neatly stacked paper-work was filed in order of importance, and coordinating stationery locked firmly away in her desk drawer.

Jennifer pushed open the door, casting an eye at the clock on the wall. It was a choice between arriving at work unwashed and on time, or suitably preened and late. She glanced at her colleague DC Dunston, guessing he had gone for the first option.

Will threw her a weary look. 'You've missed briefing.'

'Tell me something new,' she said, pointing at the yellow stain on Will's tie. 'Eggy soldiers for breakfast?'

'Egg McMuffin, if you must know.' He patted his beard to dislodge the errant crumbs in his blond whiskers.

'McDonalds at this hour?' Jennifer pulled a sterile wipe from her bag as she crossed the room to inspect his tie.

Will sighed as she picked away at the offending stain. 'For God's sake, you're worse than my mother.'

'If I was your mother, I'd be down the pub every night drowning my sorrows. Now, what jobs have we lined up for today?' Jennifer threw the wipe in the bin and rubbed her hands on her skirt.

'A grievous bodily harm. They're finally trusting us with something decent.' He handed her a wad of paper bound together with a large black clip.

'How come?' Jennifer's eyes greedily scanned the page. Like any typical police station, Haven had a pecking order, and Jennifer was no longer given precedence when it came to serious crime.

'Steph's assisting the others with a raid so they're tied up for the morning.'

Jennifer was glad her sergeant was out. Steph was a stickler for timekeeping, and Jennifer's lateness had got up her nose on more than one occasion.

Jennifer stared in disbelief at the file. 'Is this a wind-up? Johnny Mallet's been nicked for stabbing Mike Stone?'

The small town of Haven had changed when 'Man Mountain' Mike Stone took up residence. An ex-boxer well known in the criminal underworld, he was purported to have retired from the drug scene, having amassed his fortune. But the pull seemed too strong, and his newly opened nightclub, Klass, covered for an increasing network of users in the area. Users like Johnny, a scrawny lowlife who funded his drug habit through petty crime.

Will grabbed his interview folder. 'Apparently Mike called around there to recover a drug debt, and Johnny shanked him. We've seized a knife. The forensics aren't in yet, but Steph suggested we interview Johnny to see if he'd cough to it.'

'Have you read through the package?'

'Yep,' Will said.

Jennifer clipped the papers back into order and grabbed a notebook and pen. 'No time like the present then.'

'Don't you want to go through it?' Will asked, downing his coffee.

'I've seen enough. You lead the interview, I'll pick it up along the way.' She strode down the narrow corridor, her heels clacking on the thinly carpeted floor. A faint smell of cannabis tainted the air, a seized harvest from the day before.

Will half walked, half trotted to keep up. 'I wish you'd wear flat shoes. It doesn't do much for my ego when you're towering over me every day.'

'It's not my fault you're a short arse.' Jennifer grinned.

'I'm taller than you if you wore proper bloody shoes.'

Jennifer didn't miss a beat. 'Is that with or without your Cuban heels?'

Will feigned indignation. Their banter was a coping mechanism. It had seen them through probation as idealistic eighteen-year-olds, then through the never-ending nights investigating what followed; broken victims, fractured lives, and the brutal violence that lingered, surfacing lead-footed in the dead of night. They had joined the job to save the world, and twelve years later had settled for keeping the streets of Haven clean. But even that was a battle, and as Jennifer approached the custody block, she hoped that today she would be on the winning team.

She pressed her tag against the scanner on the wall and pushed the heavy custody door ajar. A film of water glistened on the freshly mopped cement floor, and she narrowly missed colliding with the yellow hazard sign.

'All right, Sarge?' Jennifer nodded at the harassed-looking custody sergeant. His platformed desk lent him an air of authority, and the clear plastic screen protecting his computer was a necessary precaution against prisoners that either wanted to spit at or punch it, depending on the charge against them.

He replied without taking his eyes off his computer screen, his glasses perched halfway down his nose. 'Mallet's in cell nine. He doesn't want a solicitor, so he's all yours.'

Will followed the detention officer to the cell, while Jennifer made three cups of watery tea in the custody kitchen.

Walking down the narrow corridor to the interview rooms, Jennifer juggled the polystyrene cups, a pen in her mouth, and paperwork under her arm. She leaned against the door with her bottom, pushing it open. Shaking the spilled tea from her fingers, she placed the cups on a small wooden table in the corner of the pokey room. Looking around the windowless space she found an air freshener. Voices echoed down the corridor outside, and she quickly squirted a burst of lavender and lily into the air.

Will wrinkled his nose as he entered with his prisoner.

'Johnny. Nice of you to grace us with your presence today,' Jennifer said, trying not to inhale the smell as sweat and cheap air freshener assailed her nostrils.

No answer. Johnny stared at the floor. His pockmarked face turned downwards in a scowl, as he stood rooted to the spot. A pathetic creature, he stood at five foot five and weighed about seven stone.

'C'mon Johnny, you know the drill. Have a seat.' Will gestured to the padded chair in the corner. Bits of yellow foam peeped through the blue material, holes picked by nervous suspects. Johnny pulled back the chair and glanced furtively around the room as if someone was going to jump out on him.

Jennifer pushed the tea towards him, hoping it would calm him down. She leaned into Will, pulling her seat close. 'He's a bit jumpy. Has he been checked by the FME?' The force medical examiner was kept busy with the steady stream of drug users and mental health cases that graced their custody block.

'Yeah, they said he's fit for interview. Doesn't seem himself though.'

Jennifer noted that Johnny was born the year after her, which made him thirty-two, but his pale-lipped gaunt face appeared twenty years older. 'Are you OK, Johnny? Can I get you anything?'

He smiled, revealing a row of rotten teeth with the breath to match. 'Fuck off, bitch.'

Fuck off yourself you ugly sod, Jennifer thought, as she turned on the tapes.

Johnny gave a short laugh, raised one buttock, and broke wind. A stench of rotten cabbage filled the already stinking room.

Will clenched his fists. 'You dirty ...'

'Right!' Jennifer interrupted. 'This interview is being tape-recorded. My colleague is going to explain the process, read out your rights and entitlements, and then we can talk about why you're here.'

Jennifer leaned back in her chair as Will went through the pro forma that preceded every interview. Jennifer rubbed her arms as the cold bit through the sleeves of her jacket. The beat of a headache began to throb, and she kneaded her forehead to ease the building pressure.

'Johnny, I said, "can you confirm you are happy to proceed without a solicitor?"' Will took a swig of his tea and made a face that said he wished he hadn't.

Johnny's eyes set firmly on Jennifer. 'Fuck you.'

She looked at her watch. At this rate, it was going to take forever. She gave Will a nudge. 'Just carry on Will, um, DC Dunston. Johnny has given his reasons for declining a solicitor on the custody record.'

Will continued his interrogation and Johnny answered every question with a profanity.

'Is there anything else you'd like to say before we end the interview?' Jennifer said, having exhausted her armoury of questions. 'As I mentioned, we'll have the forensics from the knife so you're better off coming clean.' She returned her hand to her head. A feeling of dread grew as an insistent dark energy tapped into her senses.

'Well DC Knight, to be honest I find this all very tiresome. Do you think we could get rid of your ineffectual sidekick in order for me to speak to you alone?' Johnny's sudden change of accent was relayed with such eloquence it was as if someone else had entered the room.

His words hung in the air as the room fell silent; the only noise the faint squeaks of the tapes turning in the battered machine. The unnatural voice threw Jennifer off guard, and she replied with an automatic response.

'The time is nine-fifteen. If there's anything you'd like to say relating to this offence, then do so now, before we conclude the interview and my colleague switches off the tapes.'

'You are *so* masterful, just like your mother. Elizabeth sends her regards, by the way.' Johnny straightened his posture and crossed his legs, resting his clasped hands on his knee.

Jennifer flinched at the mention of her dead mother's name. She sat back, at a complete loss for words.

'This interview is concluded,' Will said, hastily switching off the tapes.

Jennifer felt a trickle of anger mounting within. 'What the hell is wrong with you, Johnny?'

'Have I touched a nerve? Sorry, it was not my intention.'

'C'mon, back to your cell. We've got more than enough to charge you anyway,' Will said. But the spell inside would do nothing more than provide Johnny with a decent meal and bed for the night.

'Because I could not stop for Death, he kindly stopped for me,' Johnny said, in an oddly cheery manner.

His words echoed down the corridor as Will returned him to his cell.

Will met Jennifer back in the office after he had updated the custody sergeant with the results of the interview. Her wavy brown hair shadowed her face as she sat at her desk, poring over the paperwork.

Will squeezed her shoulder. 'Don't let him get to you. He probably wants to be declared unfit for interview.'

'Emily Dickinson.' Jennifer said, pushing her hair back off her face.

'What?'

'What he said earlier, it was a quote from a poem by Emily Dickinson. How would he know that? He can't read or write.'

'He probably planned it to mess with your head. Don't waste your time worrying about it.'

'I suppose you're right,' Jennifer replied. 'Have you got any painkillers? I've got a stinking headache.'

Will searched his drawer and pushed two tablets out of a foiled pack. 'Here. Anything else I can do for you?'

'There is. Can you come with me to take a statement from the victim? I've rung the hospital, he's fit to see us now.'

Will scratched his beard as he glanced over at the growing stack of paperwork on his desk. 'Yeah sure, paperwork can wait.'

. . .

Jennifer was glad of the respite as they drove the battered Ford Focus to Haven Hospital. Will tapped the steering wheel as he hummed along to the tunes provided by their local eighties station. It was certainly more cheerful than the built in police radio competing for their attention. Crime was on the increase in Haven, and she felt for the uniformed officers putting their heads above the parapet. But shoplifting and break-ins were minor compared to the worries weighing heavy on her mind. A cloak of foreboding had consumed her since Johnny's interview. She wound the window down an inch and breathed in the cool winter breeze. But it could not dismiss the feeling of unease growing inside her.

CHAPTER TWO

FRANK – 1966

The tin bucket wobbled beneath his feet as Frank reached the ledge in his father's shed. The smell of damp rotting wood made it unique, and the dimly lit hovel was his favourite place in the world. Reaching over to the muddied window, he gripped his small chubby hand over a fly and felt it angrily buzzing against his palm. It tickled. His face screwed in concentration, he opened his fingers enough to detach one wing, then two. Its remains scattered on the ledge, the protesting fly joined the other insects in various stages of dissection. Frank leaned over the body of a legless fly, cupping his ear to listen for the tiny buzzing sound that indicated life. In the darkness of the shed, he was the ruler of life.

His mother had nicknamed him 'Casper' due to his ability to sneak up on her without making a sound. He liked that game. It gave him a warm feeling inside. Mummy had just bought him some Casper comics for his sixth birthday that he would hide under his pillow and read when everyone was asleep. He shifted the numbness from his bottom as he sat on the stairwell. He had only come inside to use the toilet but peeping down through the banisters at his parents below, he sat entranced as the drama unfolded before him. They were shouting because Mummy wanted to buy nice things and Daddy had to work too hard to pay for them.

The papers shook in his father's hand as he waved them about. He had his coat on, which usually meant he was on his way out. Mother, or Viv, as she preferred to be called, stood next to some pink shopping bags with her hand clasped to her chest. Strands of dark brown hair fell loose from her bun, which was held together with a diamond-encrusted pin.

'How can I be expected to pay all these bills when you're off shopping every day? It's no use, you'll have to return it all.'

Viv smiled, but it was a cold smile, through bared teeth and narrowed eyes.

'You expect me to look like those tired old women across the street? With curlers in my hair and an apron around my waist? I'm telling you now, it's not going to happen.'

'Of course not, darling, but if things don't improve soon, we may lose our home.'

'Can't you tap your mother up for some money?' Viv's hands rested on her hips, her long talons flashing red against her black dress.

'Mother's barely on speaking terms with me. How can I ask her for money?'

'I don't see why not. She can afford it.'

'It's not an option ...'

Frank craned his neck forward as his father lowered his voice. He could barely hear him as he took Viv's hands.

'If I got promoted, we'd have a lot more money to play with ...'

His mother snatched her hands away. 'I know where this is going and the answer is no.'

'I'm just saying. You know my boss has really taken a shine to you. He told me he'd do anything for a night in your company. I was shocked when he suggested it but as you say, you're a charming woman. It's not surprising men would fall at your feet.'

Viv softened at the compliment. 'Please Charles, can't you get promoted without my involvement?'

Charles shook his head. 'Burke can't choose between Jeffery and me. The only thing that would swing it in my favour is you. He told me as much.'

Viv folded her arms and sighed hard, looking down at her nice new patent shoes.

'You'd be able to keep all these things and even buy that handbag you've always wanted,' Charles coaxed.

'Wouldn't you be jealous? The thought of me ... with someone else.'

'Of course I would, I don't want another man touching you. But if it was just the once ... and I mean, it's not as if Burke is looking for a relationship, he's a married man.'

Viv sighed. 'I ... I don't know.'

Charles lay a hand on each of her shoulders, softening his voice. 'For our family's sake. Look at Frank, he's growing so quick, he'll need new clothes soon.'

Viv's face contorted into a sneer. 'It's a waste of money buying nice clothes for him. He only gets them covered in mud.'

'I know, sweetheart. But it would get us out of a jam. And then we wouldn't have to bring these back to the shops.' Charles picked up the bags and raised them to get his point home. 'But if it's asking too much ... maybe I should just these refunded.' Charles walked towards the door and Viv grabbed him by the forearm.

'No, wait. Leave the bags. Call Burke and tell him I'll do it. It'll have to be quick, before I change my mind. And tell him ... tell him I want to be taken out for dinner first.'

Charles dropped the bags to the floor and embraced his wife in a bear hug, swaying from side to side as he lifted her off her feet. 'Darling, you've just saved this family.'

Frank wondered what they were talking about. Saved the family? By going out for dinner? His mother passed him on the stairs as she brought her bags to her room, barely giving him a second glance.

The next night was hot and sticky. Frank was unable to sleep, despite his father trying to coax him with some dark gloopy medicine he did not need. A car pulled up outside. He peeked through the net curtain onto the street below. Sounds of laughter filtered through the air as his mother stepped out of the car with a tall, broad man, bigger than his father and smartly dressed. It had been a long time since he had seen his mother laugh. She looked pretty in the tight-waisted dress. His father's footsteps creaked on the landing and Frank jumped into bed. Snoring softly, he pretended to be asleep as his father entered the room. He planted a kiss on Frank's dark hair, which lay in contrast to the whiteness of the starched pillow underneath. Frank continued to snore as his father gently pulled the door behind him, leaving the faint smell of cigars lingering in the air. The muffled voices downstairs piqued Frank's interest and he bided his time until he slowly turned the doorknob and crept onto the landing. The upstairs bulb was gone, so they would not see him. Frank smiled at his ingenuity. The dark was safer than the light. It harboured you, while all the light did was sting your eyes and leave you exposed.

A deep voice boomed from the downstairs hall. 'Charles,

Vivienne has been the most pleasant company this evening. I really am quite taken with her.'

'Thank you, Mr Burke. I see you've had a drink, Vivienne.'

Viv giggled and ran her hand across Mr Burke's arm. 'What if I did? I had a lovely time and I gather it's not over yet. So if you'd like to make yourself scarce?'

Charles coughed. 'Yes. Of course. If you're quite sure ...'

'Yes, Charles, I am quite sure, now off you go. Frank, is he ...'

'Yes, fast asleep. I gave him the medicine. He's out like a light.'

Frank grimaced. He had spat the foul mixture into a tissue when his father wasn't looking. His mother wasn't as easy to fool.

Charles paused and Mr Burke leaned towards him, speaking in a low voice. Frank shuffled towards the stairwell to hear.

'Don't worry, Charles, I'll take good care of her. And your promotion is secured. I'll announce it in the morning.'

Charles shook Mr Burke's hand and smiled. 'Thank you,' he said, shrugging on his coat as he went. Frank tiptoed back into his room. His mother ran upstairs, squealing with delight as Mr Burke slapped her on the backside.

'Now get up there you, it's time for some fun.'

Viv stopped at her bedroom door and Mr Burke pulled her to him, kissing her hard on the mouth. Frank scowled as he peeped through a crack in the door. His mother was acting very strange indeed. Mr Burke's big hands were squeezing her all over, and as quick as a flash she pulled him into her bedroom and slammed the door behind her. Frank yawned as he went back to bed and dragged the covers over his shoulders. More giggling came from the room next door. They must have been playing the squeezing game again.

· · ·

Mr Burke visited his mother lots more times after that, sometimes bringing presents. She seemed much happier, while Charles grew more withdrawn. Frank knew that if he pretended to be asleep by eight o'clock he did not have to take the medicine. It was hard to sleep with the noise in the room next door and most nights he clasped a pillow over his ears to block it out. Then one evening Mr Burke brought over a friend and things became very loud indeed. His father came home and punched Mr Burke square in the face. Mr. Burke never came back.

The arguing between his parents ended the night his father packed a case. The familiar sound of his father's footsteps approaching his room made Frank pull the covers to his face and turn to the wall. Charles slouched on the edge of his bed and sighed. The bed seemed to sag from his weight, as if it carried his burden. 'Son, are you awake?'

Frank sensed the anxiety in his voice. He sat up in bed and stared at his father's haggard face. 'Son, Daddy has to go away for a while.'

Frank stared unblinkingly.

Charles forced a smile. 'Daddy's got a new job in a place caused Australia. They have kangaroos there, you know.'

Frank gave a little gasp, the life flickering into his eyes. 'When are we going, Daddy?'

Charles lowered his head and rubbed his face as if he wanted to wash something dirty away. 'Well ... Daddy has to get a place set up first. Then I'm going to come back and get you.'

'Is Mummy coming too?'

'No, Mummy wants to stay here. Mummy has new friends.'

Frank heard a little catch in his father's voice as he stared at the floor.

'Be a good boy for Mummy and I'll be back soon. Can you do that?'

Globules of tears filled Frank's eyes and he blinked them away. The thought of being left alone with his mother fired a strike of terror into his heart. He must have done something bad to make his father leave him behind.

'But I want to come. Please Daddy, I'll be good.'

'I'm sorry son, you can't. But I'll come back for you. I promise.' Charles wiped the tears from Frank's freckled cheek with his thumb. 'Frankie, listen to me. I know Mummy doesn't always say so, but she loves you, really she does. And it's not forever, as soon as I get us a nice place to stay I'll come back for you. OK?'

Frank pulled the covers over his head and buried his face in his pillow to choke back the sobs. His father kissed his head. 'Bye son, I'll be back, I promise.'

Frank knew he was on his own.

Charles's footsteps thudded dully down the stairs. Frank rubbed his eyes and sat up in his bed, his teddies staring accusingly through button eyes from the shelf on the wall. His mother would not allow him to sleep with them, they were expensive and just for show.

Frank crept to the crack of light coming through the door and listened. His father had long since given up telling Viv to keep her voice down in case he heard.

'Said goodbye to him, have you? Happy now?' His mother shrilled, taking a gulp from the glass of wine in her hand.

'You know I didn't want any of this,' Charles said, picking up his briefcase. 'I'll be back for him as soon as I get settled.'

'You're welcome to him. Just remember you owe me.'

'How can you be so cruel? Frankie's up there crying his eyes out.'

'More fool him. And don't turn this around on me. All I've ever done is try to please you. On and on you nagged me for a baby. I told you I wasn't ready, but oh no, "It will be good for our marriage," you said, and now look at you, abandoning him to travel halfway across the world.'

'That's not the reason I'm going and you know it. I told you I couldn't bear you sleeping with other men. How could any husband be expected to put up with that and keep his dignity?'

Viv took another swig from the glass. 'And whose idea was that? Oh yes, it was yours. What was it you said when I gave in? Oh yes, "You've just saved the family."'

'I know what I said. I just didn't expect you to enjoy it so much.'

'Oh, so you would have preferred it if I were raped, then.' Viv slurred, her voice growing louder.

'Of course not. You're twisting it.'

'It's not my fault you couldn't satisfy me.'

The couple stood face to face as Charles spit out his words; 'My mother said I couldn't make a silk purse out of a sow's ear.'

'Get out of my house.' The hurt was etched on Viv's face.

Charles turned to leave. 'Just go easy on Frank and try to show him a bit of affection. I know it doesn't come naturally to you.'

Viv swigged the contents of the glass and threw it at the wall, narrowly missing her husband's head.

He looked back in disgust. 'You're pathetic, you know that?'

'Just get out.'

Charles paused, looking at the top of the stairs.

'I said get out!' Viv screamed.

'I'm sorry Frankie,' Charles said, his voice resigned.

Viv pushed him out the front door and slammed it behind him, rattling its hinges. Leaning against the door, she slid to the floor and emitted a choking, gasping sound as she sat amongst the remnants of glass. Frank walked out of the shadows and tiptoed downstairs.

'Mummy? Are you OK?'

Viv swallowed and wiped her nose with the back of her hand. Her mascara drew runny lines down her face as she snivelled in the dim light. 'Get up to bed will you, I'm fine. And call me Viv like everyone else. It's just you and me now.'

CHAPTER THREE

Will peered at the ward map. 'Now let me see ... down the end of this corridor and turn left.'

Jennifer led the way as she strode down the antiseptic-infused corridor. She could not understand why people complained about the smell of hospitals. It was a damn sight better than the delightful aroma of a custody block. A grey-haired man wearing blue striped pyjamas gave her an appreciative smile as he shuffled towards her, wheeling his drip with one hand, and clutching a bent up packet of cigarettes in the other. Jennifer flashed him a smile and he returned the gesture with a delighted wink.

'Looks like you have an admirer. He must have come from the psychiatric ward,' Will whispered.

'Charming. Let's hope I can work my magic on Stone,' Amy said, fingering the paperwork. 'Here it is – Mike Stone, aged fifty-two, lives in one of those big houses in Fleetwood Avenue.'

'Who says crime doesn't pay?' Will spoke with a hint of envy in his voice.

A hulk of a man, Mike Stone lay in bed next to the

window on a shared ward, snoring loudly through his once broken nose. His hospital gown gaped open at his broad chest, revealing a scorpion tattoo peeping out from under a large blue bandage.

Jennifer bumped into the cradle holding the IV line.

'Should I wake him?' she whispered. Will replied with a shrug, reluctant to disturb the sleeping giant. Tentatively, she touched his hairy arm, which jolted in defence. Mike wheezed a cough as he awoke, resting his eyes on Jennifer with the same appreciation as the elderly man in the hallway. His expression fell when she produced her warrant card.

'I'm DC Knight, this is my colleague DC Dunston. Are you all right to talk?'

Mike winced as he tried to sit up. 'Have you nicked the bastard that did this to me?'

Will glanced around the ward, aware that they had become the focus of attention. 'I'll just pull the curtains for privacy,' he said, drawing the thin blue material around the bed.

Mike pointed to the water on the bedside locker and Jennifer handed it to him. He sucked greedily through the straw.

'I can assure you Mr Stone, the suspect is in custody. I'm just waiting on your statement.'

'I ain't giving you no statement. I can't have it getting out that that little weasel almost done me in.' Mike coughed and groaned at the sudden movement. He pressed the button in his palm for morphine and lay back as it took hold.

Will flipped open his pocket notebook and began to write. 'Can you tell us what happened? He's not admitting to anything.'

'He owed me some money ... so I paid him a personal visit.' Mike's voice slurred as he settled back into the morphine-induced warmth. 'I'm gonna ... kill him.'

Jennifer and Will exchanged glances. She leaned over Mike, keeping her voice soft and low. 'I'm not being funny, but you're a big bloke. How did he overpower you?'

'He was strong ... saying all this weird stuff ... He pinned me down.' Mike pressed the morphine button again. 'I'm gonna ... kill the bastard.'

Will raised his eyebrows, not wanting any more grief that day. 'Mr Stone, remember who you're speaking to.'

Mike closed his eyes as the shot of morphine continued to spread through his veins. 'Yeah, whatever.'

'Mike, we'll be in touch in a couple of days about a statement when you're up to it.' Jennifer left her card on the bedside table and pulled back the curtains. Mike's breathing slowed as he fell asleep, his hand clasped over his bandage. Something gnawed at the back of her brain. She pulled the car keys from her bag and handed them to Will. 'Here, can you drive? I need to think.'

Will nodded as they left the ward. 'My pleasure. High as a kite, wasn't he? Pity we couldn't have got some intel from him.'

'There's only one thing I want to know. How the hell did Johnny manage to stab Mike Stone and get out in one piece?'

'You'd be surprised what people can do with a sharp knife and the right opportunity. I don't suppose Mike thought Johnny would have the balls to go for him like that.'

Sergeant Stephanie Cox cornered Jennifer back at the station, her face patterned in red blotches. Stiff peaks of plum-coloured hair stood to attention on her head, refusing to comply with the damp patches of gel. 'You missed briefing this morning. When are you going to get your act together?' She perched her plump bottom against Jennifer's desk and folded her arms.

Jennifer bit her lip. 'Sorry Sarge. It won't happen again.'

'It better not. Now get down to custody and have a word with your prisoner. I don't know what you said to him this morning, but he's going mental. Can you hear that?'

The shouts of disgruntled prisoners often echoed down the hall from the custody block to their office. Today they had one shoplifter, an alleged rapist, a juvenile drug user, and Johnny, who was making more noise than the rest of them put together. It was a small nick, with just fifteen cells, and one noisy prisoner was enough to disturb the whole building.

Jennifer stopped at the vending machine outside custody and bought two bags of Maltesers; one for her and one for Will. She shoved the bags of chocolate into her jacket pockets before making her way through the heavy metal door.

A shift change offered a new custody sergeant, who gratefully waved her through to attend cell nine. Jennifer did not like speaking to prisoners alone as it left her vulnerable to complaints, but the recent installation of CCTV helped protect her from any false allegations.

Johnny's voice echoed down the corridor and a husky voice bellowed from the cell next door. 'Will someone shut him up, I'm trying to get some kip here.'

'Get out, get out!' Johnny screamed, banging on the heavy metal door of his six by eight feet cell. Cubes of light from the reinforced window highlighted the smooth concrete floor.

Jennifer flipped down the small square hatch in the door, pausing to stand to one side. She wasn't in the mood for having her new black suit paint-balled in green phlegm. A scuffling noise in the far corner signalled that she was safe.

She peered into the cell, crinkling her nose at the odious smell.

Johnny paced, his jagged whispers coming intermittently. 'No, leave me.' He scratched at his head and began to pull his greasy hair. 'I want you out ...'

'Are you all right?' Jennifer said.

Johnny sank to his knees, still clutching his head, 'No, please, it hurts.'

'What's wrong? Do you need a doctor?'

He froze and his eyes darted towards Jennifer. A menacing grin spread across his face and his voice changed into the same distinctive prose as before. 'You should have let me talk to you today. I may have spared him. Never mind, we'll meet again.' He licked his lips, then crawled towards the cell door and disappeared from view.

Jennifer paused, wondering if she should call for a medic. The room fell silent and she leaned towards the cell door to listen. The open hatch rattled as Johnny's face slammed against it, making her jump backwards.

'Please, help me,' he whimpered, spittle flying.

Jennifer raised a hand to her nose to avoid the putrid smell. 'Calm down, I'll get help.' She waved towards the CCTV, reluctant to leave her prisoner. Asshole or not, if anything happened to him under her care, questions would be asked.

Johnny's black fingernails clawed into his neck. Tiny rivulets of blood seeped through his skin and his bloodshot eyes bulged in a frenzy. 'Get out, I want you out.'

The broad shadow of the custody sergeant was a welcome sight as he walked down the corridor towards her, flanked by two uniformed officers. One, who looked about sixteen, was holding a blue padded 'suicide suit' and the larger, more rotund officer had limb restraints and cuffs at the ready.

'We'll have to restrain him until the doctor gets here. You go Jennifer, we'll take over now.'

Johnny continued to gouge his neck. 'Best get your gloves on, lads,' the custody sergeant said, pulling on the rubber PVC with a satisfying ping.

Jennifer inhaled some deep cleansing breaths as she pulled the door open to the outside yard. Dealing with human misery was part of her job, and she had learned to cope with it over the years. But this was different. The sinister voice, Johnny's evident pain; something had gotten its teeth into him and wasn't about to let go. The screaming sirens of an ambulance grew louder as it sped through the rear security barrier. Jennifer followed them inside, the hairs on the back of her neck prickling as Johnny's strangled cries filled the air.

CHAPTER FOUR

'Nice to see you on time for once,' Steph said, shaking the rain from her umbrella. She plodded over to her desk, the vertical stripes of her shirt wobbling in zigzag lines as gaping buttons fought to close over her expansive chest.

'I've been here for ages,' Jennifer lied. Lately her cleaning obsession was driving her mad, and she had only got away from home on time today because she had started an hour early. She used to be able to leave the house after it had been dusted and polished, but now she couldn't settle unless the floors had been mopped too. Her home was like a showroom, but still the need for order itched. OCD tendencies her doctor called it, not as bad as full-blown obsessive compulsive disorder, but enough to make her anxious if things weren't just right.

Detective Inspector James Allison strolled out of his office, looking crisp and clean in his tailored navy suit. His silver-grey hair offset his light blue eyes, and regular workouts in the gym helped battle the paunch developing around his mid-section.

'Morning,' Susie chimed brightly, blonde waves bouncing

as she walked. Nicknamed 'Slack lips Sue', the buxom young DC was everyone's friend, but Jennifer had had bitter experience of her gossip-mongering.

'My car wouldn't start, I had to get a lift in with the custody sergeant,' she said breathily.

'Come in together, did we? People will talk,' Steph said, a hint of sarcasm in her voice.

'Oh goodness no, I don't go after married men, Sarge.'

A blush reddened Steph's face as she turned to DI Allison, who was now standing beside her. 'It's good to have you with us, gov. I know how busy Westlea keeps you.'

DI Allison smiled. 'Thank you, Stephanie, I like to pop in when I can, see how you're all doing.'

Will nudged the door open, his tray rattling from the array of teas and coffees for morning briefing. Intelligence was swapped and jobs dished out. The usual tale of burglaries, domestics, and drug-related crimes were more than enough to keep the small team of detectives on their toes. Known as the poor relations to the dynamic Westlea CID, Haven's resources were not enough to combat the crime wave engulfing their town.

Jennifer retreated to her desk. She had hoped to spend some time investigating the Johnny Mallet case. Their interview the day before had earned her a restless night's sleep. Reluctantly she read through the domestic incident they had been delegated to deal with. 'We've been given a quality domestic,' she said to Will as she flicked through the paperwork. 'An argument over the remote control. He wanted to watch the footie on TV so she lumped him with an ashtray, giving him a black eye.'

Will wasn't listening. He'd just got off the phone to the custody sergeant. 'Johnny Mallet was taken to "The Rivers" mental health unit yesterday and given a full assessment.'

'I should think so,' Jennifer mumbled, her head bowed over her paperwork.

'Yeah but get this. Psychiatrists assessed him as having a personality disorder and released him a few hours later. He's been bailed with conditions to sign on while we progress enquiries.'

'Jesus. Well on their heads be it. I'll put a sixty-one on the system.' An intelligence alert would at least warn any unsuspecting police officers knocking on his door.

The domestic incident in custody was dealt with quickly. After meticulously cleaning her desk, Jennifer used the spare time to do some digging on Johnny Mallet. 'He has a girlfriend. Fancy paying her a visit?' She lifted an eyebrow at Will, averting her eyes from the coffee stains that had returned to his desk by magic.

'Only if you promise to help me with my paperwork later on. It's all right for you, starting here with a fresh slate. Some of my files are so old they're growing mould.'

Jennifer grinned, her dimples breaking out. 'Will, you've been behind on your paperwork for as long as I've known you.'

'Best I stay and get on with it then.'

Jennifer rolled her eyes. 'OK, I'll help. Johnny's due to sign on at the nick, so if we go now, he won't be with her.'

'Make control aware. The last thing I want is a showdown with one of Mike Stone's cronies if he decides to pay a visit.'

A brisk winter wind whirled as they walked to the flat. 'I don't know why we couldn't have taken the car,' Will said, dragging his feet over the foot-worn pavement.

'Stop moaning, we're nearly there. Besides, you could do with the exercise.'

'Bloody cheek, I'll have you know I'm in very good shape.'

'Yeah,' Jennifer giggled, 'round is a shape.' Will opened his mouth to retort but was interrupted by a gang of kids sitting on the wall outside the dingy block of flats where they were heading.

Leers of 'I smell bacon' came from a boy with dirty blond hair sitting next to a skinny girl in emo clothing. Jennifer had dealt with him for drug offences in the past and he had not forgotten her face.

Jennifer leaned over him. 'And I smell dope. If you're still here when I come out, I'll be stop-searching you both for drugs.'

The boy drew his breath and stubbed out the roll up on his shoe. 'All right babe, chill out. We're going.'

'Yeah? And pull your pants up while you're at it!' Jennifer shouted as they swaggered up the street.

Will grinned and swept his hand forward to allow Jennifer through the front door of the building. 'After you madam, the trade buzzer appears to be working.'

'It's a long time since a tradesman has graced this dive,' Jennifer mumbled.

Will took the lead, climbing up the cement steps to the tune of rap music blaring obscenities from a neighbouring flat. Jennifer hovered her hand over the sticky metal banisters.

The door of number fourteen displayed the tell-tale indentations of a police enforcer, the battering ram also known as 'the big red key.' She knocked hard on the door and it creaked open.

'Hello,' she said, poking her head through the door. 'Anyone home?'

A skinny woman with wiry blonde hair shuffled towards

them, her long painted toenails poking out of the holes in her mismatched socks. Jennifer guessed from the intel picture it was Shelly. Her low-cut top displayed her prominent chest bones which was decorated with brassy necklaces that disappeared in the gap between her breasts.

'If you've come looking for money, I ain't got none,' she cawed.

Will flashed his warrant card. 'Police. We need to ask you some questions.'

The woman waved them into the gloomy room. Will and Jennifer silently followed. Without a warrant, Shelly was perfectly entitled to make them leave. Jennifer chose her steps carefully to avoid the empty beer cans and used hypodermic needles littering the floor. Chinks of light spiked through tears in the yellowed curtains, and Jennifer grimaced at the sticky fly tape hanging from a single bulb, littered with its victims. The room reeked of cigarette smoke and judging by the overspill of the dirty ashtray on the sofa, Shelly was a chain smoker.

'We want to talk to you about Johnny,' Will said, eyeing the open bedroom door that revealed a hefty looking black man lying face down on a dingy single bed.

Shelly spoke through the open door, not bothering to lower her voice. 'It's the filth.' The man moaned into his pillow in response.

'Have you seen Johnny lately?' Jennifer said.

'I ain't seen him.' The thin black elastic of a G-string was slung over Shelly's hipbone and she hooked her thumbs through her belt buckle to hitch up her jeans.

'Are you aware he's been involved with the police?' Jennifer said, unable to give too much away.

Shelly sucked a cigarette and her words peppered with smoke as they left her mouth. 'Everyone knows about that.

Mike's cronies showed up here looking for the money he owes.'

Jennifer found it difficult to muster sympathy. 'How's Johnny seemed to you? Has he been himself?'

Shelly snorted a laugh. 'Ain't that something? The filth wants to know how he's feeling. He's acting all weird, that's what. Even tried to take a bite out of me.' Shelly offered up her bony arm for inspection. A faint round bruise dappled her paper-thin skin.

Another moan emanated from the bedroom. 'What's he on?' Will asked, changing the subject. Amy knew her colleague didn't care what cocktail of drugs the man had shot into his veins but the last thing he wanted was an assault job to deal with. A mobile phone chimed from the bedroom.

Shelly retrieved the phone from the dresser and jabbed her guest in the side. 'Hop it. I'm busy.'

Jennifer guessed what busy meant, as she peeped in through the open bedroom door to see various sex toys strewn around the grimy room.

Shelly spoke into the phone in her most alluring voice. 'Hello Wilfred. Just give me five minutes, dear.'

Will whispered to Jennifer, 'As much as I'd love to stay and watch, we really should be going.'

Jennifer nodded vehemently.

Shelly nodded towards the door. 'Now if you don't mind, I'd like you to sling your hook.'

'Just a minute,' Jennifer said. 'Do you want to make a complaint about that bite?'

'Don't you think I've seen enough of your lot today? Nothing happened, now leave me alone,' she said, bustling them towards the door.

Jennifer sighed in exasperation as she left. 'One more question. Did Johnny ever recite poetry?'

Shelly responded in a shrill cackle, 'Poetry? Don't be

fucking stupid.' Her laughter rang through the door as she shut it behind them.

Clack ... clack ... clack; the noise of a walking stick echoed in the stairwell. An old man, steadily making his way up towards Shelly's flat, passed Jennifer on the landing. A slight smile crossed his lips in a look of anticipation.

'Must be Wilfred,' Jennifer whispered, 'I hope she gets rid of her guest first, can you imagine that for a threesome?'

'Yuk. I hope I'm never that desperate.'

'You can't be too fussy now you're single, Will.'

'*I* can't be fussy?' Will huffed, failing to see the funny side. 'When's the last time *you* had a shag?'

Jennifer snorted a laugh as she made her way downstairs. 'Oh, touchy. At least I make an effort with my appearance. You're the one that's gone all Robinson Crusoe, with your shaggy beard and baggy suit.'

Will stomped down to the car.

'Are you annoyed?' Jennifer giggled, opening the car door. 'I was only joking, mate. I like your ... beard.'

Will slammed the car door and clicked his seatbelt into place.

Jennifer helped Will with his paperwork in the hope he would stop sulking. It wasn't her fault he had let himself go since his wife left him. Sensitivity wasn't her forte and if he wasn't up for a piss-take then he was in the wrong job.

Five o'clock came, and she grabbed her coat from the rack and slid it on. It was rare to escape work on time, and she didn't feel like staying late. 'See you then,' she said. A chorus of goodbyes rang from her colleagues, all except Will, his eyes fixed on his computer screen.

'Bye then, grumpy drawers,' Jennifer shouted over. A two-fingered salute flew up as a response. All was forgiven.

. . .

Tesco metro was Jennifer's usual haunt when it came to picking up chocolate for her nephew, Joshua. The thought of seeing him warmed her, and a few minutes with Josh could chase away the stresses of the day. She aimlessly wandered around the small supermarket, throwing bottles of cleaning fluids and random food items into her basket. Avocado, chicken slices, rice, and pasta. Cooking for one was boring, but she couldn't bring herself to eat a 'ping' meal every night of the week. She picked up a bag of apples from the shelf. The days when she had scraped around for leftovers to feed her and her little sister while her father disappeared on one of his benders were long gone. While most ten-year-old girls played with make-up and secret diaries, Jennifer had spent her time concealing her neglected home life from children's social care. Displaying enough food in the cupboards in case they came around was one of the methods she employed, and on the nights when Amy cried for more food, she would ration out bowls of cornflakes, shaking the box as she wondered if she could spare a few more. If they hadn't been taken in by their Aunt Laura ... it did not bear thinking about.

Not that her sister remembered any of that now. Jennifer scanned her food at the self-service till. It was doubtful she would be asked to stay for dinner – Amy had a thirty-minute tolerance, after that she began checking the clock on the kitchen wall.

Jennifer drove into the small housing estate just as the street lamps flickered on.

The blue glow of the television shone through the nets of the front bay window of her sister's house. She knocked loudly to overcome the sound of a crying baby inside. A harassed-looking Amy opened the door. Splodges of food painted her sweatshirt and something sticky matted her hair.

'Come in,' Amy said in a flat tone.

Jennifer followed her in, observing the sag in her sister's shoulders. She had offered to babysit numerous times to give her some respite, but Amy seemed determined to go it alone.

'Jenny!' her four-year-old nephew grabbed her legs tightly in a hug. He looked positively angelic, his light blond hair complimented by his cobalt blue eyes. The magic was broken as she realised hugs did not come for free. 'Auntie Jenny, did you bring me anything?'

She knelt down, breathing in his little boy smell.

Jennifer handed him the bag of giant chocolate buttons, and his eyes twinkled as he peeped inside. 'Oh, Mummy doesn't let me have these!'

'Thanks Aunty Jenny, yes, Josh has eaten his supper.' Amy scowled as she looked into the bag. 'Josh, you can have half now and half later.' Sighing, she waved them into the living room. 'Now why don't you show Aunty Jenny the picture you drew for her?' Amy turned to Jennifer. 'It's like he knew you were coming. He always draws a picture just before you turn up.'

Jennifer found a clean spot on the couch and sat down. Her niece was laid in a Moses basket under the television, which was playing reruns of *Teletubbies*. Her tiny fingers grasped at the air as she cooed at the sounds.

'She's a bit young to be watching TV, isn't she?' Jennifer said, instantly wishing she had engaged her brain before her mouth.

Amy rolled her eyes. 'If you've come around here to criticise my parenting skills, you can leave now.'

'Blimey. It's only been ten minutes,' Jennifer said, 'I'm due another twenty minutes yet!'

Amy creased her forehead, 'What are you on about?'

'Nothing. Where's David?' Jennifer asked, noticing Amy's husband appeared to have vacated the building.

Amy tried running her fingers through her hair, but they stuck in something halfway through. 'He's gone down the pub. Got fed up of watching *Teletubbies*.'

Jennifer's voice softened. 'You look shattered. Why don't you let me watch these two while you have a nice bath?'

Amy looked at her sister doubtfully. 'I suppose I could have a quick shower if you're offering. Lily's been fed, just don't shake her, or she'll throw up on you like before.'

There was no fear of that; the last thing Jennifer wanted was baby vomit all over her Karen Millen suit. Not to mention her shoes. Jennifer stared at the ragged bunny slippers gracing Amy's feet. 'You should let me take you shopping, buy you some nice new clothes.'

Amy gave a cynical laugh. 'Look at me, I'm two stones overweight, I've got two kids, and as you said, I look like shit. What's the point?' She marched out the door before Jennifer could reply.

Jennifer hated seeing her sister so upset, but everything she said came out wrong.

Joshua tugged at her sleeve, holding a picture. 'I drew this for you, Jenny.'

She examined the drawing. It consisted of a skinny woman in a black dress wearing spiky shoes and carrying a handbag. A yellow moon nestled in a night sky clouded with black blobs and intermittent stars. 'That's lovely, is that me?'

'Yes,' Joshua said proudly, his dimples melting her heart. Funny how they were the only ones in the family to have them. 'And is that my shadow?' Jennifer said, pointing to a black figure behind her.

Joshua's face clouded over as he frowned. 'No, that's the bad man.'

'Is that one of the baddies Auntie Jennifer is putting in jail?' Joshua was slowly beginning to understand the concept of her job.

'No,' Joshua said, shoving a handful of buttons into his mouth.

Lily's cries shrilled as the programme ended. Her little fingers were balled into tight fists, and her face grew redder with each wail. Jennifer looked at Joshua. 'Do you know how to put on another one?' she asked, forgetting her parental advice to Amy earlier. Joshua shrugged and stood over Lily, waggling his finger. 'Naughty Lily, be quiet for Auntie Jenny.'

Jennifer grabbed the TV remote, but the programme would not restart. The noise of Lily's screaming was deafening. She slipped off her shoes and putting them aside, took off her jacket and grabbed a towel from the arm of the sofa. 'Shush Lily, shh.' Slowly reaching under the warmth of her body, she lifted Lily from the basket and cradled her on the sofa. The crying continued, and she stood up, pacing the floor. Minutes felt like hours as she paced up and down, cradling the screaming baby. 'She needs to burp,' Joshua pointed out.

Jennifer threw the towel over her shoulder and raised the baby, who gave an enormous burp. 'Well done Josh, you're a clever boy, aren't you?'

'That's what Mummy does,' he said, smugly, a dribble of chocolate creeping down his chin.

Jennifer found a dummy and slipped it into Lily's pink mouth. She sucked greedily, and after a few seconds relaxed in her arms and drifted off to sleep. Jennifer kissed her forehead before placing her gently in the basket. Putting her finger to her lips, she gestured to Joshua, who wiped a sleeve over his mouth.

Amy came downstairs, pink from her shower, towel drying her damp hair. 'Sorry for snapping, I know you're trying to help. Why don't you stick the kettle on while I run a brush through this?'

Jennifer nodded, following her into the kitchen through

the open double doors. The pair of them chatted, Jennifer about work, and Amy about the pressures of raising a family. Their lives were poles apart, and Joshua seemed to be the only thing keeping them together. She watched Amy brush her long brown hair, teasing out the tangles, just as Jennifer had done for her when she was a little girl.

'Remember when Mum used to brush our hair?' Amy said, smiling at the memory.

Jennifer sat on the high stool, her face haunted from the past. 'I remember a lot of things. I remember her leaving us to fend for ourselves.'

Amy frowned. 'Why do you always have to spoil it? Every time I talk about Mum, you bring up the bad stuff. Don't you have any happy memories at all?'

'I have memories. Mine are different to yours, that's all.' Jennifer blew the steam from her coffee before taking a sip.

Amy lay down the brush and began to braid her hair into a plait. 'You need to move on with your life.'

'You're probably right,' Jennifer said, wishing she could.

As Jennifer drove home, she wondered if her sister even liked her. She had never expected thanks for taking on the mothering role, but lately all she felt from Amy was simmering resentment. Now that Amy was married with a family of her own, Jennifer was not sure what part she played in her sister's life anymore.

CHAPTER FIVE

FRANK – 1973

Frank could not find the words to tell Gloria he didn't like being touched. Her fingers bit into his shoulder as she spoke.

'It's a bit late for you to be out alone. Is your mum at home?' she said, smiling with lipstick-stained teeth.

Frank nodded in response. He liked sitting on the steps of Haven's town hall. Faded posters of variety acts hinted at better days. But the theatre had long since closed its doors to the public, who preferred the advent of television to stage shows.

'Has your mum got ... visitors?'

He stared, willing her to go back to the other women on the street opposite. Back to the kerb-crawlers. Frank was almost thirteen and knew all about sex. He knew about everything. He chewed his nail. She just stood there, smiling patiently, waiting for him to answer. Her dark bobbed hair and black lined eyelids masked a ghostly white face, tinged by a faint bruise above her cheekbone.

She ruffled his hair. 'I'll take that as a yes.'

Frank nodded, pushing his skinny hands into the sleeves of his jumper to stop the biting cold numbing his fingers. A newspaper clung to the lamppost in the winter breeze, and Frank shivered, feeling like a gutter rat with no place to go. The last few years had not been kind, and he had taken to the cobbled streets to escape his mother's temper.

Gloria dropped her gaze and sighed. 'It's not right, you being out here alone at this time of night, with no proper coat. You go home to bed. I'll speak to your mum tomorrow.'

Gloria turned to the others. 'It's Viv's kid. Look at the state of him. She needs a good telling off, letting him out in this weather.'

'Well he shouldn't be here, should he? We ain't no social services.' The young woman laughed as she joined them. A teenager herself, her dishevelled blonde hair framing her sharp features. She knelt down, her breath stinking of ciga-rettes and alcohol. It was his mother's signature aroma.

'Come back in a couple of years when you know what to do with it.' She cackled and Frank blushed furiously as the anger spread from his gut to the rest of his body.

Gloria pulled her away by the scruff of her leopard print coat, almost knocking her off her high-heeled feet. 'Get lost, Tina, he's only a kid.'

The beam of a car's headlights illuminated the path as it slowed.

'Fuck's sake Glo, you nearly had me over there!' Tina found her balance and brushed herself off as she sauntered over to the car, her hips jutting from side to side.

Gloria produced a coin from her coat and pressed it into the palm of Frank's hand. 'Here, get a bag of crisps and a drink for yourself on the way home. The newsagent on the corner should be still open.'

Frank pushed the coin in his pocket. He ran home, taking the maze of short cuts he had become accustomed to. He stood solidly as he knocked on the door, his cheeks stained red from the cold.

His mother's sharp face stared from under the hairnet stuffed with curlers, and she ushered him into the narrow hall before bolting the door. 'I hope you've not been getting into trouble. You'd better not bring the police to our door, you hear me?'

Frank frowned, fingering the coin in his pocket. He could give the money to his mother, but did she deserve it?

'And I asked you to clean this dump. You best do it tomorrow or you won't be going anywhere.'

Frank bound up the worn lino stairs. It wasn't a dump to him. Their two-up two-down house was just as good as anyone else's on the terrace, it was his mother that made life difficult. He remembered her wailing the day she had moved there. He couldn't understand it. At least the neighbours didn't make snide remarks and look down their noses at them. Nobody really cared what they did.

The week passed without event. He kept his head down, went to school. Leaving private school for state had not been that hard. The dumber the other children were, the easier they accepted whatever persona he presented to them. The best way of keeping a low profile was to immerse himself in the mundane. Act like them, talk like them. A smile, a joke was all it took – at least during the day. The night was his own.

Frank woke to the sound of a woman's raised voice from downstairs. It sounded like Gloria was paying his mother a visit. But Frank's mind was not Gloria, it was on the spoils from his burglary the night before. Ducking his head under the bed, he pulled out a cardboard box containing the red leather bag he had stolen. His habit of waking up at two a.m. served him well. He was able to reach the outskirts of Maple Avenue in twenty minutes if he ran without stopping.

He pulled the stiff gold clasp of the bag open and rifled through the contents. Hair clips, a tissue, a comb, lipstick, papers, a few loose coins, and five pounds! Frank kissed the crisp note and threw the bag back into the box under the bed. At least he wouldn't have to listen to his stomach grumble today.

He smiled, wondering if the owner would miss her handbag. What did she expect, leaving it in full view on the kitchen table last night? Frank had been shocked to see the old man with his nose in the fridge. Frank's heart had felt like it was going to pound itself clean out of his chest as he hid behind the long velvet curtains in the living room. The old geezer was lucky he didn't cave his head in with his crowbar. The cold solid metal had felt good in his hands. He would have smashed his skull to pieces for sure. He began to imagine standing over the old man's body as crimson red seeped into the patterned swirls of their expensive carpet. But in the dimness of the light, the old coot was either blind or too stupid to see him.

Frank's attention was brought back to the voices from downstairs. They grew louder, relaying the same old story. Gloria arguing with his useless mother, telling her to look after him better, and Viv reeling off a bunch of excuses as to why she couldn't give a shit.

'When are you going to sort your life out? You owe it to Frank.' Gloria's muffled voice filtered through the bare floorboards. Frank squirrelled away the five pounds with the rest of his spoils, some coins and trinkets of jewellery hidden in a box on top of the wardrobe. It was just as well he could look after himself.

'Sort your own life out before you start coming around here preaching at me. At least I'm not sticking needles in my arm!'

Touché, mother, Frank thought, although it was a shame, Gloria had gone downhill lately.

'I've been clean for three weeks, I'll have you know.'

'Don't give me that. Look, Frank is fine. We are both fine, now sod off. We don't need you to tell us what to do.'

Gloria replied something Frank could not make out. He crept downstairs, feeling six years old again as he peeped through a chink in the kitchen door at his mother, framed in a cloud of cigarette smoke.

Her response to Gloria was sharp and to the point. 'Now you listen to me. If you call social services we are finished. What's more, I'll make it that everyone knows you're a grass. You get that?'

'I'm just saying he needs to be with people who will look after him.'

'What's the social going to do for him? Only throw him in a home full of people he doesn't know! You think he wants that? You ask him. You see if you're doing him any favours.'

'I'm fine, honest.' Frank stood in the doorway, his long arms dangling from the shirtsleeves two sizes too small for him.

His mother sat at the table, wearing the same old silk dressing gown, frayed at the edges. Gloria was standing over her, arms folded, with a scowl on her face. Smiles were rare in this house. Smiles had to be bought and paid for.

'Aw sweetheart, your mother and I were just – having a talk. Nothing to worry about,' Gloria said, pulling out a chair and sitting down.

'Stop treating him like a baby. Frank, Glo wants to call the social. You want to go into a home?'

Frank stood beside his mother and put his arm around her skinny shoulder. 'No, I'm happy here with Mum.'

His mother nodded her head, shifting in her chair to shrug off his embrace. 'Is that good enough for you? Now have you got anything to drink because I'm parched.'

Gloria rolled her eyes and slipped a small bottle of whiskey from her bag. 'C'mon then, you get the mugs.' Viv stood in the small kitchen and, as if for the first time, noticed the delicate china teacups hanging on hooks from the shelf on the wall. She had hung them the day she moved in, displayed as a symbol of hope for the future. Viv took two of the rose-patterned cups and set them on the table, dissolving any remnants of hope in the honey coloured liquid that flowed within.

Frank slid out of sight of the two women, who grew more cheerful with each swig.

Gloria stubbed her cigarette into the saucer on the kitchen table. 'You were right about what you said about the social. I've spent half my life in homes and I don't want that for Frankie. What if I take him for the summer holidays when I sort myself out? I'm getting too old for this game, I'm chucking it in.'

Frank felt a flicker of hope as his mother mulled it over.

Gloria continued. 'It would give you a break, and you know I'd look after him – fatten him up with a few home cooked meals.'

Frank bit his lip. He had stayed over at Gloria's place once before when his mother was in the hospital. Sleeping in crisp, clean sheets, waking up to hot buttered toast in the mornings. At night they read together, and when he left, Gloria had entrusted him with a hardcover poetry book. It was his most treasured possession. He held his breath now as he listened for Viv's response to her offer. If he were too keen, she'd say no, just to watch the disappointment on his face.

But half a bottle of whiskey had mellowed his mother and taken the shrillness from her voice. Frank smiled. Glo was a crafty cow; she must have planned this all along.

'How are you gonna support Frank if you give up work? You don't think I'm paying ya. I've barely got enough to support us as it is.'

Support your booze habit, more like, Frank thought bitterly.

'Well, you know Mr Wallace? He's one of my best clients. He said he could get me a little job down the bingo halls in Lexton as a cloakroom assistant. It wouldn't be much, but I've been putting some money aside. You could have Frank weekends when I have to work and I can look after him during the week.'

'Sounds like you've worked it all out,' Viv said, raising her cup for more. 'There's only one problem, isn't there?'

The sentence hung in the air. Glo leaned forward and whispered, 'He doesn't have to know.'

'And how is that gonna happen? You think Osborne is gonna let one of his best earners go, just like that? Off into the sunset, "Ta ra Glo, I'm gonna miss you!"' Viv extended her fingers in a tinkly wave to demonstrate her point. 'If he finds out what you're up to, the only way you'll leave that place is in a box.'

Gloria looked around. Frank pulled back behind the door, holding his breath as he strained to hear.

'Mr Wallace is going to rent me a flat over the bingo hall. It's not much, but it's a start. There's a spare room and everything, Frank would love it there, it looks over the town, all the lights, you can see for miles. If we travel down on the train, we can get Frank here to you every weekend. I might even be able to get him a little job so he can help you out with the bills. It's about time you started taking it easy.'

Viv lit another cigarette and looked at Gloria coolly. 'This Mr. Wallace; married, is he? Planning on paying your rent in kind?'

Gloria sighed. 'Maybe, but he's a good man that wants to help. Osborne will be none the wiser until it's too late.'

'Glo you can plan all you want, take Frank with you, I don't care. But you listen to me ...' Viv grabbed Gloria's forearm hard. 'Osborne won't let you go. I've seen what happens to girls that try to leave. Why do you think I've never walked the streets? You and I may have our differences, but I don't want anything to happen to you.' Viv's cigarette bounced on her bottom lip. 'If you're leaving, you plan it good. And don't tell anyone. You get me?'

Gloria nodded sombrely. 'I won't tell a soul. When I'm settled, I'll come and get Frank. That's if he wants to come.'

'Of course he will. I've not been much of a mum to him. Since his dad left, life has been hard. Some days it's all I can do to get out of bed.'

'You try your best Viv, but I think a little break will do you both good. You know I would never have called the social on you. I may be a lot of things, but I'm no grass.'

Frank counted down the days to the summer holidays. The weeks passed and as the chill left the air, he dreamt of the day Gloria would come for him. Once he left, he would never come back to this dive again.

Thump, thump, thump. The headboard vibrating against the wall in his mother's room distracted him from his thoughts. Old Andy O'Leary was paying a visit. Shouldn't take very long, although he always shouted to God when he was nearly finished. He wasn't a churchgoer as far as Frank knew.

Faster; thump thump thump. It gained momentum. He

really should try to fix that headboard. Wedge something to stop the noise. 'Oh God, Oh God, Oh ... GOD.' Frank imagined ramming a large cloth in Mr. O'Leary's mouth and taking him down with his crowbar. That would grant him his wish to meet God for sure. After a few minutes, the bedroom door creaked open and Mr. O'Leary padded downstairs, exiting through the back door into the night. Frank looked out his window to the garden below to see the small Irishman swivelling his head from side to side as he checked the coast was clear.

'Frank, come here!' His mother shrilled from the bedroom next door. Frank got back into bed and pulled the blanket over his head. An object hit the adjoining wall. 'Frank, you come in here right now.' Frank dragged himself out, cursing under his breath as his feet hit the hard wooden floor.

'I'm trying to sleep, I've got school tomorrow.' Frank opened the door to see his mother spread on the bed, a pillow covering her waist as she rested an ashtray on it. 'For God's sake Viv, cover yourself up, will you?'

'Why? It's only tits. You've seen them plenty of times before.'

Frank rubbed his eyes, wishing he could erase the vision from his memory. His mother had changed after his father left. 'Reverted back to self' was what his grandmother said. Not that they saw much of her these days. One thing was for sure, mothers weren't meant to go around flashing their tits like that. It was disgusting.

'What do you want?' Frank said, in a voice older than his years.

'Go downstairs and get me my bottle of gin. It's at the back of the bread bin.'

'Go and get it yourself, you lazy bitch. I'm going back to bed.'

Viv picked up the ashtray and threw it at him. It whizzed

past his ear, clanged against the door and scattered its contents on the floor. 'After everything I do for you. Go and get me that bloody gin before I tan your arse.'

Frank stared at his mother in defiance as he imagined shutting her up once and for all. It was not the first time such a thought had entered his mind, and they were becoming more frequent.

'Don't you give me the evil eye,' she said, unrepentant.

'I can't wait to leave this place, and when I do, I'm never coming back.' Frank spat the words festering in his mouth.

Viv pulled on her dressing gown and swung her legs from the bed. 'Oh yeah? Where are you gonna stay?'

'I'm moving in with Glo. I heard her say so. She must have her place ready by now.'

Viv whispered under her breath, pushing her feet into her slippers. 'You stupid boy.'

'I know where it is, over the bingo hall in Lexton. I'll pack my stuff and go there tomorrow.'

'You can't.'

'I can. You just watch me.'

'You can't – because she's dead.'

Frank stepped backwards, failing to mask the horror on his face. 'You're lying.'

Viv shuffled towards him with as much sympathy as she could muster. 'She died of a drug overdose last week. I wasn't going to tell you.'

Tears welled in Frank's eyes. 'No. I don't believe you.'

Viv put her hand on his shoulder. 'Son, why would I lie?' She patted him twice on the shoulder and walked through the door, her words following behind her. 'You can't rely on anyone. Life is shit and people are shit. Sooner you know that the better.'

Frank's voice broke into a sob as he followed his mother out to the landing. 'I thought she was off the gear.'

'She was. But you best let it drop now,' Viv turned, pointed her finger in a warning, 'I don't want to hear of you talking about this to anyone else. Not if you know what's good for you.'

Frank wiped his tears as fresh hatred grew within him. Osborne. He was responsible for Gloria's death. He closed his eyes and took a deep breath, and when he opened them, he knew what he had to do. His days of crying were over.

CHAPTER SIX

Johnny paced the confines of his narrow bedsit, rubbing his clammy hands on the back of his sweat-stained jeans. A raging temperature coursed through his body, and he ripped off his t-shirt and threw it on the bed. His sudden fever was the least of his worries as he listened for signs of the men who had threatened to take his life. As much as he hated his neighbours, he preferred their company to being the only person left in the block of flats. Pulling back the net curtain, he peered out the grime-streaked window. Apart from some kids leaning on their bikes, it was all clear. He patted the reassuring outline of his phone in his jeans pocket, trying to work out how long he had to call the filth should the door be forced open. Not long enough. Stretching onto his toes, he ran his fingers over the doorframe until he felt the outline of the knife. *They'll never get through the double bolts,* he thought. Like a rat in a cage, he paced from window to door. But he knew. If the people working for Mike Stone wanted a way in, they got a way in, even if it meant dressing up as Santa fucking Claus and coming down the chimney.

. . .

It was no surprise that Shelly had refused to take him in. They were hardly love's young dream. But with his mates too scared to speak to him, there was nowhere else to go. Johnny sat on the bed and rocked as he held his head in his hands. They were coming. He could feel it. By stabbing Mike Stone he had signed his own death warrant. 'I'm as good as dead,' he whimpered in the silence of the room. Mike was building his empire and wouldn't let Johnny show him up. Then there was the matter of the two grand debt. If he paid back Mike the money he owed, he might have taken a beating and left town. But Johnny was skint, and the money he got pimping Shelly had dried up along with her looks. A wave of dread washed over him. Daylight was rapidly evaporating, and with it, any hope of survival. Under the cover of darkness, the hunters would come. His shoulders shook as he wept, tearing his nails into his skin in an act of reproach. A dribble of saliva fell from his mouth as he cursed the root of his problems.

The ouija board had seemed like a bit of fun when he had discovered it on the wardrobe of his flat. He had used them as a kid and knew how they worked. But this one didn't work like the others. It brought the voice. It brought the Grim Reaper. Johnny used to pretend he couldn't read or write. It was his way of protecting himself from signing anything the coppers put in front of him. But his literacy was good enough to pick out the words which came with each slide of the glass over the smooth varnished wood. HELP. REWARD. LISTEN. ACCEPT. YES.

After one active ouija board session, he invited it in. He didn't need the board to communicate anymore, because after that, he heard the voice in his mind. It said it was the Grim Reaper, but not to be afraid because it wasn't coming for him.

Johnny had a job to do, and he accepted being fully controlled by the Grim Reaper in return for the gifts that appeared in his wake. A puppet, that's what Johnny was – and he was not the only one. It was no different to a good hit, losing hours of his time. But just like drugs, the good times did not come for free. The Grim Reaper took what it wanted and gave little regard for its host. Like a virus, it extended feelers in the gloom, preparing its next infection. More and more voices were filling his head, snapping at his heels like hungry rats. He hoped it would move on; leave him alone to pick up the pieces. But it never had any intention of letting him live, and when Johnny realised he had stabbed Mike Stone he knew he was living on borrowed time.

Johnny jerked as he opened his eyes and realised the room was in complete darkness. *Please not again*, he thought, pushing the button on his phone to check the time. The backlight shook beneath his trembling hands, and he blinked as he struggled to focus his blurring vision. Razor sharp pain speared his stomach and he bent, clasping his sides. He couldn't remember the last time he had eaten. He couldn't remember anything.

Johnny's knees gave way and he dropped to the floor as a seizure overtook him. Footsteps made their way into the room as he writhed amongst the mouse droppings in the space between his bed and the wardrobe.

'Poor Johnny, are you suffering?' a voice crooned from above.

Johnny's eyes opened into two painful slits, allowing him to make out the hooded figure. It was not Mike Stone. He recognised the face from somewhere but his thoughts were jumbled. Had he just let them in? Flecks of foam shot from his mouth as he muffled a cry for help, and he kicked and jerked as his body convulsed out of control. His was hoisted into a sitting position against the narrow single bed, head lolling to one side like a rag doll, blood trickling from his mouth where he had bitten his tongue. After a few hoarse breaths, Johnny turned his eyes to the person before him. 'You?' he croaked.

Johnny's ragged fingernails screeched against the floorboards as the figure dragged his limp body to the hall. He knew there was little point in fighting, but his body kicked out just the same; a frail attempt at self-preservation.

Johnny's eyes swivelled upwards to see a thick hemp rope hanging from the top banister. A rickety chair caught its shadow from where it was parked underneath. His heart, which was straining to provide him with the most basic functions, began to bounce in his chest as raw fear flooded his system. He realised then, that in the cold paint chipped corridor amongst the mouse droppings and the cobwebs, this was where he was going to die.

There was no sympathy from the cold-hearted figure propping him to his feet. Having prepared for his demise, the Grim Reaper silently left the building, and tears streamed down Johnny's face as he found enough strength to walk to the back door and bolt it behind him.

Johnny's legs weakened and he plopped heavily on the chair. His hair hung limply around his face as he stared at his bare feet, considering his options. Either he said no and the Grim Reaper would kill him anyway, or he could wait for Mike Stone's men to find him. He shuddered as the breeze tickled his back. Johnny had heard all sorts of rumours about what happened to people that crossed Stone, including torture by amputation. Even if he survived this, he would most likely die soon. Johnny stood on matchstick legs as he grasped the back of the chair for support. He could smell the toxicity seeping through the air like poison. He lifted one foot up on to the seat, then the other, and reached for the rope. He could just go to sleep now. Go to sleep and the pain would all be over. The whispers were gentle now, calming, like a lullaby. Trance-like, he pushed his head into the rope and closed his eyes. Soon, it would end.

CHAPTER SEVEN

The lights of the marina twinkled as Jennifer drove across the river bridge. The marina was a multi-million pound project, boasted to help the historic tourist town. But all it did was segregate the population of Haven into the haves and have-nots. The marina hosted yachts, luxury townhouses, and a variety of fine dining establishments. Not the sort of places the homegrown residents of Haven could afford. In the east of England, at just over an hour's commute to London, Haven was a reasonably priced base for the bankers and brokers that commuted from the flats overlooking the Blakewater River.

Bolting the front door behind her, she switched on the hall light and rested her coat on the banister. The feeling of foreboding had followed her home, and she reprimanded herself for allowing Johnny's words to play on her mind. Returning to an empty house intensified her growing apprehension. She flicked up the heat and took the post from behind the door. She had lived in the house for two years, yet never fully relaxed within its walls. It had everything she could have wanted, including a newly fitted kitchen in black granite with gloss white walls and rows of gleaming spotlights overhead. The black and white theme continued throughout most of the house, except for the dark wooden banister, which matched the original flooring in the hall. A cream carpet in the sitting room meant guests had to take off their shoes, and her favourite part of the house was the under floor heating which kept it warm all year around.

She tried to relax as the mundane chatter of a TV chat show played in the background. But peace evaded her, and she shifted in her armchair, trying to deny the thoughts filling her head. They were calling her.

Jennifer clasped her hands to her ears as whispers began to run unbridled through her mind. *Who's there? Annabel, is that you?* An old man whispered.

'Go away,' Jennifer said, grasping the remote control to turn up the television.

An insistent woman's voice broke through. *There's no Annabel here, you silly sod. What about me? One minute I'm making a nice cup of tea and the next I'm looking at myself, lifeless on the floor. Young lady, I need to speak to my daughter, do you hear me? I insist you fetch her this minute!*

As a child, Jennifer had tried to help, but it always came to the same conclusion. The people the voices sought so desperately could not be found, they were from a different time, or they just didn't want to know. And then there were the others – dark energies masquerading as weeping children, looking for a way in. Their sinister intentions were fuelled by hatred and anger that drove their host to the brink of despair. If it weren't for Father Kelly ... she shuddered. The family priest had patiently taught her to channel her energy, deflecting the cries of the lost souls roaming the void. He explained that by listening she was keeping them grounded, stalling their need to relinquish earthly ties. She had joined the police to help the living, plagued by guilt because she couldn't help the dead. But now they were flooding her consciousness in uncontrollable waves. Curling up in her chair she pressed her fists to the side of her head as she steadied her breathing. Just what the hell had started this off again? It didn't matter what the clinic told her, the whispers were real. The restless dead. All searching for something.

Jennifer recalled the look of disbelief on DI Allison's face when she had first told him she had had a way of knowing things since she was a little child. But confiding in people was a bad idea and James had insisted she received treatment for her 'mental illness', which was followed by counselling when she disclosed that she was hearing voices. *Stress can do funny things to you. There is medication that can help. Soon you will be back to your old self.* Jennifer turned up the television and drowned out the whispers with several glasses of wine.

Shafts of morning light broke through the stained glass, casting her hall into a colourful glow of greens and reds. A cold breeze kissed her skin as she approached the kitchen. Jennifer pulled her dressing gown tightly together and checked the dial on the wall. *Why is it so cold?* She froze, adrenalin kicking in at the sight of her back door, which was wide open. Her breath fell shallow as she listened for sounds of an intruder. But all she could hear was the jingle of the milk cart whirring down the street outside. Her eyes scanned the room. Had she been burgled? Her iPhone lay on the counter, untouched. Her panic diluted in the absence of scuffmarks or forced entry. Had she really gone to bed and left the door open? The night before was a blur; she barely remembered taking herself up to bed. Slipping out the door, she padded to the shed at the bottom of her small garden. The soles of her woollen socks absorbed the dampness from the dewy blades of grass, and her eyes scanned the garden for signs of disturbance. The combination lock on the shed door was still in place. Frowning, she returned inside and hung her socks on the radiator to dry. 'Better lay off the wine for a while,' she mumbled, reaching for the mop bucket and bleach. It was time to clean the house before she got ready for work.

A small crowd littered the pavement outside the police station, smoking cigarettes and cracking jokes. Probationers. Jennifer could spot them a mile off. Their enthusiasm could only be matched by their optimism for what lay ahead. 'Job pissed', Will called them. Young people high on the excitement of becoming real life detectives, with no idea of what lay ahead.

DI James Allison was putting on his coat as she walked into the office. 'You look smart. Can you spare time to attend a suspicious death with me?'

Jennifer patted the bun in her hair, held with a silver-edged black clasp. It matched her suit perfectly, and she hoped the dark circles under her eyes did not betray the last few nights of unease. 'Sure thing, boss. How come the duty inspector isn't attending?'

'He's held up elsewhere. And besides, it's one of yours – Johnny Mallet.'

Jennifer's eyes widened. 'Seriously? What's happened?'

DI Allison checked his watch. 'I'll tell you on the way.'

Jennifer pulled her shoulder harness from the locked drawer, slapped a fresh battery into her radio, and attached herself to the incident with the control room. It was one of the things she loved about her job. She never knew where her day would take her.

Raindrops clacked against the roof of the unmarked Ford Focus as Jennifer turned the ignition. 'Where are we going?'

'Twenty-three Wilbur Way, it's off the Barrington estate. There's a unit on scene waiting for us. They don't think it's anything suspicious but given his run-in with Mike Stone, I thought we should attend.'

'Of course,' Jennifer said, her mind running back and forth, like the wipers fighting to keep up with the sudden downpour of rain. Her phone vibrated in her pocket and she chose to ignore it. Not because she was driving, but because it was the third silent call she had received that day.

DI Allison gave her a cursory glance as she remembered to try to stay within the speed limit.

'How are you today?'

'I'm good, why do you ask?'

'You look tired, that's all. Everything alright?'

'Fine and dandy,' Jennifer said, trying to sound nonchalant. The last thing she wanted was to go over old ground. She was grateful to have woken with a clear mind and wanted to keep it that way. Keeping her eyes firmly on the road, she fixed her thoughts on the job ahead.

The Barrington estate was flanked by two blocks of flats on either side. Nicknamed 'The Crack Estate,' the appearance of police was something the residents resigned themselves to. DI Allison nodded to the PC on duty as he opened the door to allow him inside. The PC straightened his posture as the DI approached him for a quick briefing. 'We had to force entry, gov, as the premises were secure. A wallet is on the table with money inside, and keys are in the back of the door, which was double bolted. There doesn't appear to be a suicide note.'

'There won't be,' Jennifer said. 'He couldn't read or write.'

The officer nodded and carried on. 'A concern for welfare was called in by a Shelly Easton after he failed to turn up at her address. When there was no answer, she looked through the letterbox, and saw him swinging in the hall. Given the intelligence on the system, we left him in situ just in case anything cropped up. I can cut him down when you've looked him over.'

'Good job PC—'

The young man glowed, 'Clarke, sir.'

Jennifer frowned. 'Why wasn't he found by other residents?'

'I've spoken to the landlord; the flats are undergoing redecoration before the next set of tenants move in. He let Johnny stay as he had nowhere else to go.'

It made sense. Shelly would not have wanted Johnny cramping her style.

'OK, I'll shout for you in a minute,' the DI said, walking inside.

Jennifer followed him into the hall towards the limp body hanging from the banisters. A damp patch patterned the crotch of his jeans, and a dense, sour smell clawed at the back of her throat. She winced at the sight of numerous scratches dragged down his shirtless torso. Pulling on a pair of gloves from her back pocket, Jennifer handed an extra set to DI Allison. The mottled skin of Johnny's stiff hands suggested he had been dead overnight at least. The dried blood under his nails also suggested the scratches were self-inflicted. White foam edged the corner of his blue lips, which drooped to one side. Jennifer glanced at the rickety wooden chair, which lay on its side on the tiled floor.

'His neck's broken.' DI Allison's voice snapped Jennifer from her thoughts.

'Do you think Mike Stone had anything to do with this?' Jennifer said, wondering if there was anything she could have done to prevent Johnny's premature death.

'If he were going to do anything, he would have sent his

cronies around to give him a pasting. Besides, Mallet wouldn't have opened the door to anyone. Double check the rest of the flat, but I doubt anyone has gained entry.' The DI called for PC Clarke to cut the body down. Jennifer prepared herself, knowing she would be elected to hold the dead weight as it was released to the floor.

A black van turned up outside with 'private ambulance' in white letters on the side. Neighbours gathered as two grim looking men in black suits wheeled a trolley towards the door, complete with a body bag. The short police community support officer that attended to assist seemed thrilled at having something more interesting to deal with than ticketing people for allowing their dogs to foul on the pavement.

'Want to have one last look inside, Jennifer? We're almost wrapped up here,' DI Allison said, beckoning the PCSO.

Jennifer nodded, making her way through the open door of Johnny's tiny bedsit. Like an itch she could not scratch, a distant nagging urged her to investigate the pitiful box space. She squeezed between the bed and kitchen unit on the other side, its sink belching plates caked in dried food. Walking past the wardrobe to the yellow-netted window, she sniffed the bottle of sour milk and empty cider cans littering its frame. The timber was crusted with emulsion paint and impossible to open. She glanced through the window to the houses across the street. Front entry was too visible. Someone would have seen an intruder under the glare of the street lamps. They may not have been keen on speaking to police, but Johnny was well known by local residents and an anonymous call might have been made if anyone was seen trying to force entry. She checked the bed, picking up a discarded t-shirt and dropping it again as the smell of sweat assailed her nostrils. A rolled up duvet served as a pillow, and the green horsehair blanket made her feel itchy just looking at it. Jennifer had seen them before, being given out to the homeless by the Salvation Army.

She froze as the wardrobe behind her opened with a creak, revealing a single metal hanger. It's just a breeze, she told herself, straining to check the top shelf. Nothing. *You'll get a better view if you stand on the bed.* Jennifer considered the thought before standing on the spongy mattress. The bed frame wobbled as she stretched her fingers across the top of the wardrobe. It was clear apart from a piece of flattened board, which she grasped between finger and thumb. She ran her finger across the arc of letters and numbers in black ink. The words 'Yes' and 'No' flanked either side. 'What's he doing with this?' Jennifer said to the empty room. The fact that Johnny was messing around with the occult did not come as much of a surprise, given his behaviour in the interview room. A cold breath whispered into her ear, sending goose-bumps down her arms. 'Yes.'

Jennifer jumped at the contact and spun around.

The DI leaned against the doorframe, smiling wanly. 'You all right there?'

'Oh yes, erm … did you just say something?'

'No, I was just about to tell you we're ready to leave. What have you got?'

'It's a ouija board.' Jennifer held out the board for inspection.

DI Allison raised his eyebrows. 'Bit soon for a séance.'

Jennifer gave an uncomfortable laugh. 'I haven't checked the rest of the building yet.'

'It's been done. The meat wagon's taken the body away. There'll be an autopsy, but I don't expect they'll pick up anything unusual. We're good to go.'

She sighed, relieved she had managed to avoid helping with the aftermath. She had enough dead body memories to last her a lifetime. Dropping the board on the bed, she followed the DI outside. The wind whipped errant strands of hair into her face and she pushed back the misgivings that were plaguing her mind.

DI Allison's phone rang and he nodded for Jennifer to go ahead to the car. 'Yes, that's taken care of. We're heading back now.'

Plucking off her gloves, Jennifer fished for the car keys in her bag. She needed to focus on her job and keep a clear head; she was a police detective, for God's sake. She should fall back on her training for answers, not musings of ghosts and whispers. The truth would come out in the end, without the help of the supernatural.

CHAPTER EIGHT

FRANK – 1978

Frank watched Tina jig as she stood on the pavement, elbows clamped to her side as she dragged on her cigarette. Her legs, bare and mottled, were a pathetic sight. Questions ran through his mind, the same ones he had asked five years ago when he was thirteen years old, watching Tina from the refuge of the shadows. Why did Gloria have to die? Why couldn't it have been Tina? The monsters inside him scurried like unwanted rats demanding attention. They had grown. They were fat and greedy and wanted to be fed. He pushed the thoughts to the back of his mind. Impulse had no place here. He could not afford to mess this up.

'Fancy a good time?' Tina's voice was slick as she walked towards him, jutting her denim-skirted hips, the same as before.

Frank realised he was clenching his fists and relaxed his face into an alluring smile. 'Tina. You don't recognise me.'

Tina's eyes narrowed as she looked around. 'Are you a cop?'

'No. I'm Frank. Viv's boy.'

Tina frowned in puzzlement as she tried to recall the name.

'A friend of Glo's.'

Her eyes widened, and she stubbed out her cigarette with the heel of her boot. 'Glo's dead.'

'I know. How much?'

'How much for what?'

'A tour of the city – what do you think?'

Tina smirked. 'Bit of a comedian, aren't you? What'cha got?'

Frank waved a couple of notes before her.

'Have you got somewhere we can go?' Frank said.

Tina glanced at the notes and smiled. 'Well, if the alley ain't good enough, my mate lets me use his flat.'

'I know somewhere quieter,' Frank said.

Tina cocked her head to one side. 'I don't know. I'm not sure if I trust you.'

Frank's nails bit into the palms of his hands and his voice deepened into an impatient growl. 'Do you want the money or not?'

Tina swore as she tottered through the wet leaves, bowing to avoid the low branches on the narrow path.

'Where are you bringing me? We've been walking for ages.' The bones in her fingers dug into Frank's forearm, and he resisted the urge to push her into the briars.

'Quit your moaning, we're here.' The beam of his torch lit a derelict house. The torch was for Tina's benefit. His eyes had long since adjusted to the night, and he knew these paths well.

'Stinks a bit.' Tina wrinkled her nose as Frank pushed open the back door. The scent of soot still hung in the air, remnants from a partial house fire. The original occupants of the house had long since fled.

'Sorry, I forgot you're used to the Ritz,' he said, lighting a fat roman candle and carrying it through to the sparsely furnished room. A porcelain doll lay on the thinly carpeted floor, its arm outstretched, searching for the owner that abandoned it. Tina removed her high-heeled boots and tiptoed over to the burgundy sofa in the corner. She made an effort to drape herself seductively on the damp material. 'Well, come on then. Let's see your money so we can get started.'

Frank hesitated, somewhat tempted as she began to undo her blouse and hitch up her skirt. He waved the cash and left it on the table.

'C'mon my lad, let the dog see the bone,' she said, hitching her knickers to one side.

Christ, what was he thinking? Yet there it was, laid out on a plate in front of him. He had only intended on getting her alone to question her, but it was too good an opportunity to miss.

The candlelight flickered against her bare breasts as she pressed them together in an effort to hurry him up. Frank moved towards her, his plans changing by the second. He undid the buckle of his belt, his heart beating hard in his chest. 'Turn around,' Frank said, enjoying the feeling of empowerment. Grabbing a fistful of Tina's hair, he satisfied himself until his plans were temporarily forgotten.

'You got a fag?' Tina said, appearing indifferent to it all.

'I don't smoke.'

Tina shrugged and took a pack out of her bag. 'Maybe now you've popped your cherry you can start. It's good after sex. You should try it.'

Frank stared at Tina as the circular orange glow of her cigarette punctuated the darkness. He imagined stubbing it out on her face. How dare the dirty slut talk down to him? He bit down hard on the inside of his cheek, a small trickle of blood leaking a copper taste into his mouth.

'Aw c'mon, what are you looking so mad about? You got what you wanted. Now show me the way back. It's fucking freezing in here.'

'Sit down,' Frank said, his voice deep and low.

Tina sniffed. 'Look, I don't know what's going on here but I don't have time for it. Are you going to show me the way back or do I have to find it myself?'

Frank took two strides towards her, and placing both hands on her shoulders, pushed her back against the sofa. Tina yelped as her head hit the corner of the tattered armrest. Frank leaned over her and pressed his finger to her mouth. Fingering the knife in his jacket pocket, his words came slow and deliberate.

'You want to get out of here in one piece, you listen to me.'

Tina's eyes widened as a panicked look flashed across her face. Her eyes darted towards the door and back at Frank. She nodded, edging herself backwards.

'Where's Osborne?'

'Who wants to know?' Tina's chest heaved up and down like a frightened bird.

'I would have thought that's pretty obvious,' he said, relishing the power he held over his frightened captive.

'He's not on the scene anymore. Now let me go or I'll scream.' She straightened herself up defiantly, but her large, frightened eyes betrayed her.

'You make one move and I'll slice you from ear to ear.' Frank drew the hunting knife from his pocket and admired the glint of candlelight on the blade.

Tina sank back into the chair. 'Look, I don't give a shit about Osborne, but if it gets out I'm a grass, I'm finished around here.'

The serrated edge of the knife left an imprint on Tina's face as he pressed the cold blade against her cheekbone.

She flinched, recoiling from the blade. 'OK, don't hurt me, I'll tell you. He's squatting somewhere in the old Barnes estate. He meets his dealer every Thursday night and goes back there to score.'

'You better be telling the truth ... because if you're not ...'

'I am, I swear!'

Frank stroked her face with the knife. 'What happened to Gloria?'

'It's a long time ago, but rumour on the street was that he overdosed her. Go and shank the old bastard, I don't care, just let me go.'

Frank gripped the knife and stared intently at the veins bulging on her neck. What would it be like to slice into it? To watch as her lifeblood drained away. But not yet. Not when he had so much work to do. 'If you tell anyone about this, I'll be back to finish the job. Understand?' He pushed the blade further into her skin and a film of blood seeped red.

Tina drew a sharp breath at the sting of pain. 'I swear, I won't say a word.'

Frank reluctantly lowered the blade. 'Go on, get lost. Just remember what I said.'

With shaking hands, Tina grabbed the cash on the table before gathering up her things and running barefoot out the door.

In all of his eighteen years, Frank had never felt so alive. He walked with silent footsteps as he stalked the dark alley, waiting for Osborne to appear. Frank slung his rucksack on one shoulder, the anticipation lending him a heightened sense of perception. This was no practice run. This time it was for real, and he was ready for it. He had been ready all his life.

The thin, shabby figure crossed the road towards him, his black beady eyes cast greedily over his drugs purchase. If his routine played out as normal, Osborne would go inside the derelict building and shoot up. In about ten minutes, he would be sky high.

Completely oblivious to his stalker, Osborne's feet splashed carelessly through the dirty puddles leading to the rear of the large vacant house.

Frank's breath quickened as he followed, each footstep bringing him nearer his prey. He had tried to stem these feelings, as society taught him they were wrong. But the exhilaration as he finally surrendered to the monster inside him was like no other.

Frank's hands trembled as he waited outside and pulled the plastic covers over his boots. The back door was barely on its hinges, and Frank pushed his shoulder against the chipped paintwork. He picked his way through the debris littered on the floor.

A rat scuttled past an empty milk bottle, causing it to spin. Frank moved only to grip the knife in his pocket. If Osborne came out to investigate, he would be ready for him.

Frank steadied his breath and walked into the remnants of a living room. The ceiling blossomed with black damp spores, which reached out to a glass chandelier, a hint of the grandness this house had once harboured. Splinters of wood cracked and spit from the fireplace, casting light into the dingy space. The damp pores invaded Frank's lungs. He resisted the urge to cough.

In the corner of the room Osborne lay on a mattress, his head tilted back as a soft moan emitted from his lips. A rubber band wrapped around his skeletal arm confirmed that he had taken a hit. Frank stared at the pimp intently, years of frustration fuelling his hatred. The feel of his leather gloves lent him a certain satisfaction as he clenched his fists. How good it would feel to end his worthless life.

Osborne lay with fingers extended and eyes closed, still holding the empty needle.

Adrenalin pumped through Frank's veins as he strode towards him, and Osborne raised his head, squinting in the flickering light.

'Whatdaya want? I ain't got nothing.' The man's voice echoed haplessly and was greeted with silence as the dark figure above threw his rucksack on the ground.

Frank worked swiftly. Pulling the heavy hemp rope from his bag, he threw it over the beam. He tugged it twice, satisfied it would hold. His hands worked purposefully as he knotted the top half into a loop. The noose was already lovingly prepared. The legs of the wooden chair dragged on the thinly carpeted floor as he pulled it into position. It was a good thing one chair had escaped the fire, although Frank would have found a way if things hadn't gone to plan. He was twice the size of Osborne to start with. He smirked. It would be like snapping a twig.

Osborne dropped the needle and forced himself to sit up. He flailed his arms in an effort to chase away the intruder. 'I said, fuck off and leave me alone.'

Frank's lip curled in a sneer. Kicking the bag out of the way, he marched over to the man. Osborne's eyes grew wide as he pushed his hand under his mattress, grasping for something that was no longer there.

'Looking for this?' Frank said, waving the knife in front of him. 'I took it yesterday. Now be quiet and this won't be too painful.'

Osborne tried to stand, but his useless legs crumpled beneath him. Using one hand, Frank grabbed him by the throat and lifted him up. Osborne's eyes bulged as he fought to breathe, clawing at Frank's muscled arms. Frank punched him in the mouth, knocking out two of his front teeth. 'I said, be quiet. Now, do I need to tell you again?'

'Pleath messr, pleath don't hurth me.' The words whistled through the bubbles of blood, pouring from his gums into his ragged beard.

'Did Glo say please?' Frank said, shoving him into the mattress and binding his wrists. Frank wiped his brow. He flipped Osborne around and shoved a rag into his mouth.

'Did Glo ask you to stop as you pinned her down and injected your poison into her?'

He pulled Osborne up and held him at arm's length.

Osborne almost looked pitiful – but it was too late. Frank had seen the guilt in his eyes.

He dragged him to the centre of the room and placed the noose over his head.

'Blindfold? No? Glo didn't have a blindfold when you killed her, did she, you murderous bastard.' The irony was completely lost on Frank as he pulled a length of rope tighter over the rafter, stretching Osborne to his full height.

'Guaarghh,' Osborne gurgled, his bloodied tooth nestled in his greying beard. Frank wrapped the rope around his arm and lifted Osborne onto the chair. He flopped like a fish out of water, fighting his grip.

'Let's see how long you can keep your balance.' Frank said, as he pulled the rope tighter over the beam, tying a double knot. He giggled manically as his fantasy reached fruition. Somewhere in the back of his brain, a voice spoke to him. It was his father. *You don't have to do this Frankie, it's not too late. Just cut him down and tell him you were teaching him a lesson. He won't tell a soul.*

Frank stood back and took one last look at the man, dancing on his toes on the chair. The truth was, he didn't want to back out. He had imagined the scene so many times, it had already happened. With one swift kick, Frank sent the chair skidding onto the floor. Osborne's body jerked and wriggled as Frank burned the image into his memory. Soon the only noise was the creaking rope as the body became limp and swung from side to side.

Taking out a pair of scissors from his rucksack, Frank cut the binding from Osborne's wrists. He tutted at the red marks they left behind. The bloodied nose, the red wrists – Osborne had fought more than he had expected. He paced the room, mumbling under his breath. He gathered up the bindings and bloodstained blanket from the mattress, throwing them onto the fire. It roared into flame and he stepped back, still holding the gag. A trickle of sweat ran down his back as he decided what to do with it. Frank shoved it in his pocket. With any luck, the body would not be discovered for weeks, maybe months. By then the bruises would not show.

He ran home, expecting to hear sirens screaming behind him. The faint glow of the upstairs light could be seen from the road, which meant mother was awake. Frank panted heavily, rooting for his back door key buried deep in his jeans pocket. He had to get inside without arousing suspicion. She was his only alibi.

He peeled off his damp sweaty clothes and lit the gas hob for the kettle.

'Frank? Is that you? Where have you been?'

Frank quickly slipped into the spare set of pyjamas he had hidden in the clothes basket. Racing up the stairs, he flicked on his mother's light, gaining some satisfaction as the 100 watt bulb hurt her eyes.

'What do you want?'

Viv rubbed her eyes and turned on the bedside lamp.

'Turn off that effing light, for starters. Where were you? I called for you and you didn't answer.'

Frank rubbed the back of his neck. 'Yes well, call louder next time, I didn't hear you.' There was nothing wrong with his mother's hearing as she cocked her head to one side at the noise of the kettle whistling on the hob downstairs.

'Be a good boy and make your mother a cup of tea, my legs are giving me gyp tonight.'

Frank nodded and closed the door behind him. He paused as the floorboard creaked under the weight of his foot. He would have to get that fixed. Couldn't have her waking up again, not when he was going out on the prowl.

Fixing her tea, he smiled to himself. He'd done it. He'd actually killed that pathetic excuse of a man. He wondered if his mother would be pleased when she heard. His heart skipped a beat as he recalled the scene. Not exactly how he had rehearsed it, but close enough. He had been careful. Nobody had seen him. And nobody would see him the next time.

CHAPTER NINE

Jennifer ignored the rattle of the cell door from down the hall as she waited in a queue to speak to Sergeant Greaves, the custody sergeant. A jolly man, his tufts of grey hair spiked the edges of his bald patch. He smiled mischievously as he encouraged a young probationer to search the ginger-haired male he had just arrested for shoplifting.

'Don't forget the scanner.' Sergeant Greaves handed the large black wand over the counter to the officer.

'What's that for?' the prisoner asked, as the officer waved the metal detector over him.

'It's to make sure you aren't lying.' Sergeant Greaves replied with a twinkle in his eye. The prisoner stiffened, then realised technology had not advanced that far yet and relaxed his posture.

Jennifer rolled her eyes to Lara, the detention officer who was removing cigarettes from her trouser pocket for a sneaky puff outside. The short stout woman gave her a weary look. 'Can you sort your mate out? He's a right pain.'

'My mate? For goodness sake, who is it now?' Jennifer asked.

Lara scratched her head. 'It's em, what's his name ... Charlie, that's it. Charlie Taylor. He's been asking for you all day. Said he's a friend of yours.'

Jennifer's mouth gaped at the mention of the name. 'No ... it can't be. What's he in here for?' Another murderous scream from the custody cell. The young prisoner gulped nervously.

'Bet you wish you hadn't stolen that Twix bar now, eh mate?' Sergeant Greaves interjected, positively enjoying the look of terror on the young boy's face. 'I've heard that chap is lonely, fancy keeping him company?'

The prisoner paled. 'Don't I get a cell to myself?' he croaked, removing his trainers for the searching officer.

'That depends on whether you tell the truth or not,' Sergeant Greaves said with a wink.

'Oh for God's sake Greavesy, give the kid a break,' Jennifer laughed. It was like watching a game of cat and mouse.

'He knows I'm only joking. Now can you please go and see your angry friend? He's only been nicked for breach of the peace, but we can't let him out until he calms down a bit.'

'Anything for you Sergeant, as long as I don't lose my place in the queue.' Jennifer turned and walked down the stale smelling corridor, passing empty cells one and two.

Silence descended upon cell five as she approached it. Jennifer took the keys she had borrowed from Lara to open the door; quite happy that her old school teacher would never harm her. She cast her mind back to the dinner parties her parents used to have for Charlie Taylor and his wife, and how happy they had all seemed to the outside world.

The temperature dropped with each step Jennifer took towards cell nine. She strained to listen outside the metal door, not wanting to catch him on the stainless steel toilet that graced the corner of the cell. 'Mr. Taylor, it's Jennifer. Are you OK?'

No response. She put the key in the door and paused. Something wasn't right. Looking through the peephole, she made out the figure of a man crouched whimpering in the corner, his face hidden from view. She removed the key from the door and undid the small serving hatch instead.

'Charlie, are you OK?'

The man turned around, his voice weak and feeble. 'Jenny, is that you?'

Overwhelming sadness bore down on Jennifer at the pitiful sight before her. Tears stained the man's face. He pulled together the filthy rags that passed for clothes and shivered. Charlie had always described himself as a happy alcoholic, and he normally kept himself reasonably clean and fed. His usual cheery expression was replaced by a look of bewilderment, as much out of place as the silvery white hair, which was now dirty and unkempt.

'What's happened to you?'

'I shouldn't have listened, why did I listen?' he whispered as he threaded his fingers through his hair.

'What are you talking about? Has someone hurt you?' Jennifer's face was etched with concern.

Charlie sat on the bench, his breath coming thick and fast. He grabbed his head in his hands and let out a blood-curdling scream.

'Calm down,' Jennifer said. 'We'll get you a doctor, then you can be released.'

He emitted a low moan. 'I don't want to die,' he snivelled.

'It's only a breach of the peace, you're not facing the firing squad. Don't worry, I'll be back in a minute.'

As she turned to walk away, a voice snaked through the air, 'Jenn-i-fer, I told you we'd meet again.'

It was the same slick voice that had spoken through Johnny as it enunciated her name and felt like grease against her skin. She turned back to the open hatch.

Charlie wore a smile of contempt. His dark stare was hypnotic, and Jennifer felt the pull, deep into another world. 'Charlie, tell me what's happened to you.'

The man growled a response. 'You know this isn't Charlie, you little bitch.'

'I ... I don't know what you're talking about,' Jennifer said as the hairs stood sentry on the back of her neck.

'Don't lie to me. If you want to play games, I have ways of making you listen,' he hissed.

The man in the cell clicked his fingers and grinned wildly. 'I know, like for like. What about that?'

'Have you lost your mind?'

'Why don't you open that door and we can find out.' Charlie's yellowed teeth flashed in the dim cell.

'Not until you explain what's going on.'

'Relax, it's me, Charlie, I won't hurt you,' he purred.

Jennifer wasn't talking to Charlie anymore. She shot a look down the empty corridor, and back to the man in the cell. 'Who are you?' She whispered. 'What do you want?'

'Oh Jennifer, you know who I am ... now stop being coy.'

Jennifer rubbed her forehead. Her veins pulsed under her fingers as stabbing pain made her head feel like it was in a vice. 'I don't have time for this. Whoever you are, just leave Charlie alone.'

'Or else what?' Charlie laughed. 'You? A slip of a girl afraid to let down her defences? You're only good for one thing.' Charlie's gaze travelled down the length of her body. 'Just think, if I can give you a headache just by talking to you, what I could do if I were ...'

'I'm not listening to this shit anymore.' The door hatch slammed shut and Jennifer turned on her heel and walked away.

The voice echoed down the corridor as she walked. 'The

frost makes a flower, the dew makes a star, the dead bell, the dead bell. Somebody's done for.'

Jennifer strode to custody, leaving the keys on the counter. 'I don't know what's wrong with him, but he's not the Charlie I used to know.'

The jukebox in the corner sang out 'Don't You (Forget About Me)' by Simple Minds and Jennifer wondered how she had allowed her shift partner Will to talk her into a drink after work.

'C'mon, what's say we go out on the lash? You could do with letting your hair down,' he said, his grin embellished by the coffee froth clinging to his ridiculous beard.

'I'm sorry, mate. I've just got a lot going on right now.'

'Jennifer, you're single. You're financially sound and you have no dependents, not even a cat. What do you have going on in your life that is so important you can't stay a bit longer? We could go for a bite to eat, my treat?'

Jennifer's worries were bubbling over, threatening to spill out at any moment. But confiding in Will brought its own set of problems. Not least of which was that he was a die-hard sceptic and refused to open his mind to anything that wasn't grounded in science.

Will wasn't stupid, and if Jennifer wasn't going to tell him what was wrong then he would come to his own conclusions. 'Are you ...' he lowered his voice to a whisper, 'hearing voices again?'

Jennifer felt a stab of pain as Will jumped to the conclusion that her mental health was at fault. But she desperately needed to confide in someone, and a sympathetic voice was better than none at all. Her eyes flicked around the empty bar and she nodded slowly. 'I'm trying to keep them out, but it's so bloody hard.'

'You should have said. Are you worried about work finding out?'

She chewed her lip. 'Something like that. You can't breathe a word or I'll lose my place on the department.'

'There must be something we can do. Have you tried ignoring them?'

'That's easy for you to say. You don't hear these damn whispers when you're trying to sleep at night.' Jennifer took a breath to elaborate but decided against it and looked out the rain-dappled window instead. Blurred outlines of people milled by, all wrapped up in their own problems.

Will placed his hand on hers and to her surprise, she turned her hand palm upwards and wrapped her fingers around his. The warmth of his skin seeped comfort into her soul. It had been a long time since she had felt the touch of a man and she relaxed into it. Perhaps it was time to trust him with the truth.

Will squeezed her fingers. 'You've had a tough childhood. It's possible you suffered post-trauma. The mind is an amazing thing, you think you're coping really well then bam, it hits you out of the blue.'

'Yeah, that's pretty much it,' Jennifer said, withdrawing her hand and looking at her watch.

Will stared at her, willing her to carry on.

Jennifer opened her mouth to speak and was interrupted by the vibration of her mobile phone. She frowned as she put it to her ear. 'Hello? ... Hello? Anyone there?'

'Everything all right?' Will said.

She rejected the call and slid the phone back into her pocket. 'I've been getting silent calls. It feels like I'm being watched, but I've nothing to back it up.'

She massaged her forehead. 'I've got a pounding headache, do you mind if I call it a night?'

'No problem. It's probably stress related. Why don't you give your counsellor a call in the morning?'

Jennifer forced a smile as she delivered a lie. 'I've already set up an appointment. Are you all right getting home?'

'The rain doesn't bother me, I'll walk.'

Jennifer finished her drink and placed her glass on the table. 'In that case I'll be off.'

'Want me to walk you to your car?' Will said, pushing his chair back under the table.

'I'm parked right outside, you numpty,' Jennifer said, giving him a peck on the cheek, his soft bristles tickling her lips.

Will held her elbow briefly. 'Any problems, give me a call?'

'I'll be fine, and not a word to anyone.'

Jennifer watched through the windscreen of her parked car as Will loped down the dimly lit street, leaning against the splatters of rain. Curling her fingers around the door handle, she leaned forward to offer him a lift when an icy whisper drew her back ... *Jenn-i-fer* ... She stiffened as a thin frost crept up the inner windows, sealing the doors and cutting her off from outside world. ... *Jenn-i-fer* ... The deathly whisper spoke with decaying breaths, immobilising her body as corpse-like fingers caressed the nape of her neck. *It's not really there, it's not really there,* she whimpered, gulping back breaths as her heartbeat thundered in her ears. A chill froze the back of her neck as she repeated her mantra, her limbs trembling under the weight of malevolence. Seconds passed, each one an eternity She exhaled in relief as the sensation ebbed. Another brick in her defences crumbled into dust.

CHAPTER TEN

Long shadows fell in the living room of the ex-teacher who had given up on life. His house was a shrine haunted with memories. The small golden carriage clock ticked from its place on top of the large box-shaped television. Each second that passed brought him closer to oblivion and that suited him just fine.

Charlie Taylor gazed lovingly at the faded photograph, flicking it over to re-read the blue inked inscription. *Rosie, aged four, Frinton-on-Sea*. It didn't matter that the photo was in black and white. To him, it was alive with colour. He could almost smell the sea as they sat underneath the buttermilk sky. Seagulls crying overhead, the salty wind catching his deckchair as he lowered himself in. Shrieks of laughter as it collapsed in the sand. Charlie's heart ached as he relived the memories, the pain tightening his throat as his body shuddered with another jerking sob. But still the memories came, each one striking a dagger into his heart. Charlie blinked as he focused on the picture of his daughter, her tongue catching the dribbles of ice cream trailing down her chin. Photographs of his only child were so precious, if only they had more … or a portrait … a portrait would have been nice. He closed his eyes as the pain created fresh tears. He lost part of himself when his daughter died, on this day so many years ago. Since then, he had become fragmented, piece by piece crumbling away like a cliff edge under the weight of the hammering sea. He tried to carry on, but life pounded against him in waves, and he just couldn't take it anymore.

'Your daughter has leukaemia.' *Bam!* 'I'm leaving, Charlie … I don't love you anymore.' *Bam!* On and on it went, eroding his soul until there was nothing left but sand and water. And still the clock ticked. It was three years since he had welcomed the news that his drinking would kill him within twelve months. Three years on, and he was still alive. Others had passed before him, people who deserved to live. But the world wasn't finished with him yet. His wounded soul was an attractive meal to the vultures circling overhead.

The figure watched from the hall as Charlie drank himself into oblivion. It would have been easy to leave him to finish the deed. But the plan was not to watch a man drink himself into the arms of death. The plan was to send a message. It was just like old times. The thought of sending the old fellah up in flames sent a thrill of delight through the watcher's festered soul. This time it would be easy. Matches or accelerant were not necessary. Spontaneous combustion was a gift from the realms of the supernatural. The cloaked figure grinned as they cracked their knuckles. They promised they would send a message. And they kept their promises.

CHAPTER ELEVEN

ELIZABETH – 1978

Elizabeth picked a piece of cotton from her uniform skirt as she listened to the woman at the front counter. She would be of more use on the streets than sitting here, taking complaints. Being volunteered for desk duties was the thanks she got for catching up with her work so quickly. She couldn't wait to start her new role, which would make her the youngest female sergeant in the county. The raspy voice of the woman on the other side of the counter interrupted into her thoughts.

'I know he gives me nothing but grief, but I'm worried. Ozzy usually taps me up once a week and I've heard nothing from him for a month now. Can't you find him?' Maude broke into a cough. She was small, fierce woman, with deep-set eyes and wiry hair dragged into a bun.

Elizabeth discreetly inched herself further away from the wheezing woman. 'Maude, usually you're in here making reports that he's stealing from you. I would have thought you'd enjoy the peace and quiet. It's almost Christmas. Make the most of it while you can.'

The woman pointed a nicotine stained finger in her direction. 'There's something wrong. I can feel it in my bones. Now are you going to take my report or not?'

'I never said I wasn't. But how do you expect us to find him if he's homeless? Do you know where he sleeps?'

'Last I heard he was sleeping in that derelict house in Burkley Road, off the old Barnes Estate, number 104. I'd go down there myself, but with my arthritis ...' Maude spit into a hanky and wiped her mouth. 'My legs aren't what they used to be.'

'You need to give up the ciggies before they kill you. Look, officers are busy but I'm finished in a minute. I'll go down there myself if I have to.'

Narrowing her eyes, Maude grasped the handles of her handbag and leaned forward. 'Good. And if you see him, tell him not to waste his time looking for money. I don't have none. I just want to know he's all right.'

'Yes yes, now you go off home and make yourself a cuppa. You look like you need it.'

She watched as Maude shuffled out the door, dragging her shopping trolley behind her. Speak to people in their own language was a rule Elizabeth went by, and people respected her for it. It was one of the things she loved about being a uniformed officer. A detective role wasn't for her, it would take her away from the streets she loved. But she couldn't wait to rise in the ranks as a female uniformed officer and she wore her uniform with pride.

Elizabeth smiled at the burly police officer that took her seat. 'I've had all sorts here today, I'll be glad to get some foot patrol in for some air.'

'Two hours left on your shift; it's hardly worth it.'

'That,' Elizabeth grinned, 'is why I am in fine shape, and you are not.'

'Get out of it!' the officer smirked as he flapped her away with his clipboard.

The full moon shone down on Burkley Road as Elizabeth approached number 104. PC Hargreaves had arranged to meet her there, but she guessed he had been called away as there was no sign of a police car at the address. A group of boys pedalled past, fascinated by the sight of a lone female police officer walking down their estate. Elizabeth stood tall, refusing to be intimidated. She knocked on the door of the end terrace house which was shrouded in darkness. The last tenants had long since vacated, and the owners had yet to spend money on making it habitable again. In the meantime, it was a haven for squatters and errant teenagers. She gave up rapping on the front door and walked through the overgrown vegetation to the back, frowning at the sight of the unhinged door.

She exhaled in relief as car headlights lit the front of the two-story building. PC Hargreaves was not going to let her down after all. She flashed her torch to draw his attention. The break in was most likely caused by Ozzy, but she trusted her senses, and they were screaming at her not to enter the building alone.

The officer's familiar broad figure came around the corner, stamping his heavy boots through the vegetation. 'What's up, Liz?'

'I came to check on Ozzy. His mother reported him missing. I was going to go in, but something didn't feel right.'

'Good thinking. A young girl like you shouldn't be going in places like this alone.'

Elizabeth fought the urge to say that female officers were just as capable as male officers on the beat. The look of concern on his face softened her response. 'The back door is insecure. You ready to go in?'

'Sure.' He led the way through the back kitchen, their feet crunching on broken glass. Slowly, they crept into the hall, listening for sounds. He flicked the light switch, but there was no response.

Elizabeth gripped her torch. She would use it as a weapon if she needed to, although it would take a lot to get through PC Hargreaves. If there was one officer you wanted in your corner when things got rough, it was him.

His voice broke the silence in a whisper. 'If he *is* here, he must be frozen to death.'

Elizabeth raised a hand to her nose. 'Smell that? You may be right.'

The officers followed the smell into the vacant living room. Their flashlights beamed on a figure hanging from the rafters.

'Ozzy, you bloody idiot.' PC Hargreaves murmured as he approached the body.

Elizabeth scanned the room while PC Hargreaves called it in. His voice blended into the background as she looked over the dirty mattress and used needles.

'Yes sir, it looks like suicide, but we would be grateful if you could visit, as entry to the building appears to be forced.' PC Hargreaves absently nodded his head as he leaned into his radio, 'Yes, he is a well-known drug user ... no sir, no sign of a disturbance apart from forced entry ... we've checked his pockets and there's some cash in there ...'

Two rats scuttled in the corner of the room, startled by the beam of the flashlight. No doubt there was a nest of them nearby. It was probably a good thing he had hanged himself. If he'd died on the bed ... Elizabeth shuddered.

'Too cold for you, lassie? I can wait for the undertakers if you want to get off.'

'Isn't the inspector coming out?'

PC Hargreaves clasped his hands together and rocked on his heels. 'It seems not. He's busy on another job and doesn't deem it to be suspicious.'

'That's a bit chancey isn't it? After all, it's forced entry.'

'Aye maybe, but Ozzy's a squatter. He didn't exactly let himself in with a key. With the money in his pocket and drugs still under his pillow, it's unlikely anyone else was responsible.'

'All the same, I'll feel happier if I search the rest of the house. I won't be long.' PC Hargreaves shrugged his shoulders as he lit a cigarette. 'You won't find much up there apart from rats and spiders but be my guest. If you need me, just shout.'

'Don't worry, I will,' she said. PC Hargreaves was a nice man, but his view that a woman's place was in the home was painfully evident. It was nothing new for Elizabeth, who fought hard to prove her worth in the team. It wasn't that she didn't want to settle down and have children someday. But she couldn't see any reason why she couldn't have both. She even had the names of her children picked out. Jennifer after her grandmother, and Joseph if she had a boy. Amy was nice too. Lots of women managed to juggle a career with children, why couldn't she?

The wooden stairwell creaked as she climbed upwards, shining a light onto the upstairs landing. Mottled wallpaper hung off the walls and dangled onto the floor. The damp spores caught in the back of her throat and she stifled a cough.

The layer of cobwebs covering the loft hatch was a welcome sight. It meant she did not have to climb up there to investigate, because nobody had been up there recently. Pushing open the bedroom doors, she stood to one side and flashed her torch before entering. Her police training had taught her not to enter head on in case someone was waiting on the other side. She listened for the slightest sound as she entered each room. This house had sheltered a family once, but there was no sign of children here now. It was abandoned to decay and ruin, its only occupants an army of rats, spiders and a decaying body hanging from the rafters downstairs.

A car door slammed outside, most likely the undertakers. She returned downstairs, vowing that when she was made an inspector she would attend every death she was called out for. Ozzy's demise had all the trademarks of a suicide, but it didn't sit right, and she knew it would churn in her thoughts when sleep evaded her.

Elizabeth volunteered to deliver the agony, feeling guilty for being so dismissive to Maude earlier on. Informing family of the death of a loved one was termed by police as an 'agony' for a reason. For all her bravado, Elizabeth knew Osborne's mother would be heartbroken with the news.

'He's dead, isn't he?' Maude said, in response to Elizabeth's presence at her doorstep. The little cottage was nicer than Elizabeth had expected, and she wondered what had happened in Osborne's life to make him cause so much trouble.

'It seems that way. I'm sorry Maude.'

'Seems that way? He is or he isn't,' Maude scowled.

Elizabeth removed her hat and swept a hand across her hair. 'May I come in?'

Maude opened the door allowing Elizabeth inside. The smell of stew hung in the air and Elizabeth's stomach rumbled. Family photos graced the fireplace of the cosy home, and three ceramic ducks were displayed on the wall overhead, frozen in flight.

'Drugs, was it?' Maude asked, as Elizabeth perched on the small green sofa. It was low to the ground and she moved forward to balance herself. 'No Maude, it seems as if he hung himself.'

'Nah, he wouldn't have done that. Not Ozzy. Are you sure it was him?'

'We identified him from paperwork in his trouser pocket. I'm afraid he'd been there for some time, but ... it does seem to be him. The coroner will examine the body in due course.' A cat rubbed itself against her legs, covering her black tights in a pattern of grey hairs.

'In due course? Well, I can save them a job. He would never have hung himself. Never. He was too much of a coward.'

'I'm sorry, Maude. Drugs can make people act out of character. We'll keep you updated with the coroner's report. But you should brace yourself for the worst.'

'Worst? I'm over the worst. At least now I'll get some peace. The little sod, why ...' Her voice choked into a sob and Elizabeth rested a hand on her shoulder.

Maude's words rang in her ears when the coroner's report came back. M. Osborne. Male died of asphyxiation. Secondary injuries consisted of a broken nose and fractured wrist. The injuries may have been obtained prior to his death and due to body decomposition it was impossible to tell if foul play was involved.

An open verdict was called. Elizabeth stared at the paperwork, the far-reaching consequences of Osborne's demise beyond her comprehension.

CHAPTER TWELVE

Jennifer fell into a fitful night's sleep. Her first thoughts went to Charlie. How she could solve the mystery unravelling around her? Who had spoken to her from the confines of the cell? The conversations with both Johnny and Charlie were vague and rambling but interconnected in ways she did not yet understand.

Rifling through her wardrobe, she pulled out a knee length black skirt, which she offset with a mink top. She dragged a brush through her damp hair, vowing to check their custody records when she went into work that afternoon. Such records could be accessed on the force computer long after the prisoner had left, and they held all sorts of useful information, such as what they ate, what they said, and any medical examinations. She wound her hair into a bun. If anyone asked, she would say she was checking to see if her contact with the prisoners had been recorded. It wasn't as if she was lying.

. . .

The office bustled with people and a sense of excitement filled the air. Steph approached her with a look of determination. 'Jennifer, can I see you for a minute in the inspector's office? Something's come up.'

'Never a dull moment,' Jennifer mumbled under her breath as she followed Steph, whose swift waddle was causing her trousers to strain at the seams.

Jennifer took up a spare swivel chair next to the expansive wooden desk. Despite being a sergeant, Steph was not granted an office of her own, and she shared the DI's space when private matters needed to be discussed. The fluorescent strips overhead cast a gloomy light. A battered filing cabinet in the corner housed personnel records and, it was rumoured, a bottle of scotch in the bottom drawer. It was more for posterity than anything else, a throwback to the time when a drink and a cigarette after a long day's work was acceptable. Jennifer sat, wondering why DI Allison never displayed any family photos on his desk.

'Have I done something wrong?' she asked Steph, who was looking through the blinds to the adjoining CID office.

'Apart from being a shit magnet, no. I've been trying to ring you all morning. Don't you answer your phone?'

Jennifer reddened. She had switched off her phone the previous night to stop the silent calls. 'Sorry. 'What's wrong?'

I hear you were one of the last people to talk to Charlie Taylor in custody.'

Jennifer's heart pounded a little faster. Either she was in trouble or Charlie was in danger. 'Yes, I was, why?'

Steph sighed. 'I'm afraid he was found dead in the early hours of this morning.'

'No. He can't be ...' A lump grew in Jennifer's throat. It felt as if her anxiety had formed into a ball and wedged in her neck.

'Sorry Jennifer, I didn't think you knew him that well.'

Charlie's death was a shock – another broken link from the past. Jennifer reached for a tissue as tears welled in her eyes. 'He was my teacher in school. My parents used to invite him around for dinner parties. After my mum died, he stayed friends with my dad. Well, when I say friends, more like drinking buddies.'

'God, I would have broken it to you gently if I'd known. You don't make it easy for people to know you, Jennifer.'

The comment was harsh but accurate. Jennifer nodded, twisting her tissue.

'Have the undertakers collected his body yet?'

Steph hovered uncomfortably. 'It's not straightforward. There was a fire. His death … it wasn't natural causes.'

Charlie's pleas for help replayed in Jennifer's mind. *I don't want to die.* Why hadn't she listened, instead of walking away? The realisation was too much to bear. Another voice sang in her memory, a slick, sneering reprisal. *The dead bell, the dead bell. Somebody's done for.* The walls began to close in. She needed to get outside. Grasping the desk, she tried to stand. The air left her lungs as she fell into depths of confusion. 'This isn't real. None of this is real,' she whispered, as blackness descended on her, weakening her legs and loosening her grip. Steph shouted for Will and he bundled through the door, dropping his belongings on the floor.

Steph ushered him in. 'Help me get her onto the chair, I think she's fainted.'

Jennifer blinked as she came to seconds later. Will exhaled in relief and Steph put the phone back on the receiver.

'Are you OK? We were about to call a medic.'

Jennifer rubbed her face as she tried to conceal her embarrassment. 'Sorry. Low blood sugar. I'm fine,' she lied.

'Will, can you stay for a few minutes? I have to go to briefing,' Steph said.

'Of course.' Will dragged a spare chair to sit beside Jennifer, who was cradling her head in her hands.

Steph briefly returned to give Jennifer a cup of hot sweet tea and closed the office door as she left.

'Do you know what's happened to Charlie?' Jennifer asked, taking slow, controlled breaths.

'I do, but I'm not sure if telling you is a good idea,' Will replied.

'I'm going to find out anyway, it may as well be from you.'

Will sighed. 'He shouted for a while after you left, then it all went quiet. CCTV showed him standing, staring at his cell wall. He refused a medic and his clock was running out, so they had to let him go.'

Officers were only allowed to keep prisoners for as long as necessary and twenty-four hours was the maximum amount, unless an extension was granted, and only for very good reason.

'About an hour later, a call came in about a fire at his address. When the firefighters got there, the house was fine, but Charlie ...' Will paused.

'Tell me.'

'It was as if he had been set alight, but nowhere else was affected, not even the chair he was sitting on. His legs ... all that was left was his legs, from the knees downward. Everything else was soot. It's very grisly. The people who found him are being offered counselling.'

Jennifer looked up, a depth of emotion behind her eyes 'Did he have any implements, anything that could have lit the fire?'

'No, nothing, but they're launching an investigation as it's still counted as a death in custody because it was so soon after release. PSD may need to talk to you, as you spoke to him.'

Jennifer blotted her face with a tissue, her stomach churning at the thought of being interviewed by the Professional Standards Department. What on earth was she going to tell them? She looked at her watch. 'Right, well, I'm off to briefing. Now if you'll excuse me.' Jennifer pushed back her chair, hoping the briefing would provide her with some answers.

Will grabbed her arm. 'Jennifer, wait.'

'I'm OK. It's just the fire...' Jennifer cleared her throat. 'When I was young, we lived in a boathouse, a wooden cabin beside the river. One night it caught fire. Amy and I were upstairs asleep and dad was downstairs, drunk. We got out just in time.'

Will gently placed his hands over hers. 'Sorry, I didn't know.'

'It was my fault. I asked for it.' Jennifer's words were cold and flat.

Will was about to speak when Steph opened the door. 'The DI said you're to take the day off. He'll brief you tomorrow.'

'But...' Jennifer began. Steph was having none of it. 'You can't go to briefing, conflict of interest and all that. I got into hot water just for suggesting you should attend.' She turned to Will.

'Pair up with one of the guys on attachment. There's lots of prisoners to be dealt with. C'mon Jennifer, get off home.'

'Are you OK to drive?' Will said, his eyes cloaked in concern.

Steph's shrill voice interrupted the scene, her patience having reached its limit. 'Of course she's OK, and you need to get cracking. You've got a three handed domestic to deal with.'

'I'll go to my sister's, I'll be fine,' Jennifer said, ignoring Steph's outburst.

Will rested a hand on her forearm. 'If you need anything, call me.'

. . .

Jennifer steered her car onto the gravel drive of St. Michael's church on her way home. A visit to the graveyard was long overdue. The fragile sun reflected off the leaves dancing in the cold crisp breeze. She walked through the headstones, the damp grass leaving trails of dew on her boots. Her mother's grave was shaded under an oak tree, which made a gentle rustling sound in the summer, but the bare frozen branches gave no such comfort today. Three pots of pansies quivered in the breeze, and a drawing of an angel held firm under a rock. She picked it up and brushed off the dirt. Joshua was such a sweetheart. It was a shame he had never got to know his grandmother. Elizabeth would have loved him.

Jennifer returned the picture to the grave, her brown eyes misting with unshed tears. She strained to remember the good times. They must have been happy once. Living in the boathouse, fishing and playing in the water. But each happy memory was tainted with a bitter taste; being pulled out of the river when her father was too drunk to watch her, putting Amy to bed because her mother was working another twelve-hour shift, then later, trying to bring up her sister at ten years of age because her father had fallen apart.

Footsteps broke the silence and Amy smiled as she pushed the pram towards her. 'I didn't expect to find you here.'

Jennifer brushed off her clothes as she stood up. 'I've got the day off. Where's Josh?'

'Playgroup. He's excited about starting school, so I send him a couple of afternoons a week to make friends.'

'He's a bright spark, that one. He won't have any problem there.' Jennifer peeped in at Lily, her tuft of red hair visible from beneath the soft pink blankets.

'She's so sweet. You look nice today, going somewhere?'

Amy looked every inch the content mum in her blue knee length dress, cream pumps and tan cardigan.

'Thanks. I don't always look like crap you know. I'm meeting David after work then we're going for a bite to eat after we collect Josh.'

'That's nice. So, how's the retail trade?' Jennifer asked, grateful for her sister's good mood.

Amy laughed. 'Sis, you are no more interested in the inner workings of a supermarket than I am. Still, it pays the bills.'

Jennifer smiled. 'You've got me there. I'm glad you and David are happy together. He's good for you.'

'He is.' Amy said, her eyes wandering to the headstone. 'You know, mum would be happy to see us together like this.'

Jennifer nodded. 'I think she would.'

Amy pulled an empty carrier bag from under the pram and began to pick up bits of debris from the grass. 'Teenagers come down here sometimes, you find all sorts of crap lying about.'

'Time I was off.' Jennifer turned to leave.

'Wait,' Amy said. 'Is there something wrong? You don't seem yourself today.'

'I received some bad news. Charlie Taylor was released from custody last night and died.'

Amy frowned, trying to recall the name. 'Taylor ... that name rings a bell.'

'He was our old teacher. You probably don't remember him as well as I do, but he was a good man. Anyway, I'll see you later yeah?'

'OK Sis, take care.'

Jennifer walked down the path, thinking of Charlie. He *was* a good man and she owed him. More than her sister could ever imagine.

· · ·

Darkening clouds threatened rain as she shoved her key in her front door. She looked over her shoulder, picking up the feeling of being watched. She peered across the parked cars and curtained houses across the road. Cursing her paranoia, she pushed opened the door and double bolted it from the inside.

She turned up the heat a notch and changed into a track-suit and woollen socks. Grabbing a spoon from the drawer, she rested it on the worktop and reached into the fridge for a tub of ice cream. This was long overdue. Jennifer stared at the spotless granite counter space. The spoon was gone. She scratched her head, muttering to herself. 'I'm sure I left that there.'

Jenny... a whisper blew in her ear. It was not the malevolent voice she had heard in the car, but a gentle call. Jennifer gasped as she spun around, half expecting to see someone standing behind her. She flinched as the chimes of the doorbell cut in, alerting her to a visitor. Cautiously she padded out to the hall to answer it. A dark shadow reflected through the stained glass.

She opened the door to DI Allison, his unshaven face appearing drawn and haggard. 'Are you all right?' he said, 'You look like you've seen a ghost.'

'I ... No, I'm fine, sorry, come in.'

'I can't stay long, I just wanted to let you know how it's all going.'

'Time for a coffee?' she asked, hoping he could stay long enough for her to gather her nerve.

DI Allison stifled a yawn behind the back of his hand. 'No thanks, but I'll have a glass of water.'

He followed her into the kitchen as she took a glass from the cupboard. Frowning, she stared at the dessert spoon on the counter.

'Something up?'

'Oh, it's just that ... the spoon ... it went missing and now it's turned up again.'

'Oh right.' DI Allison pulled back his sleeve to glance at his watch. 'Anyway. I just wanted to let you know, this business with Charlie Taylor is going to hit the press. They're coming out with all sorts of ridiculous theories. They're even suggesting spontaneous combustion.'

Jennifer nodded as she poured filtered water into the glass, reminding herself to act normally. The last thing she needed was her DI putting her on restricted duties. 'You look tired,' she said, handing him the glass.

He popped open the top button of his shirt and loosened his crumpled tie. 'I got called in at three this morning and I've not stopped all day.'

'Are you any closer to finding out what happened?'

'No. Your teacher friend blew very high in the intoximeter when he was arrested, but we don't know how he ignited. Steph told me what happened in the office. I don't think it's healthy for you to be thinking about this.'

Jennifer chose her words carefully as the lines between work and friendship blurred. 'If you're worried about my mental wellbeing you don't need to be. I've been given the all clear.'

'Good, I'm glad to hear it. I'll keep you updated about Charlie, but if the press call, refer them to the police media department.' DI Allison drained his glass. 'I've got to shoot off.'

'Sure. Thanks for calling in.'

She returned to the counter and the spoon was gone. She pulled open the drawer to find it nestled with the others. 'Maybe I *am* losing my marbles.'

. . .

Jennifer found therapy in cleaning and was in the middle of hoovering the living room carpet when the evening news flashed up on her television. A news reporter spoke of the suspicious death, which was being hotly discussed as 'spontaneous combustion'. He was flanked by a man each side, which was the channel's usual way of dealing with the case for and against whatever topic they were reporting.

Jennifer switched off the hoover and perched on the edge of her sofa as she took it in.

'What is your take on this being a case of spontaneous combustion, Professor Morgan?'

The newsroom cameras panned to the right of the reporter to a dishevelled expert they appeared to have found in a hurry. He patted his bristled hair. It had the same erratic form as his eyebrows, which were now knitted together in a frown.

'Well, a certain set of circumstances needs to exist to make this condition occur, and there have been very few genuine cases. Up until now, it has been almost impossible to measure correctly, so while it's very sad for the family involved, the police are the best people equipped to deal with this forensically.'

Jennifer bristled to hear them talk of Charlie Taylor as a throwaway piece of news. All the same, she found herself straining to hear what the red-faced man to the left of the presenter had to say.

'Ex Superintendent Jim Reynolds, what do you make of this?'

A film of sweat glistened over Mr Reynolds' brow under the heat of the studio lights. His chin wobbled as he spoke, his shirt button stifling his thick neck. 'It's preposterous; there is no reliable evidence to back up the theory of spontaneous combustion. What we have here is an unfortunate death in police custody, cause unknown. I will be waiting for the coroner's report before jumping to any wild conclusions.'

Turning the hoover back on, Jennifer attempted to lose herself in the numbness of everyday life. But she could not keep out the thoughts that demanded attention. Something had entered Charlie's body before death. No matter how much she tried to deny it, she knew it was the truth. Whatever had entered Charlie was evil and had killed him. It was most likely the same thing that had killed Johnny Mallet.

Her gut twisted in fear as she raked the hoover over the spotless carpet. She could cope with voices, and shadows could be ignored, but this thing had taken form and she was too scared to contemplate it. She was living in two worlds, never fully accepted in either of them. But she couldn't run away forever. They were calling, drawing her near. It was time to make contact. She owed it to Charlie.

CHAPTER THIRTEEN

FRANK – 1980

Frank replayed the killing so many times in his head it became like a worn rug, loved but in need of replacing. As he left his teenage years behind, his hunger for experimentation grew. The hunt was as thrilling as the kill. He wasn't one of those spree killers he read about in his magazines. He was happy to play the long game, even if it meant waiting years. That way he never got caught. Getting one over on the police made him feel invincible, and he was only doing their job for them after all. If they weren't able to bring justice to the drug dealers and paedophiles then he was happy to do it for them.

He was amused to discover he was not the only one lurking in the shadows. That evening, as he dragged his feet through the damp grass, the lone figure of a man swigging from a brown paper bag aroused his attention. The man's brown leather aviator hat obscured his face and his bulbous nose was flanked by the furry ear flaps either side of his jowls. The trees bordering the playing fields provided ample cover and Frank followed the man's gaze to the young boys playing football on the green. He had seen the old man before, leaning against the black spiked fence surrounding the local playground. The curious thing was that none of the children seemed to know who he was. Frank tilted his head and narrowed his eyes like a crow about to pick at a worm. This one was worthy of his attention. Pre-empting his next move, Frank cut through the fields and hid behind the black thorny undergrowth at the back of the boys' changing rooms. His suspicions paid off. As the game ended, the lecherous old man ambled to the back of the small brick building and peered through the gap in the open frosted windows. Frank watched, disgusted, as the man's breath quickened, hands fumbling for pleasure under his coat. Hatred rose within, tinged with satisfaction at his find. The man had sealed his own fate, and Frank was happy to take his time delivering it.

Frank was not conventionally good looking, but his wavy black hair and dark eyes drew the girls' interest, if only briefly. His new job as a delivery driver for a local shop helped him keep a low profile, and the old dears loved the person he pretended to be. There were plenty of gossips willing to fill him in on the strange man named Stanley, who liked a drink every pension day. A retired teacher who, rumour had it, had come to Haven after leaving his job under a cloud.

Stanley's crumbling cottage had an expansive back garden, dense with thickets and briars that scratched skin and tore clothes. It was set back far from the road, having been built long before the development of the town. The only access was via a narrow lane, flanked by low drooping branches, providing homes for the bats that swooped as twilight approached. The rear garden was almost impassable, backing out onto barbed wire-enclosed fields, and nightfall cloaked the house in blackness so thick you could barely see your hands.

Twice a week, Stanley trudged half a mile down the lonely road from his house to catch the bus to town, where he bought three bottles of cheap wine. On Thursdays, he picked up his pension and treated himself to a large bottle of whiskey. In his leisure time, he visited anywhere children frequented, and Frank felt a sickness grow in his stomach the day Stanley followed a young child home. It accelerated his plans and reinforced the justifications for what lay ahead.

Frank chopped back some of the thorny bushes in the back garden for access, but not so much that anyone would notice. Soon it would all be ablaze. He had experimented with fire when he was young, and it had seemed biblical; a ritual purging of the contaminated. Frank recalled the screaming rats from his childhood, their stinking fur ablaze in his father's wooden shed. It was late afternoon, pension day. The last pension Stanley would collect.

The latch on Stanley's kitchen window was old and easy to force. Frank inhaled the smell of frying pan grease which hung heavy in the air. The living room was lit by a large gold-fringed lamp, which cast a murky yellow glow on the walls. A gold carriage clock decorated the tiled fireplace, and there were no family photos to be seen. The shabby upholstered brown chair was perfectly positioned in the corner of the living room in front of the ancient television.

Frank smiled at the convenience of it all. Stanley was a hoarder and the house was filled with stacks of newspaper which would serve as useful tinder for the fire. He would be numbed by alcohol, which would prevent him putting up a fight. The thought of touching Stanley's loathsome skin made Frank nauseous.

Frank had brought enough rope to wrap around the armchair twice. He wished he didn't need to use a gag. Listening to his victim plead for his life would have given him immense pleasure, but he couldn't risk anyone discovering the body until it was too late. Small dust clouds rose as Frank settled down behind the mismatched patterned sofa, and he hoped that Stanley would not smell the canister of fuel he brought along for the party. The scratching of a key in the front door signalled Stanley's return. Frank ducked his head and steadied his breath, his heart pounding in his chest so loud it was almost audible.

Bottles clinked in a plastic bag as Stanley rattled the door shut behind him. Minutes later the pan sizzled with bacon. Frank bided his time. Stanley hummed tunelessly as he shuffled into the living room and placed his bacon sandwich on a small round table beside his armchair. The removal of his hat revealed a shock of white hair, which he patted into place before turning on the television. Ceremonially, he draped a tartan blanket on his knees as he sat down. He did not need a glass for the bottle of whiskey held lovingly in his right hand. The *Blue Peter* theme tune filled the air, and Stanley swigged his whiskey happily as it played.

The dirty bastard, getting his rocks off watching children on the television! Frank thought, as he curled his fists, willing himself to stay put until Stanley had downed the full bottle. His legs cramped as the programme ended. At last, the empty bottle fell to the floor, and Stanley breathed a regular, contented snore. Frank flexed his leg muscles as he stretched, waiting for a reaction. Stanley was out cold. All the same, he would not take any chances. The cloth would make a nice wad in the old man's mouth should he kick up a fuss. Opening his bag, he pulled out his tape recorder, a new tool to preserve the memory. He would enjoy replaying his special time. He would relish every second.

. . .

Lying in bed that night, Frank replayed events as he stared at his ceiling. Stanley's whimpers were playing over and over, a favourite song in his collection of memories. It was by far the richest reward. He surveyed the singe marks to his forearm. He hadn't expected his jacket to catch alight, but the mission had been a success. This was a moment in his life he never wanted to forget. Frank rifled in his bedside locker and pulled out his sketchpad. Poetry was interesting, but he enjoyed drawing more. The image of Stanley tied to a chair with the rag in his mouth was a memento to be proud of. Frank chortled. The dirty old bastard hadn't known what hit him.

Viv's long frail fingers turned the pages of the local *Gazette*, and she tutted in disgust. She rarely left her bed anymore and made it quite clear that it was Frank's job to support her, now she was too ill to turn tricks for a living. Years of alcohol abuse had taken its toll, and the haggard looking woman with the wiry hair was but a whisper of who she used to be.

'I see old Stanley Rogers has gone up in flames. No loss to bad rubbish,' Viv said.

Frank feigned surprise. He relished being able to talk to someone about the murder, even if he couldn't take the credit.

'Of course you know why he did it. He was a pervo,' she continued.

'Really? Who told you that?'

'The girls on the street. He liked to do it with boys, the dirty pervo. Good riddance, I say.'

'That's not very Christian,' Frank said, taking away the tray of uneaten porridge from her bed.

'Good job I ain't no Christian then, isn't it?' His mother cackled at the joke. Frank wondered what his father would think if he could see her now, with only a few years of life left in her. It couldn't pass quick enough as far as he was concerned.

The shrill ring of the hall telephone interrupted their conversation. It had been recently purchased at his mother's insistence. Frank picked up the heavy black receiver to hear Shirley's voice, cooing soft and low.

'Frank, you didn't come to see me at work last night.'

Frank sighed, wondering why he bothered with a girl-friend at all. 'I had to stay in, to look after Viv. She had a bad turn. Anyway, you said you didn't want to see me again.'

'Oh, you know I didn't mean it. It's just that some of the things you do ... You know ... it takes me off guard.'

Frank cradled the phone against his ear as he leaned against the wall, cracking his knuckles. 'Where are you?'

'I'm in a phone box. Nobody can hear me.'

'What do you want, Shirley?' Frank said, his patience running thin. Women his own age were just too immature, and he hated the pouty tone of her voice.

'That's not very nice. I thought you'd be happy to hear from me.'

Frank shook his head. It was always the same. Sleep with a girl and then all they wanted was to talk about feelings. It was boring and predictable and always ended the same way. Admittedly, Shirley was more open than the rest. Rough sex was something she was willing to participate in, but he could tell she wasn't really enjoying it − those pleading wide eyes, her pale face framed by her dark curls. Especially when he put his hands around her milky white throat. Shirley's frightened face flashed into his memory, and he felt himself become aroused.

'I'm sorry. It's been tough balancing work and caring for

Mum. I'll come and see you tonight if you like. When do you get off?'

That should placate her and make her feel guilty for being so demanding, he thought.

'Oh, I'm sorry. How is she?'

'Not good, I was up all night with her. Her new medication has kicked in so I should be able to get away tonight.' There was no new medicine. A double up of sleeping tablets would knock her out cold. Frank smiled at the irony. He was returning the favour for all the times his mother had drugged him as a child. He could see why she'd done it now. It was a neat trick.

'All right then, but don't let me down. I get off at ten, but if you come to the pub earlier, I'll serve you some drinks on the house.'

'I'll look forward to it. See you later, sweetheart.' The words stuck in his throat, but it would be worth the payoff. This had to be the last time. He couldn't trust himself with Shirley anymore, and as needy as she was, she didn't deserve to die. But one day he would go too far. No, his next kill would be worthy; pond scum like Stanley Rogers or Michael Osborne.

As Frank washed the crockery, it all became clear. The reason the killings were such a thrill was because it was his calling. The dirty leeches that preyed on the innocent did not deserve to live, and if the police couldn't clean up the town, he would. He thrust his hands in the sink of warm water, seeking out the dirty dishes. His life caring for his sickly mother was the perfect cover up. He worked hard at blending into the background, doing all the ordinary things, having a job and occasional girlfriend. But one day he would lead people willing to carry on his good work. The natural order would come to pass, and the world would be a better place for it. His father's voice pleaded in the recesses of his mind, as it always did when he contemplated murder. *Frankie don't do this; you're a good boy.* But the voice grew weak, and the image of his father's face blurred. He couldn't even remember what he looked like anymore. Frank's thoughts grew strong. He was a man now and didn't need to listen to his daddy anymore.

CHAPTER FOURTEEN

Jennifer's muscles burned as she polished the window ledges in her bedroom. She had been up since dawn, mindlessly cleaning as she tried to work things out in her head. Until recently, the work, eat, sleep cycle was something she had grown used to as one day merged into another. But the comfort of the routine came crashing down around her as her thoughts became filled with her recent encounters. It was no secret that Johnny had pissed off some very bad people, but why would anyone want to kill Charlie? The memory of his pleading told her his death was no accident. What if there were more to come? And if so, who could help her? Their family priest had advised her as a child and for that she was grateful. But there was one thing stopping her from calling for help now. He was a stickler for church attendance and may berate her for her lack of faith. For Jennifer, turning her back on her faith was a final act of defiance. But holding on to her bitterness would only hurt her in the end. She wondered what sort of a person it made her, being angry at God for taking her mother. Perhaps the sort of person a dark entity would be attracted to.

. . .

Jennifer tried to focus during her suspect interview at work that afternoon. It was a domestic abuse incident in which the suspect had tried to strangle his wife. He had already admitted to the offence and was recounting the incident in a slow monotonous voice. Will passed her a folded post it note asking if she was all right. He could read her like a book. She gave a reassuring smile and returned her attention to the remorseful suspect.

Jennifer had settled down to the post interview paperwork when Steph marched into the office, closely followed by a suited young man. 'Ah, here you are. This is PC Ethan Cole; he's on attachment for a few days. Ethan, this is Jennifer Knight.'

Jennifer nodded an acknowledgement as Steph continued.

'Everyone here is tied up, so I've allocated him to shadow you. He's thinking about putting in for his detective's exam so don't put him off.'

Graced with a confident presence, Ethan virtually dwarfed Steph at over six feet tall. His crisp white shirt complimented his almond brown skin, and he gave Jennifer a broad smile as he extended his hand. Jennifer's eyes flickered over to her colleague Susie, who was leering from the far end of the office. Jennifer flushed as she showed Ethan to her desk.

'I'm sorry you got the short straw. I'm sure you would have preferred Westlea nick to this one.'

'Not at all.' Ethan said, the corners of his eyes crinkling as he smiled. 'They don't have much time for one-to-ones. I'm hoping I can pick your brains while I'm here.'

'Good luck with that,' Will sniggered, and Jennifer narrowed her eyes in response.

'Ethan, this is my partner, Will. Ignore everything he says, or better still, do the opposite, and you will be well on your way to becoming a fine detective.'

Jennifer had mixed feelings about being shadowed. It would be nice to have the distraction of working with Ethan but having him watch her every move would make it difficult to investigate the police system for clues of Charlie's death.

'I've got some enquiries to make with regards to a robbery we dealt with this afternoon. I was about to pick up the CCTV. Would you like to help Will with his files, or come with me?'

Ethan grinned. 'Hmmm, a ton of paperwork or going for a drive?'

Jennifer threw him the car keys. 'In that case, you're driving.'

Will pulled a face and Jennifer reciprocated with a wink as she followed Ethan to the back yard.

The beeps of the central locking system directed Ethan to the job car as he pressed the key fob. Disappointed at what awaited him, he pushed back the driver seat of the battered Ford to allow for his long legs. 'I thought CID would have a decent car.'

'You're joking, aren't you? Westlea nick gets all the good motors. We're just the poor relations.' Jennifer clicked her seatbelt into place. 'We're going to Cash Savers Pawn Brokers in the town, on 52 Central Avenue. Their CCTV scans the street outside where the suspects were believed to be hanging about before they pounced on our victim.'

'I know where that is,' he said, driving through the rear gates. Ethan flipped on the wipers as the rain began to pelt on the windscreen.

Jennifer threw him a sneaky sidelong glance. He was an improvement on most of the old codgers in Haven CID.

'Have you made an appointment to pick the CCTV up?' He said, catching her stare.

Jennifer lowered her eyes. 'No, the storeowner is keeping it for us, he said we can drop by anytime. I thought we could grab it and then pop into Tesco's so I can get something for lunch.'

Ethan hesitated at the junction, tapping his finger on the steering wheel.

'It's left,' Jennifer said.

'Yeah, I know, but I left my mobile phone at home.' Ethan turned his brown eyes on her. 'Sorry to be a nuisance, but would it be all right if I quickly collect it now?'

'All right then, five minutes won't hurt, I suppose. I wouldn't want to get in the way of any missed calls.'

'There shouldn't be, I don't know that many people in the area yet.' Ethan said.

'I'm sure there's lots of female officers in Haven that would be happy to show you around,' Jennifer grinned, smoothing over her skirt.

'So how long have you been in the job?' he asked, ramming the car into gear.

'Forever. I joined when I was eighteen. You?'

'Not long, I've just finished my probation. I was travelling before that. I thought I should settle down, so I decided to give CID a try.'

Jennifer raised an eyebrow. 'So you joined when you were …'

'Twenty-five. I'm twenty-seven now.'

'Oh, you're only a baby then,' she smiled.

Ethan beamed, revealing a row of perfect white teeth. 'I've been called many things, a baby isn't one of them.'

The car pulled up onto a pretty tree lined brick drive, and

Jennifer surveyed the two-story building in wonder. 'Nice house,' she thought out loud.

'It's my mom's. She lives in America now but uses this as a base to visit.'

'Ah, I thought I heard an American twang.'

'My accent's a bit of a jumble with all my travelling. Come inside, I'll make you a coffee.'

Jennifer glanced at her watch, reasoning she could spare time for a break. 'Go on then, I'm gagging for a cuppa.'

Two white pillars flanked the wide front door. Ethan produced a set of keys from his pocket and went inside. The hall was warm and welcoming, and she followed him to the living room on the right. Beautiful trinkets from exotic lands decorated each room, and artwork delivered colourful splashes to the pale walls. Jennifer looked approvingly at the clean surfaces, complemented by the modern interior design. In the kitchen, Ethan filled the percolator and the smell of roasting coffee filled the air.

Jennifer dumped her things on the brown leather sofa and perused the titles on his mahogany bookshelf. The *Karma Sutra* stood out along with other titles on tantric sex. A row of leather bound books caught her eye. They were numbered one to ten but did not bear any title. She slowly slid one out and opened it, the yellowed paper giving off an old book smell. *The Occult – Realms of the Living Dead.* Jennifer picked out another, *The Occult, Significance of Blood.* She opened one more to reveal the title; *The Book of Forbidden Knowledge.*

'You like my book collection?' Ethan spoke behind her, and she jumped in surprise.

'Oh, sorry. This wasn't what I was expecting for a man of your age,' Jennifer said sheepishly, sliding the books back where she found them.

'They're vintage. I picked them up while on my travels. What were you expecting, *Beano* annuals?' Ethan laughed.

'No, of course not,' she replied, smiling in apology.

'I'm just teasing. Can I make you a sandwich? Chicken salad OK?'

'Yes please.' Jennifer said, as he opened the fridge door. Her mouth began to water at the sight of the sandwich on thick wholegrain bread. Slices of avocado lined the chicken and lettuce, with a covering of mayonnaise. An open bowl of kettle chips was placed beside her plate, and a saucer held chocolate brownies.

Ethan poured fresh coffee into Jennifer's cup and pushed the bowl of sugar and a tiny jug of cream towards her. She took a napkin and dabbed her lips before taking a crisp. 'This beats Tesco's.'

'It's no trouble. I can't take credit for the brownies, though; they're shop bought.'

'So, tell me, what's a successful young man like you doing in Haven? Or is that being too forward?' Jennifer took another bite of her sandwich to shut herself up.

'No, it's OK,' Ethan said 'People ask me that all the time, where I'm from, what I'm doing here. My mother is African American, and my dad is British. She met him when she was here on business. It didn't work out, so she went back to Washington. Against her advice, I came over here to meet my dad and decided to stay. I guess joining the police was an act of rebellion.'

'I can think of more rebellious things to do. Are you in it for the long haul?'

'To be honest I'm not sure, that's why I'm shadowing you.' Ethan's eyes met hers. 'What about you? Are you happy in the police?'

Jennifer chewed the last of her sandwich and washed it down with coffee that was so hot it burnt her throat. 'I can't imagine doing anything else,' she said, clearing up her crumbs. 'Anyway, time is ticking and we've got CCTV to view.' She began to feel guilty, playing lady of the manor while Will was buried in work.

They made it to the pawn shop just in time. A far cry from the organised Cash Converters down the road, Mr Marshall's dimly lit shop was a disorganised clutter mountain. Jennifer squeezed past the jumble of furniture, unwanted exercise equipment and locked cabinets, inhaling the musty smell of items long since forgotten. A stag's head glared from the wall of the back room, beside shelves piled with old books and outdated televisions. As Jennifer stared at the grainy image on the CCTV, her thoughts returned to Charlie. Perhaps she could distract Ethan long enough to make some enquiries when she got back to the office. She looked at her watch. 'Can you do the house to house enquiries while I take a quick statement from Mr. Marshall please?'

Ethan nodded as he took down details of the time of the robbery in his notebook.

Jennifer seized the CCTV disc as evidence and took a statement from the small grey-haired shop owner, who had lived in the area all his life.

Removing his horn-rimmed glasses, he rubbed the indents from the bridge of his nose. 'Poor old Ethel, she pawned her wedding ring to get that money. One of my regulars she is, Ethel has been coming in here every month since her old man died. She'd save her few pennies to buy back her ring, and then she'd get some bill and end up pawning it again. I don't have many regulars these days, not with these blooming payday loans springing up all over the place, but at least I don't rob people blind like they do.' Mr. Marshall was about to launch into another tirade when Jennifer brought his attention back to the task in hand.

'We've interviewed the suspects, but they're denying everything.'

Mr. Marshall shook his head. 'I don't know why they pulled a knife on her. She's over eighty years old. She would have just given it to them.'

'I know, it's awful. At least she wasn't hurt.' Jennifer quickly penned a statement covering the seizure of the CCTV and handed it to him to sign. His watery eyes magnified like saucers as he put his glasses on and read over it, signing the bottom of the page in a scrawl. Jennifer recollected the old Mr. Magoo cartoons she watched as a child. 'Of course, in my day they would have got a good clip around the ear. I don't suppose you can do that anymore, can you?'

'No, I'm afraid not, although I've felt like it often enough. Mr. Marshall, can you hang onto the footage from the previous few days for us, please? I'd like to ask one of our community support officers to look through it, in case we're missing anything.'

'Yes, yes of course. They know they're welcome here for a cuppa any time.'

Jennifer said her goodbyes and walked back to the car to wait for Ethan. Her phone beeped into life with two texts. The first was from Will asking for lunch. Jennifer quickly replied and moved on to the next one from Susie.

Who's the stud muffin? Is he on our team? Jennifer smiled, and quickly stuffed the phone into her jacket pocket as Ethan climbed into the car.

'No luck I'm afraid. They're all saying ... and I quote ... "Ain't seen nuffing."'

The words sounded out of place coming from Ethan and she tried not to laugh. 'Time to head back to the nick then,' she said, starting the car.

· · ·

Jennifer placed the bag of food on Will's desk. 'How are you getting on?'

Will shook his head. 'Not good. Looks like they're going to walk. The witnesses failed to pick them out from photo ID. We've no weapon and no CCTV. The only incriminating evidence is the hundred quid they had on them when they were stopped. It sticks in my gut that we'll have to give it back to them.'

'We don't even have enough to go to the CPS?'

'No, I've spoken to the DI. It doesn't meet the threshold test. He's said if nothing comes back on the CCTV he'll authorise a no further action.'

Jennifer groaned. 'I'm not happy to NFA yet. How about we bail them for a couple of weeks, issue a local press appeal and make some more enquiries?'

'Sure, if it makes you happy. But you're wasting your time. Nobody's going to come forward.'

Jennifer thought of Ethel, sitting at home alone, too scared to leave her house.

'There's no harm in letting them stew. I can justify the bail back.'

Will shrugged his shoulders. 'As long as they're answering to you. Run it by the DI and make a date.'

The rest of the working day passed without event. Will managed to rope Ethan into some mundane enquiries, and Jennifer took the opportunity to do some digging on Charlie Taylor's case. DS Trevor Lowe's phone extension flashed up on the police online telephone directory, and she punched in the numbers. They had had a brief dalliance before he met his wife and lost touch. While he progressed to sergeant, her career had steadily plummeted until she had found herself at the last chance saloon. He seemed happy to hear from her, if a bit hesitant.

'Jennifer. You only ever call me when you want something.

Wouldn't it be nice if you just called to say hello instead of asking for a favour?'

'Charming. I was only calling to say hello. How are you?'

'I'm fine thank you.'

'And the family?'

'All good. What's this really about?'

'Nothing. I'm glad you're well, just called to say hello.' Jennifer hung up the phone and grinned. She pressed the redial button, knowing her name would be flashing up on DS Lowe's telephone.

'Jennifer?'

'Detective Sergeant Lowe, I need a favour.'

'Funny. Real funny. I am quite busy, believe it or not. What are you after?'

Jennifer began to wind the phone cord around her fingers. 'It's about Charlie Taylor. I was wondering if you have any updates.'

'Ah yes, you spoke to him in custody.'

'Me and lots of other people who asked him to wind his neck in.'

'Did he say anything of interest? We've got the CCTV back, but the audio's cut out.'

Jennifer did her best to sound offhand. 'He rambled on. He seemed very drunk, shouting and crying, didn't make a lot of sense. Is it a murder investigation?'

DS Lowe lowered his voice. 'I have to be careful what I say. The neighbour who found him went to the papers and they came up with this daft spontaneous combustion theory.'

'And what do you think?' Jennifer said, twirling the phone cord in her fingers.

'Between you and me, I don't think this will be going any further. Charlie liked a drink, and given all the bottles of booze around him, it's no wonder he went up like a match.

The furniture was flame retardant and it was just lucky the rest of the house didn't take.'

'I thought as much myself.'

'Listen, can you write me up a statement on what you spoke about in custody? I'll need to dot the I's and cross the T's.'

'Sure, I'll do it today.'

Jennifer drummed her fingers on the desk as she went through the possibilities. She wanted to tell DS Lowe the truth. There was foul play, but perhaps not of the human variety. But what evidence did she have? Both Johnny and Charlie had appeared fine one minute, then as if they were someone else the next. The classic signs of schizophrenia played out in front of her. But that voice ... The words they had used, the mannerisms. If something supernatural *was* invading their bodies, how did it know so much about her? DS Lowe would not be much help with that sort of investigation. He would merely have a quiet word with her DI, and she would be back up to occupational health so fast her feet wouldn't touch the ground. For now, behaving normally was the only way to protect herself while she figured all this out.

The ladies' toilets in Haven police station left a lot to be desired. The absence of windows left them with a distinctly tainted smell, offset by the mechanical air freshener, which squeaked into life every hour. She shook her hands under the soft whirr of the dryer, and inwardly groaned as Susie walked in, her eyes wide with excitement.

'You didn't answer my text. Who's the eye candy?'

'Ethan? He's on an attachment for the next couple of weeks.' Jennifer gave up on the dryer and wiped her hands on her clothes instead.

Susie wasn't going to let her go that quickly. 'He can

attach himself to me anytime. Is he single? You'd better get in there, girl.'

Jennifer whispered, 'I've no intention of getting anywhere. He's seven years younger than me.'

'That's OK, you can be one of them, um … panthers.'

Jennifer snickered, 'Do you mean cougar?'

Barging through the door with the grace of a baby elephant, Steph's presence put a stop to their giggling, and the pair cast their eyes to the floor as they returned to work.

Jennifer remained tight-lipped as she showed the last of the suspects out, his bail sheet in hand. The pimply youth gave her a leery grin as he left via the front exit. 'See ya later, babe.'

'It's 'officer' to you, and just make sure you answer your bail date,' she said.

'I won't need to, I'll be NFA before then,' he sneered, pulling up his grubby tracksuit bottoms.

Jennifer rolled her eyes as she closed the door behind him. He was in and out of custody so often, he knew the police terms off by heart. He could have papered his walls with the 'no further action' letters that came through his letterbox, and unless a star witness turned up, this time would be no different. She checked her watch; she was late off again. Will had left half an hour ago, and she was surprised to see Ethan sitting at her desk on the phone. His soothing voice murmured comforting syllables, and he gave her a nod as he ended the conversation. Jennifer booked off duty and logged off her computer.

'Aren't you going home?' she asked Ethan as he hung up.

'I was updating the victim. She's very upset.'

'I know, I spoke to her earlier. I've asked one of the PCSO's to pop in on her every now and again.' Jennifer searched the drawers for her mobile phone.

Ethan slid it out from underneath some paperwork. 'Fancy going out for a drink?'

Jennifer paused, 'Sorry mate, I'm bushed.'

Ethan cleared his throat. 'Sorry, that sounded like a come on, didn't it? I just wanted to chat with you about the job, no ulterior motive, I promise.'

Jennifer shifted awkwardly, trying to find the right words. 'I didn't think that at all, I'm just tired. Next time, yeah? Maybe Will can come too.'

Jennifer walked to her car, cursing herself for turning Ethan down. She was acting like some hormonal teenager, when the poor guy just wanted to make friends. A chilled wind whistled around her legs and the street lamps cast a weak orange glow over the houses and derelict buildings either side of the road.

Approaching footsteps interrupted her chain of thought, and she exhaled in relief as the man behind her crossed the road and pulled out some keys to enter one of the houses. It was the same every late shift. A nearby homeless shelter brought groups of men to the area at night, and despite being a police officer, the short walk to her car made her nervous. But something told her this was different, and the image of a dark figure gripping a knife flashed violently into her mind. It was a warning; far too real to be her imagination. She pulled her car keys from her bag, threading the cold pointed metal through the first and second fingers of her clenched fist.

Don't turn around, whispers echoed in her mind, offering protection. *This is not the time for confrontation.*

Jessica's breath hitched as she recognised the voice. It was Charlie Taylor, her old schoolteacher ... but it couldn't be. Every sense switched to high alert as she pulled her coat tightly around her. Quickening her steps, she approached her car. Her legs shaking, she floored her car all the way home.

CHAPTER FIFTEEN

The maple trees in her back garden were beautiful in the spring, but tonight the bare branches conducted the wind into a symphony of howls. She pulled the curtains shut, turning to answer the phone as Amy's name lit up on the display.

'Hi Sis, everything all right?' Jennifer strained to listen over the background noise of children's TV. She was still shaken after her walk to her car and needed to hear a friendly voice.

Amy sighed, 'Oh you know, the usual. Lily isn't sleeping, I'm exhausted.'

'I'm happy to babysit on my days off, give you guys a break.'

'I'll take you up on it when she's a bit older. I'm planning her christening, Father Kelly is coming around to go through it.'

'Oh right, let me know when you decide a date as I'll need to take time off work.' The christening could be the best way of testing the waters with Father Kelly.

The baby's screams pierced through the theme song to *In The Night Garden* and Jennifer held the phone from her ear. 'Sounds like you're busy, I'll leave you to it.'

'Wait, I want to ask you something. Will you be Lily's godmother?'

Jennifer paused. 'Aww, thanks Sis, but wouldn't you be better off with someone more virtuous?'

Amy laughed. 'Thankfully, being virtuous isn't a prerequisite. You're still a Catholic, aren't you?'

Jennifer pursed her lips as she considered her answer. 'Lapsed,' she replied. Memories of being dragged to mass every Sunday came to the forefront of her mind.

'That's good enough for me, come around when you've got a day off and we can discuss it,' Amy said, ending the conversation to tend to her screaming baby.

The next morning Jennifer pulled on her jeans and sweatshirt, hoping a walk in the park would clear her head. She combed her dark hair back into a ponytail. Pulling on her jacket, her fingers wrapped around a cold, solid object in the right hand pocket. 'What the hell?' she said, pulling out a bent spoon. She searched her brain, trying to remember the last time she had worn the coat.

'*Jenny*,' a low voice whispered in her ear, its icy breath raking her skin.

Jennifer yelped as if she had been slapped, throwing the spoon to the floor. Every fibre of her being told her to run, but she forced herself to stand her ground. She wasn't just scared. She was angry. Charlie's face came to mind. Had it been like this for him? The voices driving him mad until he died? Her eyes darted to the door, ready to bolt any minute. The atmosphere became thick and heavy. Closing her eyes, she sensed oppression, hate, and ... death. It was coming too fast, it was powerful, and she wasn't strong enough to fight it. A voice whispered in her consciousness.

Let it go. It's too strong. It was a voice she recognised from somewhere beyond reach. She gripped her hand around the door handle to leave, but the metal refused to budge. 'Get out of my home,' she said, rattling the door handle for release. 'You don't have permission to be here.' Suddenly, the door flew from her grasp, banging against the adjoining wall and cracking the plaster. Fumbling in her jacket pocket for her keys, she took the stairs two at a time, escaping outside into the fresh air.

Slamming her foot onto the clutch, she shoved the car into gear. It lurched forward, jerking in protest. She pressed the accelerator, swearing as she did so. The car sped forward. She fought to control her breathing, telling herself not to panic. Whatever it was, it was gone. But she could not shake off the feeling of helplessness that enveloped her. She had to communicate to find out who it was, and what it wanted. Yet its presence was so strong, she could not deal with it on her own.

Steph was rushing out of the office just as Jennifer walked in to start her afternoon shift. 'No time to talk,' she said, brushing past her.

'What's going on? Where is everyone?' Jennifer said to Will, who sat with his chin in his hands.

'I'm really pissed off with the way we're treated in here. I've a good mind to put in for a transfer.'

'No one else will have you, sick note, now stop

complaining and tell me what's going on.' Will grimaced at the sound of his old nickname. Pulling too many sick days was what had got him transferred to Haven, and while Jennifer knew he wanted to put it all behind him, she could not resist teasing him.

'There's a big drug bust running in Lexton.'

'Oh, right.' Jennifer sighed and picked up the paperwork left on her desk.

'Is that all you have to say? I thought you'd blow your top when you heard we were being knocked back again. Even Susie and Ethan were asked to go, and they've been here no length.'

Jennifer flicked through the paperwork. 'Whatever, I don't care. How about you make me a coffee so we can make a start on these robberies?'

'I'm not making anything until you tell me what's wrong.'

Jennifer's computer monitor flickered in silence. 'You'd only laugh.'

Will forgot all about his bad mood as he took on Jennifer's troubles. 'Try me.'

Jennifer paused. Perhaps it was time to confide in Will, to give him some credit for being her friend. She took a deep breath. 'There's been some weird stuff happening in my house.' She examined his face for a change in expression, a grin, a flicker of amusement. Nothing. Will stared in stony silence. Jennifer gathered her courage. 'You know how I told you I heard whispers in my head? I thought I had it under control, but now I'm getting headaches every time I try to block them out.' Jennifer looked around the room, making sure they were alone. 'But now it's in the house. At first, I thought there was a break in, or at least someone messing around, moving things, making noise. But it's not.'

Will frowned. 'What do you think it is?'

'I can't make sense of it. Sometimes I hear the faintest

whisper, like someone calling my name. Not in my head, I can actually feel their breath on my face. I'm not imagining it.'

'Blimey girl, that *is* weird.'

'I'm not going mad if that's what you're thinking.'

'I didn't say that, but you have been through a hell of a lot.'

'Will please don't try to turn this back on me. I'm asking for your help here and all you can suggest is that I'm going mad.'

'I never said anything of the kind. I'm just trying to get my head around it. We should go back and check the place out.'

'What about work?'

'We've got plenty of time to deal with that. C'mon, we'll be there and back in under an hour.'

Will was silent on the journey to her home, his face a picture of consternation. Jennifer peeped across, trying not to make it obvious. For once she wished he would rattle on, talking about 'the injustice of it all' as he put the world to rights. But not today. Today his thoughts were hidden, secretive.

He braked at the traffic lights and stared at the road ahead. 'How long has this been going on?'

Jennifer rolled her eyes. 'Here we go … you *do* think I'm losing it, don't you?'

Will raised his hands from the steering wheel. 'Jesus, did I say that? You said you've heard voices and I asked how long. You're so defensive, I'm only trying to help.'

Jennifer nodded at the road ahead. 'The lights are green. And I'm not schizophrenic. I've heard whispers. There's a difference.'

The car lurched forward as he put his foot down.

'And quit muttering, I can hear you.'

'Sorry, Mum.' Will's mischievous grin warmed her from the inside out.

She sat back and tried to relax. At least he cared enough to check it out. Surely it meant he believed her? The tick tock of the indicator signalled they were home.

Jennifer's front door creaked as she opened it, and Will mouthed the words, 'me first,' as he placed a hand on her arm. She stood back with an amused smile, wondering what he would do if he heard something. Will checked out the living room and kitchen before walking into the dining room.

'Is it OK if I check upstairs?'

'Knock yourself out. Just keep out of my knicker drawer.'

Will blushed. 'Spoilsport.'

Jennifer tiptoed up the stairs behind Will, feeling silly. The house looked less threatening in his presence and she knew nothing would happen while he was there.

'Has anything else happened up here?' Will asked, standing on the landing with his hands in his pockets, a stance that suggested he didn't expect anything to jump out anytime soon.

She shook her head, then clicked her fingers as she remembered. 'The spoon, it should be in here on the floor.'

She strode into the bedroom and dropped on her hands and knees on the carpet, looking for the bent cutlery.

'It's gone,' she said, looking under the bed. She turned back to see Will staring dreamily at her backside. 'Do you mind?'

'Sorry,' he coughed. 'You mentioned a spoon?'

'What's the point? Let's just go.'

'Maybe you should think about indoor CCTV.'

'I'll be fine, forget I said anything. '

'If it's any comfort I can't see any signs of disturbance. It was probably some kids playing outside.'

'Yeah,' she said, brushing the carpet fibres from her

clothes. The concern in his eyes reflected that he'd been pacifying her all along. She vowed to keep her problems to herself in the future.

She returned to work and won a minor victory in the form of a charge for two robbers who had stolen a day's takings from a newsagent's shop. She sat back at her desk and stretched as Ethan breezed in. 'There you are. I was looking for you.'

'Sorry, I've been busy with some robbers. They had a plastic gun. Quality stuff.'

He swayed with his hands in his pockets, a smile creeping onto his face. 'Fancy coming out for that drink tonight?'

Ethan's very expensive aftershave called for a closer inspection and Jennifer smiled. 'It's Friday night. You should be out clubbing with girls your own age, not listening to war stories from a washed up detective.'

Will would have made a joke about it, but Ethan was not Will. He perched himself on the corner of her desk. 'You're not washed up and I like war stories. How about it?'

Jennifer sighed. Ethan was nice, but he was starting to chase her around like a puppy when she had other things on her mind. All the same, she found herself agreeing.

'Great,' he said, jumping onto his feet. He whistled as he strolled down the corridor. She just could not figure him out. Was he just looking for friendship or something else? Her attention was drawn to Will, drumming his fingers loudly on the desk as he stared at his computer.

'All right there, mate?' Jennifer asked.

'Sure. Just finishing this file and going home.'

Ethan was waiting as promised. As they walked into town, Jennifer was grateful that the rain had decided to stay away. She felt a pang of guilt for not asking Will along, but he had skulked off without saying goodbye. 'So where are we going?' Jennifer asked, following Ethan's long stride. He walked with his jacket flung over his shoulder, immune to the night breeze. 'The King's Head. It's not too busy in there. Everywhere else is full of kids.'

'Oh, hark at you, just what age are you again?'

Ethan smiled. 'I've been around a lot longer than you give me credit for.'

The walk was short and Jennifer kept her hands busy rifling in her purse. 'I owe you a drink after that nice lunch you made me.'

'No, you don't,' he said. 'You're paying me in war stories remember?'

The glow of an open fire and low-beamed ceiling made the pub a cosy haunt as soft music played.

Ethan glanced at the wine menu. 'I think you are a Shiraz lady... am I right?'

'Yes, how did you know?'

'Lucky guess.' Ethan handed the barman some money. 'A bottle of Shiraz and a Jack Daniels and ice, please.'

'I hope this bottle isn't for me, I only came out for a glass.' Jennifer said. She took out her purse, but Ethan waved it away.

'Please. I asked you out, remember?' He poured the wine and handed her a glass.

The wine was smooth and tasted delicious. A warm glow spread through Jennifer as Ethan topped up her glass. 'I'm driving, Ethan, I can't have any more than one.'

'Don't be silly, I'll have one drink and drop you home later. Enjoy yourself. When do you ever get out?'

The fact that Ethan knew about Jennifer's lack of social life surprised her. He had only been in the office a short while and already knew she was a virtual recluse. Smiling weakly, she took another sip. He was right. What else had she to go home to?

Half a bottle of wine later, she had warmed up nicely. The open fire crackled and Jennifer inhaled the scent of pinecones.

The hours passed as they swapped stories, the focus on her experiences in the criminal investigation department. Ethan was easy company and she felt a connection with him, although confused at where their new friendship was heading.

'Ever come across anything weird?'

Jennifer took another sip and smiled. 'They're all weird.'

'That's not what I meant.' Ethan shifted in his seat. 'You know I'm into the supernatural, right? Ever experienced anything you couldn't explain?'

Jennifer's defences rose. She didn't know him well enough yet to share her recent experiences, and she wasn't sure she trusted him either. 'Is this about the Charlie Taylor case? Because that's recent and I shouldn't be discussing it with anyone.'

Ethan's face fell. 'I just meant in general.'

Jennifer folded her arms. 'I'm bored talking about me. Tell me about your travels instead.'

Ethan picked at his beer mat as he told Jennifer of the places he visited, and she sensed his disappointment at her reluctance to open up to him.

As they drove to Jennifer's home, she wondered if she should invite him inside. Wine had quietened her inhibitions. She pointed out her house and he pulled up outside. Nerves bubbled up inside her as she pulled together the courage to ask him in. 'Thanks for a lovely night,' she said, noticing he was keeping the engine running.

Ethan smiled. 'I enjoyed it. I'll see you tomorrow then?'

'Yeah, good night,' Jennifer said, as she got out of the car. She pushed her key in the front door as he drove away, heat rising to her cheeks. It was her own fault she felt humiliated. Why on earth did she think that someone like Ethan would be interested in her? Throwing her keys on the dresser, Jennifer undressed for bed, wondering what the last few hours had really been all about.

CHAPTER SIXTEEN

Jennifer watched Will's fingers clacked furiously on the keyboard. It was a mean feat, given that he could not touch type at all. The quick turnover from a late shift to days was never a welcome one, and his grumpy expression suggested he would have preferred to stay in bed.

'Have a good night?' Will asked, barely lifting his eyes from the computer monitor.

'It was OK. I don't suppose you've got any painkillers?' Jennifer delivered an apologetic smile.

Will scanned the computer screen and jabbed the back-space button several times. 'No, and I don't have much sympathy either.'

Heads turned in the office as Jennifer's voice rose an octave. 'Bloody hell, Will, you spend weeks laughing at my pathetic social life, then moan at me when I go out! What am I meant to do?'

'No mate, you go out all you want. You're obviously far too good for the likes of me.'

Jennifer rested her jacket on the back of her seat before sitting next to him. Lowering her voice, she leaned over his desk. 'If I'm honest, Ethan's a bit flash for my liking. Why don't we go out tonight just you and me? I hear there's a good comedian on at The Crown.'

A smile played on Will's lips as he jabbed at his keyboard.

'C'mon, it'll be a laugh. What about it?' Jennifer said, folding her arms. It was the classic sign of shutting down. Either he agree now or she wouldn't ask again.

'OK, just don't bin me off again.' He glanced at the fresh puddle of coffee on his desk, and quickly wiped it with his suit sleeve before Jennifer started attacking him with wet wipes.

The day consisted of investigating burglaries, visiting pawnshops, and processing prisoners. Ethan was working with another team and for that, Jennifer was grateful. Her phone beeped to signal a text. *Fancy coming to The Ivy tonight? I have a spare reservation. Ethan*

She blinked at the screen. It was wasted on her. She was just as happy with fish and chips and a bottle of plonk. She texted a reply. *Sorry, can't. Going out with Will.* She turned off her phone and slid it into her pocket. She jumped as Will shouted from across the room.

'Oi, rat face, I'm going to the sandwich shop. Want your usual?'

'Yes please, and a can of Coke.' Jennifer smiled. Will knew her little habits. It was a shame he didn't believe the stuff going on in her head. To be fair, sometimes she wasn't sure if she believed it herself.

Jennifer was on hold to the CPS when Will returned with a sandwich and a box of pain killers. Such calls to the Crown Prosecution Service could take up to an hour to process. Pressing the mute button on the phone, she cast an eye over his salad on rye. 'No sausage and egg then?'

Will flicked the metal ring pull from his diet coke. 'I'm on a diet, as it happens.'

She blurted a laugh. 'You? A diet? The next thing you'll be telling me you've joined a gym.'

He reddened, and Jennifer stifled a giggle.

'You have, haven't you? Which one?'

'I'm not telling you so you can take the piss out of me, now eat your lunch and shut your gob.'

'That's a bit tricky.' Jennifer snickered.

A rolled up ball of paper came winging her way.

Jennifer was one of the few intelligence trained officers on duty and the minute she saw Samantha walk in, she knew she would not be going off duty on time. PC Samantha Hanlon was new on the prisoner processing team. A dedicated officer, she squeezed as much as she could out of prisoners before allowing them out of custody. Samantha turned her doe eyes on Jennifer as she made a request for an intelligence approach. Jennifer hadn't the heart to turn her down, especially now they had targets to reach.

Bradley Morris, known as 'Bacon Bradders,' sat in the stuffy interview room wearing a custody issue tracksuit. A sixty-five year old man with a weather-beaten face, barely a month went by before he was hauled into the custody block for petty crime. His usual M.O. was stealing packets of bacon from supermarkets, which had earned him his nickname. Such activity funded his alcohol addiction, and all the rehabilitation in the world would not change his ways. The custody tracksuits were changed from grey to bright red in the hope that they would become less popular with the local clientele, who never returned them. The garish colour also had the bonus of making them very easy to spot when they were out in the town. Bradley had no such concerns of fashion and was glad of something warm and clean to wear.

He squinted at Jennifer and she remembered him telling her he owned glasses but had given up wearing them as he was fed up with them getting lost every time he went on a bender.

'Look miss, I'm dying for a fag and I just want to get out of here,' he said, chewing what was left of his grubby thumbnail.

'Bradley, I'll give it to you straight. You give me some information and if it's juicy enough, we will tell the court you've been cooperative. It might help your case.'

Bradley raised his chin defiantly. 'I don't help coppers.'

Jennifer leaned forward, detecting the smell of stale cigarettes. 'This is about helping yourself. You must have something we can use.' She was all ready to tick the non-compliant box when he spoke up.

'I'll tell you what's dodgy, Johnny Mallet doing himself in. I reckon someone made him do it.'

Jennifer's heart quickened as she poised her pen to take notes. 'Any proof to back this up?'

'No. But he started hanging around with someone before he died. Johnny said they gave him free booze. I told him; you don't get nothing for free in this world. A few weeks later, Johnny was acting messed up, talking in some weird voice. He said Shelly was next.' Bradley scratched his head. 'It's bugged me ever since. I know everyone on these streets, but whoever seen Johnny is covering their tracks.'

'What about Shelly, have you seen her since?'

Bradley sighed, appearing desperate for a drink to fix his shaking hands. 'Well, that's the other thing. I reckon she knows more than she's letting on. That's all I can tell ya.'

'Thanks Bradley. This is worth a follow up.'

. . .

The conversation with Bradley played on Jennifer's mind as she pulled her black Converse sneakers from under the bed. She didn't need to dress up where she was going. The phone rang just as she pulled them on. It was not the silent calls that plagued her but Will. 'I don't know if I can make it tonight,' he said, without so much as a 'hello'.

Jennifer's heart plummeted. 'Why not?'

'Some bastard slashed my tyres. I can't get them replaced until Monday.'

'Oh mate, I'm sorry to hear that. Any idea who did it?'

'I don't know. I reckon they used a knife or a screwdriver. Could be anyone.'

'Have you called it in?'

'Yeah, I'll write my own statement. Uniform have enough to do. It means I won't be able to pick you up though.'

'I'll pick you up; you can have a few drinks. Sounds like you need them.'

'All right then, if you don't mind. See you in half an hour?'

'Yeah, will do.'

Jennifer hung up, and a text beeped into life. *'You gonna make me dine alone tonight? Ethan.'*

A chill ran up her spine. Did Ethan have anything to do with Will's tyres being slashed? Jennifer shook the thought away. As if anyone would do that, just to date her. She replied with a '*Sorry*' and secured the house before leaving.

The aroma of stale beer lingered in the air as Jennifer followed Will downstairs to McClusky's basement club. The place was heaving with students keen to take advantage of the Saturday night burger and beer deal. Her eyes adjusted to the dim light as Will squeezed them into a corner table.

McClusky's was their favourite haunt, and they enjoyed laughing at the rubbish acts on stage.

Will wolfed his quarter pounder, stopping only to take a swig of beer. 'I've been living off lettuce leaves all week,' he said in his defence.

Jennifer took a mouthful of wine, taking a break from her oversized burger. Recent events had suppressed her appetite, and her stomach felt like she had swallowed a brick. 'Will, what do you know about Ethan?'

Will swigged his pint and wiped his mouth with the back of his hand. 'He's just some rich kid playing at detective. Why?'

'He invited me to The Ivy, and I turned him down to come out with you.'

'The Ivy? I am honoured. Not that I blame you though, I'm not in for all that fine dining crap. What did he say when you told him you were coming out with me?'

'I didn't. I said I was out with a mate,' she lied, not wishing to plant a seed of suspicion in Will's mind.

'You don't think he had anything to do with my tyres being slashed, do you?' Will frowned.

'Oh God no. It's probably one of those little scroats you nicked last week. C'mon, forget about it. The second half is coming on.'

Jennifer dropped Will home at the end of the show and walked him from her car to his flat to ensure he got in OK. He was cute when he was drunk. He leaned forward and twirled her hair, trying hard not to slur his words. 'You look lovely tonight.'

Jennifer giggled, steering him back onto the pavement.

Will threw his arm around her shoulder as she did so. 'When are we going to get it together?'

'We are together. We're bessie mates, aren't we?' Jennifer was amused by Will's comments, but she had no intention of spoiling a good friendship with sex.

Will giggled. 'Ah now, you know what I mean.'

Jennifer fished the house key from his jacket pocket and shoved it in the door, shushing him to quieten down. 'Yes, and I also know you are very drunk.'

He kissed her on the cheek and she accepted a hug, wishing things could be different.

'Jennifer, it's Steph. Sorry to call so early, did I wake you?'

Jennifer fumbled with her phone, wishing she hadn't answered it. 'Oh, hello Sarge, it's time I was getting up. What's wrong?'

'I was just wondering if you could come in for a couple of hours' overtime today. We've had a spate of distraction burglaries on elderly residents, and we need house-to-house enquiries.'

'Right, yeah, I'll make my way in,' Jennifer rubbed her eyes. There were worse things than getting paid overtime to speak to some old dears.

If the gnomes bordering the garden of number 52 Maple Drive didn't give the game away, the mobility scooter parked at the side of the house did. Elderly residents occupied all the houses on the pretty tree-lined street, and they were rich pickings for the predators that preyed on the vulnerable. Distraction burglaries were rife in the area, and the occupants of Maple Drive were trusting. Jennifer inhaled the sweet scent of the winter beauty honeysuckle bordering the wall of the small whitewashed cottage.

She pressed the doorbell and a yapping sound signalled

her presence. 'Who is it?' a small frail voice questioned from the other side.

'Mrs Connelly, it's the police. I'm making some enquiries, there's nothing to worry about.'

'Henry, get down, go on, off with you.' The door opened, and a short white-haired lady peeped out cautiously. Her pink cardigan matched the gentle flush in her cheeks and her eyes were cloudy. Jennifer held up her warrant card.

'Come in dear, and call me Joan.' The woman beckoned her inside. 'You could be holding up anything for all I know, it's these cataracts you see.'

A small black poodle jumped up and down, a coiled spring vying for attention. 'Henry won't hurt you. If he did, I wouldn't have to worry about burglars.'

'I take it you're talking about the one yesterday evening.'

'Oh yes, I've heard all about it. Poor Mr Baxter, he only lost his wife last week. What sort of people would beat an old man black and blue for a few bits of jewellery? It's disgusting.'

'I agree. We're doing all we can to catch them, including making doorstep enquiries.'

'Have a cup of tea, dear.' It was a statement, not a question. Jennifer sat at the kitchen table as Joan busied herself warming the teapot. Fondant fancies lit up the plate in yellows, pinks and chocolate brown.

She had been to many houses like this, elderly people who were settled and happy until they were burgled, then the bubble of security burst, taking with it any sleep and filling the vacuum with a sense of loneliness. Jennifer admired the delicate china cups hanging from the oak dresser. 'Thank you,' she smiled, as she took two down, pouring a little milk and dropping in a cube of sugar with a plop.

'I'm afraid I didn't see anything, but Lillian, my neighbour told me all about it. I don't have any valuables, apart from Henry here.'

Henry rested his chin on her lap and closed his eyes as she stroked his head. He emitted a soft moan of comfort. 'He sleeps at the end of my bed.' Joan smiled warmly. 'It's lovely having a detective sitting here keeping me company. Can you spare me five more minutes of your time?'

Jennifer smiled, 'Yes, of course. What can I do for you?'

Joan's face lit up as she stood and returned to the oak dresser, pulling out a drawer. 'It's more like what I can do for you. Now, where are they, let me see ...' She rifled in the drawers, muttering softly. 'I knew when I woke up, something just told me I would give a reading today. Ah, here they are.'

Jennifer took a bite of a French fondant. In for a penny, she thought, briefly closing her eyes as the delicious creaminess melted on her tongue. She placed the empty wrapper on the saucer and drained the last of her tea.

Joan appeared to have taken on a new energy as she joined her. She allowed the deck of tarot cards to slide out of the red velvet pouch and lay a magnifying glass on the lace tablecloth. A cold breeze swept past as Joan shuffled the deck with expertise.

'I don't know if this is a good idea,' Jennifer said quietly, her eyes never leaving the gold-rimmed deck of cards, the edges feathered and worn from years of use.

'There's nothing to be afraid of, dear.' She paused. Her eyes were gently pleading as they looked into hers. 'Please? It won't work if you're closed to it.'

Jennifer slowly nodded. 'Go on, then.'

Joan returned her attention to the deck of cards that were now spread face down on the table. The only sound in the house was the soft snore of the poodle laid at her feet, accompanied by the tick of a grandfather clock in the hall.

'Pick out three cards,' she said solemnly. Jennifer tapped three cards with her forefinger, and Joan lay them face down in front of her. Picking up her magnifying glass, she studied the cards. 'These three cards represent past, present and future. We will begin with the past.' Joan slowly turned the card over. 'This is the eight of cups. It represents change and transition. Leave the stagnant past behind and face new challenges, the unfamiliar, something which will be more fulfilling in the future. But only if you can walk away from what you are holding on to.'

The words struck home. The memories of Jennifer's traumatic childhood were something she desperately needed to leave behind. Joan's magnified eye surveyed the next card. The image of a tower lay in front of her. 'This is your present. You are busy making foundations for challenges to come, but will they last? You must ensure your foundations are strong if you are to get through what lies ahead.' Joan sighed while she stared at the card, seeing more than the picture in front of her. 'This is not material strength; I see it in the form of relationships, love, people you can depend on. I fear some of your foundations may let you down when you need them the most, even work against you.'

Jennifer frowned. What had started out as a bit of fun had taken on a serious tone. 'Now we move on to your future.' Joan slowly turned over the last card, and the devil image flashed in front of her. Joan's mouth set in a thin line, with no trace of the friendliness she had worn since Jennifer's arrival.

Jennifer emitted a nervous laugh. 'We're not doing very well here, are we?'

'I don't like to see this card as part of a future reading. It is a warning. You are setting up structures in your life that attracts negative influences, users and takers. You feel you are bound but you must break free. This card does not bode well for you.' Joan scanned all three cards before her with her magnifying glass, before laying it back on the table. She shook her head and spoke in a whisper; 'The darkness is all around you.'

She closed her eyes and brought her head down. Her lips moved as she mumbled to herself, clutching the small silver cross around her neck. She lifted her head, her breathing beginning to quicken. 'Oh dear, this is not good at all. I sense a child in all of this. Do you understand?'

Jennifer nodded fervently. 'Yes, I do.'

Joan waved her hand over the cards. 'Whatever happens, keep the child safe.'

'From what?'

'You will know when the time comes.' Joan shook her head as she gathered up the cards in haste. 'I'm sorry dear, but I must insist you leave.' The dog awoke and anxiously circled his owner.

'But wait,' Jennifer said, 'can't you tell me any more?'

'It's not safe, you have to go.' Joan spoke with a tinge of panic as she rose from the table. The poodle barked sharply in agreement.

Jennifer stood to find Joan's hand rested on her back, gently guiding her to the front door. Jennifer turned 'Mrs Connelly, Joan ... are you all right?'

The elderly woman undid the clasp of the cross around her neck. 'Give me your hand.'

Jennifer opened her hand and Joan dropped the chain into it, warming her palm.

'I'm not allowed to accept gifts.'

'Please. It will shield you from the darkness.'

Jennifer shook her head to protest, but Joan firmly closed Jennifer's fingers over the chain and shuffled her through the open door. 'Wear it for protection and don't take it off.'

Joan took her dog by the collar as she saw Jennifer out. He yapped in protest, his front feet off the ground, scrambling in the air to chase Jennifer off the premises.

The door slammed and Jennifer stared at the chain sitting in her palm. What the hell had just happened? She raised her hand to knock, but something stopped her. Whatever Joan had picked up on, she had felt it too. The dark cloak of oppression. A realisation overcame her. She was validated. With shaking hands, she fastened the chain around her neck. Her shock mingled with relief as she left the house.

Jennifer glanced back at the house to see Joan standing at the window. Her shoulders were heavy, her expression fearful. Just what had she seen?

CHAPTER SEVENTEEN

FRANK – 1985

Women were more trouble than they were worth. They were leading him down a dangerous path and he wasn't ready for prison. Not yet anyway. He had come so close to throttling Shirley this time. He couldn't risk seeing her again. If her old man found out ... McCarthy was a tough bastard who would beat him to a pulp for what he did to his little girl. But he would never find out, Frank had made sure of that. He had put on a show as he begged for her forgiveness, making up some cock and bull story about being abused as a child, explaining how he had been treated so badly that now sometimes he turned on the people he loved the most. Then he had produced his grand finale, a piece of poetry written just for her. A goodbye poem to his beautiful angel, the only one who understood his anguish. Soft as butter, was Shirley, and she had lapped it up. He would be sorry to see her go, she was a good shag.

It wasn't as if it was his fault. The silly bitches just wouldn't leave him alone. The worse he treated them, the more they chased, as if they were part of some tragic love story. Sure, there were a couple of times he could have got away with it, but what was the point? When he killed it had to mean something, good killings that people would read about in the papers and say 'good riddance' about. When they discovered his identity, he would be revered. Not that the police were going to catch him anytime soon.

His job as a delivery driver helped pass the time, and volunteering for the Salvation Army was an excellent cover. It was almost Christmas, and he was on his last delivery of hampers for the needy. Mrs Harris's doorbell chimed as he balanced the box of groceries in his arms. He was tired and his feet ached. He had work in the morning, and wanted to drop the box and go home. The door opened to reveal a thick-jowled woman, her face set in a permanent grimace.

'What do you want?' she said, glaring at him.

Given that he was wearing a uniform, he would have thought it was obvious. Frank faked a smile. 'Mrs Harris? I've got your Christmas hamper, courtesy of the Salvation Army.'

'About blooming time. How do you expect me to get by with no food in the house?'

Judging by her ample bottom as she turned to let him in, she got by just fine. All the other old dears had been very grateful, some had even offered a tip with the little money they had.

Frank surveyed the room as Mrs Harris shooed her yapping dogs in the kitchen. A one bar electric heater did a poor job of heating the damp bungalow. He wrinkled his nose at the smell of the dog faeces that patterned the threadbare carpet, and pallid faces glared at him from dusty framed photographs on the wall.

Mrs Harris walked back in, eyed him suspiciously and rifled through the box in his arms.

'Where would you like me to put it?' Frank asked, his annoyance growing as the woman poked through the items of tinned food and condiments that caused his arms to ache. He could think of plenty of places to suggest, none of which would meet the approval of Mrs Harris.

'Where do you think? On the table of course. I'm just making sure everything's here. I know what you lot are like, coming around pretending to be one of these do-gooders, and next thing you know, half the stuff is missing. I've dealt with your kind before.'

Frank seethed as he unpacked the box onto the table, which was already straining under stacks of newspapers, empty cans and dusty old books. Gripping the tin of beans in his hand, he wondered if a dent in Mrs Harris's head would slow down her moaning. On and on her voice droned, while she folded her arms and tapped her slippered foot in disgust.

Frank turned to the woman, a hint of menace in his voice. 'I don't give up my spare time to be called a thief. Given that you are getting this food for free, you're in no position to complain.'

Mrs Harris's mouth gaped open. Wheezing, she shook her finger in disgust. 'How dare you! I've never been spoken to so rudely in all my life.' She dropped her hand to rub her chest, the colour draining from her face. 'You think you're something special, coming around here delivering this box of rubbish, well let me tell you ...'

Her sentence hung in the air as she gasped for breath. It reminded Frank of a broken accordion he once had; each squeeze emitted a whistling wheeze. In ... out ... in ... out, the woman's chest rose and fell as each breath became more laboured.

Searching her apron pockets, she gestured to Frank. 'Inhaler, my inhaler.'

Frank picked up a small canister from the fireplace, his face breaking out in a broad grin. 'Of course, is this it?' He reached out to the wheezing woman, then pulled it back.

His dark eyes narrowed. 'But first, tell me Mrs Harris, why are you such a bitch?'

The woman clasped her chest once again, as Frank took another step towards her, backing her up against the arm of the sofa. 'I mean, look around you. When's the last time you cleaned this place? What gives you the right to talk to me in such a manner?' Frank emitted a chortle, his eyes as cold as flint.

Mrs Harris tried to move backwards, too scared to turn her back on him. The sofa behind her blocked her escape, and Frank could see the strength leaving her body as her lungs grew tighter by the second.

'Do you think you deserve life?' Frank said, the devious smile spreading across his features. He clamped his hand on her shoulder. There was the look he loved. Terror and confusion. She hadn't seen this coming. Neither had he, to be honest, but she needed to be taught a lesson. Frank pushed her hard, toppling her large frame over the arm of the sofa, her doughy body scattering cushions and rising clouds of dust. Her arms and legs waved like a cockroach flipped onto its back. But at least cockroaches were of some value to the world. Frank thought of the satisfying cracking sound you get when you step on one. He grabbed a sofa cushion and pushed it onto her face, leaning on it with his knee. She weakly clawed at his sleeves, gasping for breath.

'What a shame you won't see Christmas. Never mind, I'll make sure your dogs won't go hungry.' He pulled back the cushion. The blue tinge to her lips suggested death was drawing near. All the while, a poem chanted in Frank's mind.

It was from his treasured poetry book, a final gift from Gloria. 'No matter what is green today, the Reaper's scythe will mow away.'

'Who ... are ... you?' the woman gasped, spittle gathering in the corners of her mouth as she struggled for air.

A satisfied smile crossed Frank's face, his eyes boring into his victim's. 'Don't you know? I'm the Grim Reaper.'

He pushed the cushion back onto her face while the dogs yapped in the kitchen. Car headlights lit up the front window and Frank froze, waiting for it to stop. His heart pounded a beat in his chest, which calmed only when the headlights dimmed and the car drove past. Slowly, he released the cushion and rubbed the beads of sweat from his forehead. Let the asthma attack finish the job, it was less messy that way. In the end, she just stopped breathing. It could have been her heart. Judging by the way she was clutching her chest, it was hard to make out. It was a shame he couldn't take credit for the death of this crabby old bat, but it was just too close to home.

Poor old Mrs Harris, dying from an asthma attack so near Christmas. He smiled, drinking in the scene before leaving the cottage, his lifeless victim splayed on the sofa, her mouth open and eyes bulging in disbelief. Most likely, it was the first time a man had ever taken control over her. The sense of power surged through him.

Whistling, Frank emptied the contents of the box onto the table and walked out the front door, saying loud 'good-byes' for any neighbours who might be listening in.

Frank liked his new lifestyle. For the first time in his life, he felt empowered. He felt a sense of pride at his new title. The Grim Reaper had a certain ring to it.

CHAPTER EIGHTEEN

Soft lighting and mellow music went a little way towards lifting the atmosphere in Jennifer's home, but it still seemed washed out, as if someone had sucked the life from each room. Night was the worst, when the house came alive in a series of creaks and taps. The silent calls had died off, but Jennifer still flinched each time her phone rang. She did her best to carry on as normal. Being proactive was the only way she knew of dealing with her problems.

She tapped the page with her pen, frowning as she compiled a list of suspects involved in Charlie and Johnny's deaths. She couldn't afford to believe their murders were down to supernatural events, not yet. Joan's warning echoed in her mind. Someone close to her could not be trusted. Jennifer could count the people she trusted on one hand; her sister, Aunt Laura, DI Allison. She started writing Will's name then scribbled it out. Will would never harm her. He was as soft as they came.

It was a blessed relief her father had moved to London, and it certainly wasn't worth adding his name to the list. His constant begging for money and turning up drunk at the police station was a source of embarrassment, but he would never harm her.

Jennifer sipped a glass of Merlot. She was about to run a line through James Allison's name but could not bring herself to do it. There was something about the way he questioned her mental health that bugged her. She added two question marks and moved on to the next line.

Ethan Cole. She added a question mark. 'Travelled abroad – interest in the occult. Motivation?' She had not known him long enough to trust him, but their friendship was developing.

Jennifer yawned and took another sip of wine. She was about to write 'Steph,' when she remembered Joan's warning. Someone close to her could not be trusted. Steph could not be described as close. Her thoughts floated back to her sister Amy; the one constant in her life. Things between them were strained, but there was no way Amy would plot against her. Why couldn't Joan have been more precise? Jennifer fingered the cross around her neck. She should give it back, but Joan had been so insistent. She balled up the paper and threw it at the bin. Bouncing against the edge, it hopped onto the carpeted floor. She wrapped her dressing gown tightly around her before picking up the paper and checking the doors were secure. She thought about brushing her wine-stained teeth, but sleep was close at hand and she did not want to wake her fuddled brain.

Sleep came quickly, as did the nightmares. Her memory of the past intermingled with her present. Jennifer was three years old again, skipping in her favourite pink dress. She recognised the boathouse, her childhood home. But the river had broken its banks and swelled across the path that led to the village. Mummy and Daddy had argued again.

Mummy wanted to live in a proper house in the town but Daddy said they didn't have the money. Jennifer didn't want to leave. She wanted to see the deer that crept shyly out of the forest to drink at the water's edge. Today the rushing water travelled with ferocity as it carried broken branches in its path. Jennifer shrieked as the wind whipped her hat, and her little fingers grasped the air as she chased it. Stumbling into the icy water, she gasped as it shocked her skin and filled her mouth. She tried to scream but it thundered in her ears as she fought for breath. Darkness enveloped her as the water filled her lungs with every silent scream. The last thing she saw was her yellow hat bobbing on the water.

And then all was quiet. She was not in the water anymore.

A firm hand reached through the darkness and Jennifer allowed it to pull her into the light. A radiant Charlie Taylor stood in front of her with no evidence of the sorrows of the past. He was not cloaked in angel wings. Instead, he wore corduroy trousers cupped at the knees and a plaid shirt that bestowed a comfortable familiarity from Jennifer's school days. 'Don't be afraid,' he said in a soft voice, 'I've been trying to get your attention for some time.'

A calmness surrounded Jennifer as she watched a toddler playing in the light, gentle hands giving her the most beautiful flowers she had ever seen.

'Is that me?' Jennifer said, pointing to the giggling child.

'Yes, it is a facet of you.'

Jennifer glanced around. Her surroundings were blurred, the only clear focus being the little girl happily playing and Charlie standing in front of her.

'Am I dead?'

'No, you're sleeping. I have a message.' Charlie rested his hand on her shoulder. 'You must be strong. I need you to know that no matter what happens, you're not alone.'

'Oh Charlie, I do feel alone. There's so much I don't understand. Nothing makes sense.'

A trace of sadness crossed Charlie's face. 'A dark energy is invading your senses. It is powerful and full of hatred.'

'Please, can't you tell me any more?'

'Look in your past for the answers, they will come.'

The light dimmed as the teacher began to fade. 'Sorry. What seems like seconds on this side can be hours on yours. Be strong Jenny, look to your past.'

A strong pull dragged Jennifer down deeper, back to herself. A child's heartbeat, fluttering in the darkness, a revival. Sirens screaming, hands pushing on her chest as she expelled water. Her mother Elizabeth clasping her little hand, praying for her life. 'Please save my baby,' Elizabeth cried, over and over. But all the while the darkness gripped her, pulling her down. Twisting to escape the gnarled fingers around her throat, Jennifer reached out for her mother's face. A voice snarled, 'You belong to me,'

'No!' Jennifer screamed and gritted her teeth in pain as fingernails dug into the back of her neck. She lashed out and the porcelain bedside lamp smashed to the wooden floor, destroying any remnants of sleep. Disorientated, she drew back her damp hair and traced the back of her neck with her fingers. A dart of pain made her draw her lips over her teeth. Slowly, she climbed out of bed. Her mirrored reflection revealed beads of blood from three scratches drawn over the back of her neck. 'Shit,' she winced. 'I must have done it in my sleep.' Fragments of her dream seeped into her consciousness. Stepping carefully through the shards of broken lamp, she grabbed the notepad beside her bed and scribbled her dream, writing until there was nothing left. Morning light streamed through her curtains. With shaking hands, she picked up the phone. It was time to speak to the only real mother she had known.

'Aunt Laura, it's me. Sorry to call so early. Can I come over to visit?'

'Of course dear, is everything all right?'

'Yes … I think so. I need to talk to you about Mum. I'm on a late shift so I can stay for a couple of hours.'

'Lovely. I'll make scones.'

Jennifer sat on the bed, trying to comprehend her dream. Had Charlie Taylor really communicated with her or was it her subconscious trying to make sense of it all? When she was young, Father Kelly had told her to suppress all psychic contact, but what if he was wrong? What if she could control her unwanted gift and use it to her advantage? The scratches on her neck reminded her it was time to step up her search for answers.

Rendham was a picture postcard village, with fetes in the summer, and Christmas markets in the winter. Living in such a location came with a hefty price tag, but luckily for her Aunt Laura, she did not have to worry about that. The gravel drive scrunched under Jennifer's feet as she walked up to the entrance to the large five-bedroom bungalow. She glanced at the rope swing, still hanging from the huge oak tree in the front garden. She could almost hear Amy yelling at her to push her higher, her little face scrunched up in determination as she flung her head back and stretched out her legs in an attempt to reach the sky.

Laura embraced Jennifer in a hug as soon she opened the door. She was the total opposite of her sister Elizabeth, with no sign of her delicate features. A sturdy woman, Laura's light ash blonde hair complimented the thick linens she wore, and each hug from Auntie Laura was accompanied by hefty slaps on the back.

'Jenny dear, it must be six months since you've come to visit,' she said, squeezing her into a vice like grip.

'I know, sorry. You know how work is,' Jennifer said, catching her breath.

'Yes, I do. Now come in from the cold and I'll put the kettle on.'

Portraits of Laura's beloved thoroughbreds lined the walls of the mahogany-panelled hall. Jennifer was grateful that the horses took up so much of her aunt's life; it kept her from becoming too involved in hers. She breathed in the smell of freshly baked scones in the large country kitchen, and the whistling kettle on the Aga transported her back to the days of Amy's flour stained face as Aunt Laura helped her bake jam roly poly for tea. Jennifer, on the other hand, had spent most of her free time in the tree house at the bottom of the garden. Laura had learned that the best way to gain Jennifer's trust was to leave her be, until step by step she would return to the fold like a feral cat cautiously slinking inside for food and warmth.

She took a seat at the dining table, her eyes falling on the old brown leather photo album before her.

Aunt Laura set a generous tray of scones on the table, along with homemade strawberry jam and a pot of clotted cream. 'You're far too thin my lady, tuck in. You can have a look through your parent's photo album if you like, I dug it out for you.'

Jennifer polished off a scone as Laura filled her in on the local gossip. As the conversation died, Laura turned her eyes to the untouched photo album.

Jennifer's chest rose as she sighed heavily, pulling it towards her. The pages made a crackling noise as she gently pulled them apart. A young couple stared back at her, smiling at the camera in mid embrace.

'I'm so glad we managed to save these photos. Your father looks handsome, don't you think?' Laura said.

Jennifer balked at the mention of her father, her face conveying her disgust.

'Jenny. I know you find your father's name distasteful, but it's about time you knew the truth. Now, are you going to listen to me or will I put this away?'

Jennifer gave Laura a sidelong glance, thrown by the sharpness of her voice. 'I'm willing to listen.'

'Well, perhaps I can start by giving the skeletons in your cupboards a good airing, then you can tell me what your father did that was so wrong.'

Jennifer nodded.

'I loved your mother, but she was very hard to please. It didn't help that our parents spoilt her rotten. Mum always called Elizabeth their "precious gift". They didn't think they could have any more after me, you see. She was their favourite by a mile.'

Jennifer raised an eyebrow, 'I'm sure that wasn't the case.'

'Oh, it was, they made it quite obvious,' Laura said. 'That's why they gave her the boathouse. It was only meant as a holiday home to keep her near, but it became a permanent fixture when she met your father. I remember the first time Elizabeth brought him back for dinner. He was so good-looking and very nervous.'

Laura stared with an unfocused gaze as she recalled the memories. 'Lewis wasn't allowed to smoke in the house, so we'd both sneak outside for a cigarette after dinner. After he joined the police, things became strained between them; she kept nagging at him to progress his career.'

'If Mum was so awful, why did Dad marry her?'

'You know why. She was pregnant with you. Lewis loved her, and it seemed the right thing to do. I tried to tell her to go easy on him, but she accused me of being jealous. After they had your sister, Elizabeth spent more and more time at work while your father took on most of the childcare.'

'No, this is wrong.' Jennifer clenched her fists. 'You're talking like Dad was a saint. Mum *had* to work because he couldn't hold down a job.'

'Let me finish. Lewis told me his sergeant had it in for him from the start. He criticised his paperwork and set him up to fail. One day he called Lewis in for overtime and wouldn't take no for an answer. Lewis had been drinking and his sergeant reported him the minute he smelt his breath. It wasn't uncommon for officers to have a drink on duty back then, but rather than have a quiet word, his sergeant took it all the way. Lewis got the sack. He was really cut up about it.'

'What was the sergeant's name?'

'What was it now?' Laura drummed her nails on the solid oak table. She clicked her fingers. 'He had a woman's name, I remember thinking it strange.'

'A copper with a woman's name?'

'Yes, what was it again? That's it! Your father used to joke about it; he called him "Alison in Wonderland." His name was Alison. But that could have been a nickname.'

Jennifer pressed her fingers to her lips. 'DI Allison.'

'No, he was a sergeant.' Laura said, too caught up in the past to notice the effect her words were having. 'Anyway, Elizabeth decided it would be better for Lewis to mind you and Amy full time while she went for promotion. To be fair, she was brilliant at her job, and far more driven. Lewis became resentful, and the rift between them grew. One night we invited them here for dinner. It was pitiful to watch them sniping at each other.' Laura sighed. 'I went outside for a cigarette with Lewis. That's when he told me what was going on.'

Jennifer nodded at her to continue. 'Go on.'

'I don't know if you're ready to hear the rest, Jennifer.

After all, the past is dead and gone and we just have to get on with our li ...'

Jennifer waved at her to stop. 'I'm all grown up now. I need to know the truth.'

Laura rose from her chair. 'I need a cigarette.'

'I thought you gave up?'

'I've got an emergency pack. Let's go outside. There's no point in having your uncle Ralph worrying about my lungs, bless him.'

Jennifer followed Laura to a wooden bench on the edge of the pond halfway down the garden. A cacophony of whinnies ensued, as the horses demanded attention from their paddock. Jennifer stared into the shallow pond, watching the carp dart in the icy water. Laura ignited her match into a flame and sucked on the cigarette. Blowing out the smoke from the corner of her mouth, she began to speak.

'It was a lovely summer's evening and we sat in this very spot. Lewis asked if he could trust me and I said he could. All along my mind was racing, wondering what he was going to say. Then he started to cry, saying their marriage was in trouble. He loved your mother but was upset because she was hardly ever at home.'

Jennifer shook her head in protest.

'Oh Jennifer, he loved you. He just wasn't able to cope on his own. He had to raise you single-handedly because your mum was never there.'

Jennifer stared at the water mournfully, feeling ten years old again. Were Aunt Laura's views tainted by her feelings for her father? 'When Mum talked about her job, she became alive. I remember thinking I wanted a job like that when I grew up, something that made me light up too.' A lump rose to Jennifer's throat.

'After Mum died, Dad fell apart. I had to look after Amy and put food on the table with the few pounds he threw me.

I was ten years old. Sometimes he would go on a bender and disappear for days. I was so scared the social services would split Amy and me up, I never told a soul. I cut myself off from everyone in school. How could I bring friends back knowing what was at home?'

Laura stubbed out the dead cigarette and placed its remnants back in the packet. 'Your father shut us all out, asking to be left alone with you and Amy to grieve. I didn't realise how much he was drinking; otherwise we would never have backed off.'

'Sometimes he would sober up and take us fishing for a treat. He would make a picnic and tell stories like other families. But by the time I was fourteen, his drinking was out of control. The local winos began coming back to the boathouse with him. I'd see them leering at me. I'd take Amy upstairs and lock the bedroom door. One night when dad was passed out, one of them tried to come in. He kept pushing on the door, trying force it open. I've never been so afraid.'

Laura's face crumpled. 'No! Why didn't you tell me?'

Jennifer shrugged. 'My old teacher Charlie Taylor used to watch out for me when he drank with Dad. He threw them all out and tore a strip off my father for allowing it to happen.'

'Jennifer, we all let you down, I just hope you can forgive us.' Laura said, wrapping her arm around her shoulder. 'Thank goodness Charlie Taylor called social services when he did.'

'Yes, but I didn't know that at the time. Dad didn't seem to care. He started drinking again. I just couldn't see any way out of it.'

Shaking her head, Laura realised that Lewis was not the man she had painted him to be. 'And then came the fire. You could have all been killed.'

Jennifer's stomach churned at the thought of revisiting the unwanted memory. 'I don't want to talk about it.'

'It's behind you now, you don't need to upset yourself like this, dear.'

'It was all my fault.'

'Don't ever think that. We should have been there for you.'

'I wanted him to die.' Jennifer sobbed, biting her forefinger as the tears drove down her face.

'Oh sweetheart, come here,' Laura held out her arms and Jennifer sobbed into her chest. Laura smoothed down her hair, kissing the crown of her head. Jennifer wanted to tell her aunt what had really happened that day, but as the tears flowed, the moment for confession passed.

CHAPTER NINETEEN

FRANK – 1985

The curves of Mrs Harris's body flowed onto the sketchpad and Frank paused to admire his work. His pencil moved quickly as he sketched the doughy body, limbs extended and eyes bulging in shocked silence. A sneer grew on his lips. She had deserved it and more. The tap, tap, tap of the front door interrupted his thoughts. He lay the sketch on the bed and sighed. Who could it be this time of the morning?

A pretty face smiled back at him as he opened the door. The young woman's long dark hair was neatly tied back, and she stood with self-assurance. It was unfortunate that she was wearing a police uniform, but not entirely unexpected.

'Good morning. Are you Frank Foster?'

Frank opened the door wider and smiled. 'Yes I am. What can I do for you, officer?'

'Sergeant Elizabeth Knight.' She raised her warrant card. 'I'd like to speak to you. Can we go inside?'

'Why of course. I'm not in any trouble, am I?' Frank gave

an amused chuckle, holding his hands up in mock surrender. The officer did not return his smile.

She took a seat on the three-piece white leather sofa near the window, which faced a full length bookshelf against the far wall. Frank followed her gaze as she took in his living accommodation. The walls were decorated with dark prints of bleak landscapes, and the smell of bleach tainted the sterile room. Frank was twenty-five years old and had lived alone since the death of his mother a couple of years previously. He wondered if his intimidating stature made the officer wish she hadn't come alone as his eyes bored into her.

She stiffened as her gaze met his. 'I'm sorry to impose on your day, but I'd like to ask you some questions by informal interview. You're under no obligation to answer my questions, and you can consult a solicitor. Should you prefer to speak to me at the police station where your interview will be recorded, you can also do so.'

Frank's eyebrows raised as he took a seat across from her. 'This all sounds very official, Sergeant Knight, but I'm happy to help in any way I can.'

'In that case I'll carry on. There's been an incident involving a female by the name of Mrs Barbara Harris at one of the homes you've attended.' Elizabeth ran through the caution with steady ease before carrying on. 'Do you understand, Mr Foster?'

Frank sat back in his chair, casually resting his ankle on his knee. He smiled. 'Of course. You have the most striking eyes. Has anyone ever told you that?'

'No,' Elizabeth said, in response to the compliment. He was trying to put her off, but it seemed he was wasting his time. Shuffling in the chair, she slid her police notebook from her jacket pocket and pulled a pen from under the rubber band, which held it all together.

'Sadly, Mrs Harris of 42 Harold Road was found deceased at her property yesterday. I believe you were one of the last people to talk to her. Do you recall attending the address?'

Frank did his best to appear surprised. 'Oh, I'm sorry to hear that. She didn't seem in very good health when I saw her.'

'So you did visit the address yesterday?'

'Yes, I did. But where are my manners? Can I get you a cup of tea, Sergeant Knight?'

'No thank you,' Elizabeth said, clenching her jaw as her patience appeared to run thin. 'Can you tell me about your visit? How long it lasted? Anything she said?'

'You say it's informal yet you're questioning me about the death of a person whom I was last to see. Am I to understand that I am under suspicion of murder?' Frank said, offering a bemused smile.

Elizabeth reddened. 'As I said, we're making enquiries.'

'Enquiries about what? Was she murdered or not?'

'There's nothing to suggest she was at this stage. But I'm sure you understand that when there is a sudden death, we follow all lines of enquiry.'

'Of course, I understand, I have nothing but admiration for the police. My father is a Chief Constable. I often felt like following in his footsteps, but I had to care for my mother, who was terminally ill.'

'I'm sorry to hear that. What force did your father work for?'

Frank shifted his weight. 'He works in Australia. Anyway, listen to me wittering on when you have a job to do. You were saying I am a line of enquiry?'

'Yes, you could say that. We're trying to trace her last movements.'

'The only movements she made were to put her groceries

away. She was wheezing and her complexion wasn't very good. I offered to call her a doctor but the old dear can be quite … erm, abrupt at times.' Frank chuckled, then his face saddened. 'I wish I'd known how ill she was, I would have insisted. But I left, wishing her a merry Christmas.'

'I see.' Elizabeth said, scribbling his response into her notepad. 'Did you know her very well?'

'No, not at all, it was the second time I had met her.'

'Did you see anyone else around?'

'No, she just had her dogs, funny little things they were.' Frank crossed his long legs, and his foot began to bob up and down.

'They created quite a racket after you went. You can't have been gone long when Mrs Harris was discovered deceased.'

Frank shook his head, his foot bouncing faster. 'Oh dear, poor woman. How sad.'

Elizabeth stared at him as seconds passed in silence. She was obviously trying to gauge his reaction. He followed her gaze to his foot, now bobbing frantically and he jumped up from the chair. 'Are you sure I can't get you that cup of tea?'

'Actually yes, that would be lovely, thank you.'

Frank stood over her. 'I'll put the kettle on.'

'White, no sugar, please. Is it OK if I use your bathroom?' Elizabeth said, as Frank walked towards the small open plan kitchen.

'Of course. It's the door at the end of the hall.'

Frank slid a bread knife from the block on the counter. 'I've got carrot cake, would you like some?'

Elizabeth paused, her eyes lingering on the knife. 'No thanks.'

'You're not one of these women who are always on a diet are you? You certainly don't need to be.' Frank said, taking the cake from the fridge and slowly cutting himself a slice.

'I don't eat on duty.' She closed the door behind her. Frank laid the knife to rest as he imagined her examining the rest of his home.

Frank spoke eloquently, but if Elizabeth had done her homework she would know that he didn't come from money. He imagined her poking around in his space. What did she think she was going to find? A body in his linen closet? A full confession in the bathroom cupboard? Surely, she wouldn't risk her career by carrying out a hasty illegal search. Frank had researched the law. Any evidence found would be deemed inadmissible. Not that there was anything left to find...he sucked in a sudden breath as he remembered the drawing pad in his bedroom. The pull to recreate the scene had been too strong to resist.

His heart drummed a beat as he crept into the hallway, listening for every sound. Drawing shallow breaths, he silently crept up the stairs. The bathroom door was open. So where was she? His wardrobe door creaked shut. His sketchpad was on the far side of his single bed, flanked with an array of pencils. Frank peered through the crack in his bedroom door, watching as Elizabeth stepped forward to pick it up.

'Your tea is ready.' Frank's voice made her jump out of her skin. Turning on her heel, she cleared her throat.

'Oh, sorry, I came in the wrong door,' she said, a flush creeping from her shirt collar to her cheeks.

Frank eyed the sketchpad behind her on the bed. The blade of the knife scratched the skin under his shirtsleeve as he considered his next move.

Elizabeth looked at her watch. 'Thank you for your time, Mr Foster, but I'm afraid I've overstayed my welcome. My colleague is waiting outside in the car.'

'Oh, that's a shame,' he said, tilting his head to one side as he stood in the doorway. 'I was enjoying your company.'

Reluctantly, he moved aside to allow her past. 'What happens now? Do I wait to hear from you?'

Elizabeth pulled a dog-eared card from her pocket. 'I don't expect you'll hear from us again. If you've any enquiries, call me on this number.'

He reached for the card with his free hand, turning it over in his fingers, 'Eli-za-beth.' He accentuated the word as he followed her to the front door.

Frank bolted the front door after she left. fighting the urge to drag her back inside. She was a smaller and weaker than him. It would take only seconds to clamp a hand over her mouth and overpower her. He bit hard on his lip, bringing himself back to reality. She was a copper. People would know where she was. The knife slipped from his sleeve and clanged to the floor, the moment lost. He walked to the window overlooking the street below. Elizabeth was sitting alone in the police car. *Lying little bitch,* he thought. He watched as she stared ahead before starting the engine. He had rattled her, all right. If she'd picked up those sketches, it would have ended up a whole lot differently and he'd have a dead police officer on his hands.

He marched to his room to tear up the pictures but couldn't bring himself to do it. Instead, he picked up his sketchpad and began to draw Elizabeth as he wanted her, with her hands cuffed behind her back. Frank became aroused as he drew the restraints on her legs. Helpless, drew her beautiful black hair wrapped around his fist. Oh, the things he could have done to her. It would almost have been worth the risk. He finished the drawing and his hand released the buckle on his trousers as his imagination took over. He went through the scenario as the ecstatic drug of power and control led to her pleading for her life. That would teach her for lying to him. If only he could make it real.

He expected another knock at the door, but it never came. Frank looked down at the empty parking space and dissected the visit. The dog must have disturbed the neighbour, who went to check. But would they have checked so soon? He picked up the phone and called his boss.

'Hello, it's Frank. Have you heard about Mrs Harris? I've just had the police around.'

'Hullo, Frank. Yes, I've just had Mrs Johnson on the phone, very upset she is. She's going to stay with her daughter over Christmas.'

'It must have been a terrible shock, finding her like that,' Frank said, not wanting to sound too curious.

'Terrible. It was the dogs that alerted her. She went in this morning and found her dead on the sofa. One of her asthma attacks by the look of it, she hadn't been well at all.'

'No, she didn't seem right when I left her. I wish I could have done more.'

'It's not your fault, Frank. The house was rotten with damp, but she was too tight-fisted to heat it. I don't know why the police were asking me about you. Mrs Johnson heard you say goodbye to Mrs Harris when you left. She told them as much.'

'From what I gather it's nothing to worry about. They're just tying up loose ends. It's a real shame.'

'You're being very kind there, Frank. Truth be told, she was a difficult woman with a sharp tongue. Anyway, never mind, these things happen.'

'Of course. OK then, I'll see you Monday evening.'

'Will do, Frank, bye for now.'

Frank dropped the phone on the receiver and cracked his

knuckles as he paced. Sergeant Knight was bluffing, and she an officer of the law! How dishonest. Back and forward he paced, going through it one more time. The bitch was trying to flush him out. How amateurish. She didn't know who she was up against. But she would find out soon enough.

CHAPTER TWENTY

Jennifer's eyes flicked to her mother's belongings in the corner of the living room. Laura had insisted she take them, and the tattered cardboard box looked painfully out of place in her spotless home. There were no unwanted gifts or unused gadgets in the drawers of her cupboards, and regular trips to the charity shops ensured her home was clutter-free.

She wished she could say the same about her mind. Charlie's death played heavily as she relived their last moments together in custody. If only she could have done more.

She returned her attention to the box, with its frayed edges and ragged bands of Sellotape, begging to be opened. It was either that or put it in the loft. And even then it would bother her, like an itch waiting to be scratched. What if it contained the answers she'd been looking for? Dragging the box to the centre of the living room floor, she ripped the tape and emptied its contents onto the carpet. Detaching herself from the fact that these were her mother's things, she worked methodically, putting irrelevant items back into the box. There would be another day for sentiment. The belongings were mainly work related; a pair of epaulettes, a worn cravat, and things her mother had kept in her desk at work.

Jennifer flicked through a bunch of photographs, stopping at a group picture dated 1980. Officers stood rigid with their hands clasped behind their backs, and amidst the sea of uniforms, five women sat, crisp and immaculate, their white-gloved hands resting on the laps of their A-line skirts. There was not a smile in sight. It was taken at a time when women had to work twice as hard as their male counterparts to prove their worth. She stared at her mother's face, wondering why she had sacrificed her family for a career. It was her family that had been left to pick up the pieces after she died; to her job, she was nothing but a number. Jennifer chastised herself for allowing self-pity to creep up on her. She boxed away the photos for another time, along with some small ornaments, a pencil case, calendars, and a jewellery box. She gently laid the jewellery box back with the other items and shook her head as she realised that all that was left was a faded black shoe-box. Pulling back the lid, she found that it revealed a bunch of yellowed newspaper clippings, tainting the air with a musty smell.

She carried the shoebox and her journal to the sofa. Tiny clippings of death notifications quivered in her hand. Jennifer made notes of the names in her journal, but she didn't experience the epiphany she hoped for. Laying the smaller clippings aside, she unfolded newspaper pages. The headlines reflected the biggest case of Elizabeth's career. Jennifer had heard about the case through Laura, who had told her how driven Elizabeth had been to ensure that the killer was convicted. Much of the credit had gone to her senior officers, but Laura recalled the case as her 'crowning glory.' Her swan song before she died so suddenly.

Frustration grew as she scanned the papers. Sure, it was an interesting case, but what had any of this to do with her? But her intuition drove her on. Jennifer traced her finger over the words. 'Killer confesses to spate of murders … Homeless man Michael Osborne found hung … police initially believed the death was a suicide until teenager Samuel Beswick alerted police … Killer Frank Foster was also responsible for the death of retired schoolteacher Stanley Rogers … died in a house fire.' Jennifer raised a hand to her mouth. Why didn't she see this before? She studied the rest of the page as she read on. 'Foster is also believed to have confessed to the death of seventy-five-year-old widower Mrs Barbara Harris, whom police believed had died of a severe asthma attack. Foster admitted to attempting to smothering the pensioner …' The words jumped out at Jennifer as the similarities became apparent. 'Foster also admitted to assisting in the death of forty year old sex worker Martina Savage …'

Jennifer grabbed her pen and scribbled down notes of the names. Could someone be creating current day counterparts?

Michael Osborne = Johnny Mallet. Both drug users, both found hung, both deaths believed to be suicides.

Stanley Rogers = Charlie Taylor. Both ex-teachers died in a house fire, both inconclusive.

Barbara Harris =?? Elderly lady found dead in her home, suspected asthma attack, murdered.

Martina Savage = Shelly Easton. Both prostitutes. Martina murdered. Shelly??

Jennifer twiddled with her chain as the names screamed from the page. This was her connection. She could feel it in her gut. Perhaps the last two murders hadn't happened yet but there was nothing to say … elderly lady? Living alone, apart from her dog … Realisation dawned as the image of Joan's face swam in her mind. 'No, not her.' Jennifer said. A sick feeling grew in her stomach. She whispered to the empty room as she spoke her thoughts aloud. 'I'll go there and offer to return the cross. Yes, that's what I'll do. Everything will be fine.' Yet as Jennifer grabbed her car keys, she was filled with dread.

Her fingernails bit into her palms as she waited for a response to her sharp rap on the door. No barking dog, no sign of life. A voice arose from next door and a woman with a bun piled up on her head poked her nose over the hedge.

'Are you looking for someone?'

Jennifer shielded her eyes from the winter sun as she turned to greet the inquisitive neighbour. 'Yes, I was looking for Mrs Connelly. Is she in?'

The woman looked down the bridge of her long nose. 'Are you a relative?'

Jennifer flashed her warrant card. 'Police officer. I needed to follow up some house to house enquiries.'

The woman's face fell in sadness. 'She passed away last week. I miss her dreadfully. She was my bingo partner.'

Jennifer stared in disbelief, trying to process the information.

'Are you all right, dear?' The woman's voice sounded as it was coming from far away.

Jennifer forced a smile. 'I'm fine. Just recovering from the flu. I shouldn't have come to work today,' she lied. 'Can you tell me how she died?'

'They think it was her heart. Her poor little dog was barking all night. Inconsolable, he is.'

Jennifer made it to her car, her hands trembling as she clicked her safety belt into place. She swore under her breath she flooded the engine in her haste. *Please start, please,* she thought, not knowing how long she could hold in the dam of tears that threatened to break. The engine stuttered into life and Jennifer focused on the road. Joan said it was dangerous having her there. Jennifer felt the blood on her hands as if it was real.

Jennifer bolted the door behind her. She had barely known Joan, but the sense of responsibility hit her hard. According to the list, Shelly could be next. She had to be warned. But how? It's not as if she would listen. Jennifer bit her fingernail as she paced the living room, wondering how she could persuade her DI to open an investigation. Could Frank Foster be responsible? It wasn't unknown for killers to shed their identity and slip back into the community, but after all these years? Or was she searching for a killer with supernatural powers? Jennifer picked up the shoebox, hearing a small rattle as it moved. Holding it up near her ear, she gave it another shake. The sound was so slight she could have overlooked it. As she stared inside the empty box, a piece of frayed cardboard caught her eye. She ripped back the thin cardboard to discover a small brown envelope underneath. Her mind raced as she dipped her fingers into the envelope and pulled out a black cassette tape. The same antiquated tapes they used for interviewing suspects. What was her mother doing with this? Frowning, she squinted at the scribbles on the label. 'Sam Beswick – 12th December 1980 – copy.' A flutter of excitement rose as she flicked through her journal. Of course! – Sam Beswick was Frank Foster's accomplice. Her aunt Laura had told her about the famous investigation, and of her mother's fondness for keeping 'trophies' from certain cases. Another thought hit her, not entirely unwelcome. She would be listening to her mother's voice. As soon as she could get her hands on a tape recorder, that was.

CHAPTER TWENTY-ONE

FRANK – 1990

Memories of Gloria brought mixed feelings as Frank gazed at the twinkling lights of town. The bingo hall had been replaced with a cinema, but the sentiment was the same. He was proud of his purchase. The night he bought the flat, he climbed the steps to the roof and spoke to the stars. 'I did it girl,' he whispered to the memory of the woman he had hoped would be his saviour. But all that remained of Gloria was the poetry book she had given him as a child, with the inscription, 'There is power in words – use them wisely.' Frank hadn't understood it back then, but he did now.

Moving into town was a wise choice and scamming lonely women from the neighbouring city proved lucrative. With a nicely cut suit and some choice words, he could be anyone he wanted; a stockbroker, property developer, airline pilot, or a doctor. He wasn't a whore like his mother. He sold the dream. He could have bought a city apartment with the money he earned, but there was something about the little flat above the old bingo hall that he liked. He could be himself here.

. . .

His friendship with Sam Beswick was no coincidence. He just made Sam think it was. He had watched the kid for some time before deciding he would be of value.

Sam Beswick was a loner. He stared mournfully from under his long black fringe each time he loped his scrawny frame into the building, usually after another session of name calling from two brothers, Joe and Edward. The Needham boys were Army dropouts who got their kicks picking on the vagrants that wandered into their 'territory.' But lately their attention was focused on the strange kid who wore black eyeliner and dressed as if every day was a funeral. Frank knew what was ahead for Sam. Another 'duffing up', with the added bonus of having his pockets rifled for loose change and cannabis. Frank had enjoyed stalking the two young men. It had been surprisingly simple to find out their names, addresses, and so much more. He'd missed the peculiar little thrill of hiding in the darkness and he smiled in anticipation as he settled behind the green bins down the damp alleyway inhabited by rats. Sam passed the men on the corner, head down, eyes focused solidly on the path. He quickened his step as he ducked down the side alley to the flat's entrance. Two sets of footsteps matched his pace, laughing and jeering as they threw stones in his direction. Sam clutched the bag of groceries to his chest and began to run. A strong pair of hands pushed him hard to the wet pavement, crushing the eggs he'd bought for his supper.

'Aw, look at that, he tripped,' Edward, the larger of the two lads said, as he drew back his boot to kick Sam in the stomach.

'Isn't this a nice gathering,' Frank said, stepping out of the shadows. Cloaked in black, his hat dipped forward, casting his face in shadow.

Edward squinted in the darkness, his expression changing to a scowl. Joe opened his mouth to speak but took a step back as he noticed Frank's considerable bulk.

'Do one mate, this has nothing to do with you,' Edward said, slipping his hand into his jacket pocket.

Frank lent a gloved hand to Sam as he scrambled to his feet, his long black coat dappled with eggshells and yellow yolks. 'Go inside. I'll deal with this,' Frank said, his eyes on the two young men walking towards him.

Sam's eyes widened as the glint of a knife flashed in the shadows from the direction of the men. 'But ...'

'I said go,' Frank growled.

Sam scurried away and Edward leered after him. 'Run, you little shit, we'll be back for you.'

'You won't if you know what's good for you,' Frank said, smiling.

Edward pushed out his chest as he marched towards Frank, his words punctuated with spittle. 'You mess with my fucking business again, I'll cut you up.'

Frank smiled as Edward sliced the air with his blade to drive his point home.

'You call that a knife?' Frank laughed, allowing the serrated hunting knife to slide down the arm of his coat into his right hand. His gloves gripped the thick boned handle. Curling his left hand into a fist, he deadened Edward's arm with a punch, sending the flick knife skidding across the ground. Frank moved swiftly, kicking it under the bins. Joe stepped forward and Frank drew back his elbow back to his face, causing Joe's nose to crack upon impact.

Frank quickly pushed Edward against the wall, kneeing him in the groin, making him shriek in pain.

Edward whimpered to Joe as Frank held the knife to his throat. 'Do something!'

Frank barely acknowledged Joe's punches to his rib cage

as he turned his head and spoke calmly. 'You have a choice, Joe. You're going to punch me until your arm weakens. Then I'm going to slice your brother's throat, and as he bleeds out, I'm going to gut you slowly and choke you with your own intestines. Or you can run. But I know where you live, so keep your head low and your mouth shut.'

Joe dropped his fist and ran without a backward glance.

Frank leaned into Edward. 'Well, this is awkward. So much for brotherly love.'

'Please,' Edward's voice came out as a high-pitched squeak. 'We were only having some fun.'

'I'm having fun too Edward, or "Eddy" as your girlfriend likes to call you. Sweet little thing she is. I'd sure like to meet up with her on a dark night.' Frank drove the blade further and the man choked a response, dancing on his toes as he was forced to stretch his neck away from the blade digging into his jugular vein.

'Please, let me go. We won't touch him again, I promise.'

Frank cocked his head to one side as he gave it some consideration. Sighing, he lowered the knife and pushed the man away, sending him skidding backwards into the puddles. 'Just remember, I'm watching you.'

Frank felt Sam's stare from his flat window, and casually made his way back inside. It was a real shame he couldn't carry his threat through, but the boys were young and stupid and not worth his time. Frank unwound the scarf from his neck and removed his hat. Unbuttoning his coat, he shoved his knife into his pocket and knocked on Sam's door.

'Yes?' Sam croaked.

'It's OK kid, they're gone. Are you all right?'

Sam opened the door as much as the chain would allow. 'Thanks for sticking up for me. But I'm OK now.'

Frank gave Sam one of his winning smiles. 'It's OK, I just

wanted to frighten them. I don't think they'll bother you again.'

Sam smiled. 'For sure. Thanks man.'

It took a few more meetings before he gained Sam's trust. A couple of weeks later Sam invited him inside. His flat stunk of weed and Frank persuaded him to ditch the wasters that turned up at his door all hours of the day and night. It soon became apparent that Sam would do anything Frank told him to. Not because he was afraid of him, but because of his deep admiration. The pair fell into a friendship, and Sam looked after Frank's flat when he went on one of his escapades to con women out of money. After a couple of months, Sam had forgotten bout the knife, and enjoyed the benefits of Frank's protection. But protection came with a price tag that Sam could ill afford.

Frank hammered with his fist on the black wooden door to overcome the heavy metal music blaring from the flat inside. He brushed the chips of paint that came off on his hand. Sam had decorated when he moved in during his Goth phase, but months had passed, and the place looked tired and worn.

The door opened. 'Your music is making my ears bleed.'

Sam gave a goofy smile, his teeth too big for his mouth. He really needed braces.

'Sorry. I'll turn it down. Come inside.'

He followed Sam in, completely at ease. 'I've brought some cans. I was wondering how you're getting on with those magazines I loaned you.'

'Cheers mate, they're here somewhere, sit down.'

Frank cleared the rubbish from the sofa and handed Sam a can of cider. Spending time in the untidy flat grated on him, and he needed a drink just to cope. Six cans later and the pair had eased into a relaxed conversation.

As Sam flicked through the pictures in the detective magazines, his eyes rested on the case they called 'The Demon.' The image of the man was chilling. Six foot five with every inch of hair shaved off his body. His pale skin offset the hollow wells of his eyes, and the report stated that even the prisoners were scared of the man made famous for killing people in occult practices. Even more sensational were his claims of being capable of resurrecting the dead.

'This guy is so cool. Imagine having the guts to do something like that, you'd be famous forever,' Sam said as he inhaled his joint.

Frank sat forward, checking he had heard Sam correctly. 'Really?'

'Oh yeah, these guys go down in history.'

'It's easier than you think,' Frank gave a twisted smile.

'What do you mean?' Sam asked, passing a joint.

Frank waved it away. 'You heard me, it's easier than you think.'

'Man, you're always coming out with stuff like that, but I don't believe you.'

'There's only one way to find out,' Frank said, the smile leaving his face.

Sam stared, then shook his head. 'You're shitting me,' he said, flicking his ash onto the floor.

'And you're scared.' Frank spoke with an icy edge to his voice. Lately restlessness had been crawling under his skin, whispering, demanding; an army of flesh-covered wants and needs. His friendship with Sam had distracted him, but the kid was of no use to him if he wasn't capable of joining in. Frank wanted someone to share the thrill, an apprentice to his murderous ways.

'No, I'm not,' Sam said. 'All that stuff I did down at the graveyard was real. You saw the newspaper reports.'

Frank snickered, 'Yeah but messing about with dead bodies isn't the same as putting them there.'

Sam drew on his joint, locking the smoke into his lungs before releasing it through the corner of his mouth. 'Look. All this time you've been hinting that you've killed people, but I'm beginning to wonder if you're not full of crap. I've spent time in police custody and nobody has ever talked about you.'

Frank felt his hackles rise. He tightened his grip on the can and leaned forward to speak. He needed to keep control. He didn't want to kill the only friend he had. The kid had potential, and could prove a useful sidekick, or a scapegoat, whichever way you looked at it.

'I didn't get caught because I'm good.'

'Talk is cheap. Maybe it's your turn to prove it,' Sam said, his bravado enhanced by the cider and cannabis invading his system.

'You think you're ready for it?' Frank said, a smile creeping back to his lips.

'What are you planning?'

'I might let you in on it. I have to know I can trust you first.'

'I'm hardly gonna tell the cops, am I?'

Sam offered the joint to Frank and he inhaled deeply, relaxing back into the sofa. 'I don't want you telling your friends.'

'I don't see those users anymore. There's nobody to tell.'

Frank clasped Sam's thigh and gave it a squeeze. It was a quick movement, but Frank knew it was enough to send a thrill through Sam, as he felt the warmth of his hand through the rip in his jeans. Frank wasn't stupid. He knew Sam had a crush on him and he was happy to take advantage of that fact.

'Well Sam, it's like this. Deep down most people reach a time in their lives where they want to kill someone, but something holds them back. Their enforced morals, feelings of guilt, fears of getting caught, or they just don't have the courage. Can you imagine if they didn't have any of those feelings?'

Sam stared, captive to the speech Frank had rehearsed in his mind countless times before.

'Animals kill, why can't we? If we're not meant to carry out such acts then why are human beings so hard to live with? The answer is that we're not here to be nice to each other. We are here to experience life in its fullest form. Death will come to the wicked and immoral. And I am more than willing to carry out their punishment.' Frank smiled. 'This is your chance to step up to the mark, Sam, to be a man. But I warn you, once you've made your decision there's no going back. You're either with me or against me.' Frank patted Sam's knee again before getting up to leave.

He'd plunged the young man into a tailspin of hormones, his admiration for Frank muffling the voice at the back of his mind that screamed murder was wrong. Sam smiled as he got up and shook Frank's hand.

'In that case, count me in.'

CHAPTER TWENTY-TWO

'Come in,' Shelly croaked, as Jennifer pushed open the door of the flat. The fact that it was off the latch made her nervous, and the feeling of foreboding grew as she entered the dingy space. Another raspy phone call from an unknown number had heightened her sense of danger, and Jennifer thought it was best to check on Shelly and see if she was okay. She made a mental note to keep the door ajar, ensuring a point of escape. The birth of a headache pounded against her temples as a stench assailed her nostrils. She had smelt it before, the last time she seen Charlie alive.

Shelly sat in a red armchair, with one leg slung over the ragged arm. Jennifer was shocked at the pitiful sight before her. She had seen better-looking corpses. Shelly's greasy hair hung down on her face, which was dotted with pus-filled sores.

'You look awful, do you need a doctor?' Jennifer said, her stomach lurching at the sight before her.

Shelly cackled as she played with the stringy length of hair, and the voice that spoke was not her own. 'Don't you think she's pretty? "When merry winds do blow and rain makes trees look fresh, an overpowering staleness holds this mortal flesh.'"

Jennifer sucked her lips back in disgust. 'Shelly, let me help you.'

'Aw, little Jenny, so thoughtful, so kind, worried about the whore.' She picked at a scab on her arm and a blossom of blood grew under her fingernail. 'It's lean times for Shelly, looking like this. Even horny old Wilfred couldn't get it up. Can you imagine that? He gave it a go, but the smell, you know.' Shelly pinched her nose and waved a bony hand in front of her face.

A cold breeze danced around Jennifer, sending a shiver down her spine. 'Who are you?' she said.

'You're hurting my feelings, pretending you don't know me, when I've been a friend of the family for such a long time.' Shelly scratched her crotch, her long nails tearing into the thin fabric of her jeans. 'It's lean pickings indeed. Perhaps you would like a go yourself?' Shelly began to circle her nipples through her orange vest, leering at Jennifer with a mocking smile.

'You're not worth my time,' Jennifer said, turning to leave. Whatever was within Shelly had a power beyond her understanding, but she needed answers and the entity would not want her to go.

Shelly's scrawny body rose from the chair, fury behind her hollowed eyes. Her limbs dangled as she stood, a marionette, in the centre of the room. 'Don't turn your back on me. Have you forgotten the debts you owe? Who did you think you were praying to, in the boathouse all those years ago?'

The colour drained from Jennifer's face. Thoughts of that night in the boathouse made her want to run outside and gulp clean air.

Shelly's eyes glinted. 'You remember that night, shame-lessly begging for your father's death! Even I was impressed. What God would answer such a prayer, as your sister slept innocently in her bed?'

'That's not true, I loved my father,' Jennifer said, guilt and shame raining down on her.

Shelly pointed fiendishly. 'Yes, you did. And the night he crept into your bed, you wanted to be a daddy's girl more than anything. But then he went and ruined it all, by crying out your mother's name.'

'No! He made a mistake! He was drunk, he didn't know what he was doing.'

'So you pushed him away and while he stumbled down-stairs, you dropped to your knees and pleaded for his death.'

'I wanted him gone!'

Shelly waved her finger in a tick-tock fashion. 'Now now, don't lie. You wanted him dead, admit it.'

'Yes.' The answer came in a whisper.

'Louder! Say it. You wanted him dead,' Shelly spat the words.

"Yes, I wanted him dead! Because I hated him. I hated him so much!' Jennifer clasped her hands to her face as tears fell through her fingers.

Shelly's body collapsed into the armchair. 'Hate is a powerful emotion, isn't it? But when you pray with hate in your heart, you get listened to. Shame your father had to spoil it by waking as the fire tickled his skin. But don't worry. It'll be our little secret – as long as you carry out your end of the bargain.'

'You want to kill me? Is that what you want?' Jennifer asked, swallowing back her tears.

Shelly cackled. 'Oh no dear, I don't want to *kill* you, at least not anymore. I want to *be* you. You and me, we're different from everyone else. To them you're a freak. But to me, you're powerful. It's time we fulfilled your potential.'

Jennifer squared her shoulders, as if preparing for battle. Jabbing her finger towards Shelly. 'Go back to hell where you came from.'

'Oh c'mon now,' Shelly cracked her neck, 'I need a decent body. These are shit. They don't last.'

'If that's what you want, why are you asking me?' Jennifer said.

Shelly sighed. 'I need you to give yourself freely. Addicts will agree to anything for a fix. But look at this!' Shelly prodded her chest, 'She's rotting from the inside. Your body would be powerful. Think of the things we could achieve if we combine our resources. Don't you want to bring the world to justice?'

'It's not going to happen.'

'Don't be so hasty. You'd be surprised what people will do for the ones they love. Take little Josh, for example.' Shelly's tongue lolled as she began to pant like a dog.

Jennifer's heartbeat quickened as fear swept through her. She didn't like where the conversation was going, but she couldn't leave now. The thought of Joshua, so sweet and innocent, having anything to do with this ... *thing* sickened her to the core. 'What do you mean?'

Shelly rolled her eyes to the back of her head and groaned. Her head fell back, mouth gaping, revealing black gaps where her teeth had once been. A gravelly moan escaped her dry cracked lips.

'I said, what do you mean? Answer me!'

Shelly baulked as her stomach enlarged. Jennifer stood, frozen to the spot, as Shelly lurched forward and vomited a putrid sludge on the fringed rug before her. She gripped her stomach and bent forward, her hair hanging thinly down her face.

'Shelly, talk to me.' Jennifer side stepped the vomit to crouch down beside her.

Shelly turned her bloodshot eyes towards Jennifer and a look of confusion flashed across her face. 'Who are you?' she groaned.

'Shelly I'm the police, you were about to tell me something.' But whatever had vacated Shelly's body was gone. Shelly was back, and in urgent need of medical assistance. Jennifer squeezed her hand as she whispered her name. 'Shelly, speak to me.'.

'Oh God, help me, I'm dying.'

Jennifer pressed the talk button on her police radio as Shelly groaned. A nasal voice came on the other line, and she requested an ambulance.

She went outside to guide the paramedics in and discussed Shelly's condition as they climbed the stairs. Jennifer scanned the empty flat on her return. Shelly had vanished without a trace. Jennifer checked the window, which was tightly closed. The only sign of Shelly was the pool of vomit on the floor.

Jennifer stood at the open office door, and DI James Allison waved her inside. 'Ah Jennifer, sorry I've not had much time to talk, I've been very busy with one thing and another.' He rubbed his face, looking tired and drawn.

'Can you spare me five minutes now?' Jennifer set two cups of tea on the desk.

James took the phone off the hook and switched his mobile on silent. 'Consider it done.'

A nervous feeling fluttered in her chest as she prepared to put her case to the DI. It felt silly, being nervous of a man who had known her all her life, but in a work setting, he was in charge. Laura's recent revelation about the problems he had caused for her father was not lost on her, but there were two sides to every story. DI Allison had the power to make or break her career, and she wasn't heading for promotion any time soon.

'I want to know about an old case mum was involved with. The serial killer known as the 'Grim Reaper'.'

DI Allison nodded thoughtfully. 'I see. What do you need to know?'

'Just some background information. I'd like to do some digging, look up old case files.'

He took a mouthful of tea. 'It was an open and shut case. If the accomplice ... oh, what was his name now?'

'Sam Beswick,' Jennifer said.

James clicked his fingers. 'Yes, Beswick. If he hadn't come forward we would never have been any the wiser. Why are you interested?'

'I'm concerned about the recent spate of deaths in our area.' She toyed with the cross around her neck. 'There's a pattern emerging.'

'It's news to me. Go on, I'm listening.'

'Well, first Johnny Mallet died ...'

'Committed suicide,' Allison corrected. 'We attended the scene, remember?'

Jennifer frowned. 'Sir, if you'll let me finish.'

DI Allison raised his eyebrows at her curtness. 'Go ahead.'

She opened the journal resting on her lap. 'Johnny Mallet died of an apparent suicide by hanging, similar to Michael Osborne, whose death was also believed to be suicide by hanging until Foster admitted to his murder. Both victims were known criminals and drug addicts.' Jennifer turned the page of her journal. 'Then Charlie Taylor, my ex-teacher, died in a mysterious fire. Stanley Rogers was a teacher, also killed by Foster, also in a house fire.' She sighed as she caught James looking at his watch. 'Next was Barbara Harris, a retired woman who was thought to have died from an asthma attack. However, Foster later admitted being responsible for attempting to smother the woman. Similarly, a woman named Joan Connelly recently died suddenly, due to a suspected heart attack.'

James opened his mouth to speak, and Jennifer raised her hand. 'I've just got one more, sir. Martina Jackson, a known prostitute. Frank assisted in the murder, and her body was discovered in a suitcase in a river. I'm worried about Shelly Easton, girlfriend of Johnny Mallet, also a drug user and prostitute. I visited her and she wasn't well at all. I called an ambulance, but she'd disappeared by the time they got there. Sir, with your permission, I'd like to open a line of investigation on this case.'

DI Allison folded his arms. 'Let me get this clear. Are you saying we have a copycat killer on our hands? Because Frank Foster is dead, and Beswick is banged up.'

'Oh. No, I ... didn't know,' Jennifer said, taken aback by the harshness of his voice. She should have researched Foster's whereabouts and been more prepared.

'May I?' James asked, reaching across the desk for her journal. He scanned the page, his frown deepening. 'Suicides are commonplace when dealing with our customers. And as for Charlie Taylor, he was also an alcoholic and most likely set himself alight. As I remember, Stanley Rogers was a paedophile, and this was the main reason Foster cited for killing him.'

DI Allison scanned the names written on the page. 'Foster killed Osborne for revenge. Barbara Harris died of natural causes. Foster wasn't charged with her murder, despite the fact that he tried to take the credit for it. How old was Joan Connelly?'

'Eighty-five,' Jennifer said in a very small voice.

'Eighty-five! I take it she died of natural causes?'

Jennifer nodded, wishing the ground would swallow her up.

DI Allison shook his head. 'As for Tina, Sam Beswick was responsible for her death, not Frank Foster. There's no link to Shelly, who, as far as I'm aware, is still plying her trade. I don't know why you're wasting my time with this when you've got better things to do.' DI Allison slammed the journal down, his face flushed in annoyance.

Jennifer took a deep breath. She had one more question that needed answering. 'Sir, you mentioned Tina. Are you referring to Martina Jackson?'

'Of course I am.' James pinched the bridge of his nose. 'I'm sorry for snapping, but I want you to move forward and concentrate on the cases in front of you. It's not that long since you were on restricted duties and given the number of probationers chomping at the bit, you're very fortunate to have a role in CID. Now forget all this nonsense and you'll be back dealing with proper jobs before you know it.'

'Of course, when you put it like that ...' Jennifer bit her lip as she gathered up her courage. 'It was just... when I talked to Johnny, Charlie and Shelly they spoke in a similar voice and said stuff about my past that nobody else could have known.'

'It's called a personality disorder, lots of our suspects suffer from it,' the DI said. 'You're not going to start talking about this hocus pocus stuff are you, because if I'm honest, I'm getting a bit worried about you.'

Jennifer took the journal and curled her fingers tightly around it. 'No, of course not. Investigating my mum's case made me feel closer to her. I guess I got carried away. Nothing to worry about here, I promise.'

The DI sighed. 'It wasn't even her case; she just thought it was because she got dragged into a couple of interviews. This isn't your fight. It's easy to get the sack for misuse of the PNC and I don't want that to happen to you.'

Jennifer knew only too well that unauthorised use of the police national computer could lead to her dismissal.

DI Allison's mobile phone vibrated on the table and Jennifer stood up to leave. 'Of course. Thanks for your time. I'll let you get back to work.'

Jennifer strode back to her desk. Susie scurried over, her cleavage overflowing in her tight pink dress. Jennifer's cheeks still burned from her telling off, and she wished Susie would go away.

'I wish I could have intercepted you before you went in. He's in one hell of a bad mood,' Susie whispered, revelling in the drama. 'What's wrong? Want to talk about it?'

Jennifer glared at Susie. 'Why? So you can satisfy your own curiosity?'

'Charming, well I won't ask again,' Susie flounced back to her desk.

Chance would be a fine thing, Jennifer thought. So much for reopening the case. Doors were slamming in her face at every turn. Her only hope now was the taped interview that lay sealed in the bottom of a shoe box.

CHAPTER TWENTY-THREE

The hooded figure stood in the shop doorway, grinning at the bony woman huddled under the frayed cardboard on the ground. The empty retail unit occasionally housed Haven's homeless in its generous double doorways. It offered little protection from the winter nights, but in an area free from visitors it was safer than the squats under the rule of the scourge overpowering the streets.

'Why are you here?' Shelly hissed, shifting into a sitting position, the smell of urine rising up with her.

'Now is that any way to speak to an old friend?'

Shelly stiffened, her mouth gaping open. 'It's you?'

'Yes, it is. Clever, aren't I? Some would call me the master of disguise.'

Shelly had experienced the Grim Reaper in other forms but never in the body of the person before her. With trembling hands, she put a match to the rolled up cigarette pinched between her lips. She sucked on the thin spear until the threads of tobacco caught alight.

'What do you want?' She said, blowing out a thin stream

of smoke barely discernible from her frosted breath. 'I can't take you again. You nearly killed me the last time.'

'Alas, I fear that is true. One more embodiment and you're likely to keel over. I take it you've used my gifts?'

'Have you got any more?' Shelly said, her eyes alight at the prospect of another hit. She scurried to her feet. She had left her flat with only the clothes she wore. Her elbows clamped against her sides, she jiggled on each foot.

The dance lit a memory in the Grim Reaper's eyes. 'You are a hungry little steed, aren't you? Why don't we take a walk and I can show you what I have in mind?'

Shelly stared at the inhabitant of the long dark cloak. 'But you're ...'

'What? You don't like my new mount? Are you ashamed to be seen out with me?'

'No please, I'll do whatever you want.'

'Yes. I should think you will. Now come along. It's not as if anyone's going to see us at this hour.'

Shelly's companion looked every inch the Grim Reaper, gliding into the arms of the desolate night. It was strange how an embodiment, even a temporary one, could transform the features of the person it inhabited. Shelly barely recognised the person she knew. But she had little time to care about them, because she was up to her neck in it herself.

Her companion chortled as a street lamp popped and fizzled overhead. 'Can you feel it, Shelly? The darkness is all around.'

Shelly stared forlornly at the frost-glazed street, an obedient dog following its master. They walked past the shuttered windows and ragged flyers, out of the streets onto the weed-infested shortcut that led to the riverbank. Their footsteps brought warning to the water rats that slid on greasy bellies into the reeds.

'Haven't you had enough of life?' The figure spoke as it approached the bridge which towered over the river below. 'Look at you. What's the point in going on?'

'I don't know.' Shelly sniffed, her bloodshot eyes fixed on the ground as she walked ahead. Making eye contact with the Grim Reaper was like staring into a nest of maggots.

The cloaked figure advocated suicide as they walked, each word delivered with menace.

'I want to go back. I'm tired,' Shelly said, limping from the stone which had found its way into her shoe.

They walked the wide bridge that overshadowed the Blakewater River. It was a cold metallic monster which offered no shelter from the wind. 'See how the water reflects the darkness?' the figure said. 'Isn't it welcoming?'

Shelly leaned on the steel bridge. 'I want to go back.'

Her companion spun around, clasping her throat. The veins on Shelly's neck bulged as the cloaked figure lifted her body inches from the ground. 'It's time you followed Johnny's example and said your goodbyes to this world.'

'No,' Shelly rasped, clutching at tense arms as she fought for breath. 'Please, let me go.'

The glove-fisted hand relinquished its hold and threw her to the ground. 'Why? Because you've so much to live for? What about Amber and Alisha? Have they anything to live for?'

Shelly wobbled as she picked herself up from the ground. She wouldn't cry. She wouldn't give them the satisfaction. 'You said you'd leave them outta this. You promised.'

'I'll give you a choice. The test of a mother's love. Either you jump from this bridge and save their souls, or I'll pay them a visit and you can have enough coke to ride a rocket ship to the moon.' The words were followed by an unmistakable cackle of laughter.

'No, you can't do that. They're just kids.'

The figure cracked their knuckles, savouring the moment. 'Then it's time you made a choice. Your life or theirs.'

'What choice do I have?' Shelly said, tears now cascading down her wasted face. The Grim Reaper's threats were filled with promise. She knew there was no way out.

'Good. I'll leave you to it. I'm going to get a front row view. I'll be underneath the bridge waiting for your grand appearance as you hit the water. Up you get.'

Shelly jerked as the figure lifted her onto the cold steel and threw her legs over until she was sitting facing the water below.

Shelly was still sitting on the bridge when car headlights lit up the night, music blaring in the Mini Metro. Her heart flickered as the car slowed, and curious eyes peered through the fogged up windows. Seconds later the engine roared into life, wobbling across the road markings as the orange glow of the taillights disappeared from view. A wave of weariness overcame her and she lay to one side, legs dangling. She rested her face on the cold metal. Her skin felt clammy but there was a chill from deep inside, and her body shivered as the hell of withdrawal approached. In the beginning, when she could get high for a tenner, smack made her feel nice. Nice was good. Nice took her away from the childhood in which she was forced to the streets as soon as her mother could find clients to take her. Nice made her forget the pain from the beatings. Nice took away the fact her children were in care. But now it took a lot more than a tenner to sustain Shelly, and the nice feeling was replaced with fear of the withdrawal that made her flesh crawl. And that was just the start. Her benefits had long since run out and there was no money in whoring when you looked like you'd just climbed out of a coffin. She wondered about the chances of getting another hit. Her teeth began to rattle as she shivered, and she tried to focus on her daughters. Shelly sat back up and stared unblinkingly at the water. She heard shouting from under the bridge but everything felt so far away. She couldn't remember her little girls' faces. What age were they now? The information escaped her, because all she could think of was the contents of the coat pocket of the hooded figure, which she would get if she sacrificed the children she barely knew.

'I can't do it,' she whispered to her children's memory. 'I'm sorry, I can't do it.'

But the choice was already made as a pair of gloved hands rammed into her back, sending her screaming into the icy depths below.

CHAPTER TWENTY-FOUR

A hot beverage was placed on Jennifer's desk in the absence of a white flag. 'Safe to approach?' Will said, 'You've torn a strip off Sue already and our shift hasn't even started yet.'

Jennifer almost spat her drink out. 'Ugh, what *is* this?'

'Green tea,' he smiled. 'Thought it might detox some of the depravity out of you. But I guess we'd need more than one cup for that.'

Jennifer turned to reply and momentarily forgot her problems. 'Bloody hell Will, you're looking well. Had a makeover?' Slim-line black trousers replaced his baggy chinos and his new white shirt fitted his form perfectly. Even his shaggy beard had been trimmed to an attractive stubble.

'I thought it was time I smartened up.'

'Well, I like it, and the haircut suits you.'

Will smiled. 'No Ethan today?'

'He'll be in later, he's on a prison visit or something.'

Will took a Cadbury's Creme Egg out of his drawer and placed it on the table in front of her.

'I bought it for you, but now you can give it to Susie to say you're sorry.'

'Why?'

Will grinned. 'Because she needs a partner for her suspect interview.'

Jennifer rolled her eyes as she stood. 'Not until I've cleaned our desks. Look at them.' Spraying and wiping she polished the worn wooden desks before starting on the computers, turning the keyboards upside down and tapping them as they released a shower of crumbs. She was glad Will didn't ask her about her conversation with the DI. She had no intention of sharing until she had something tangible to go on. 'Did you bring in that tape recorder I texted you about?'

'Yep, it's in my new man bag. You can have it later. Be a good girl and I might even let you have a peek inside,' Will said, with a mischievous grin. Jennifer was itching to listen to the tape at work, but the only available tape machines were in the interview room. Questions would have been asked if she booked it for her own use.

Shelly's disappearance nagged at the back of Jennifer's brain. In her downtime she emailed a referral to the mental health team to make them aware of the missing woman's deteriorating condition. Without Shelly's co-operation, there was little else she could do. What had she meant when she mentioned Joshua? It wasn't as if she could pick up the phone and ask the entity his intentions. She would have to wait until his next contact. He had made his demands clear. He wanted her. If she did not give herself freely, he would hurt Josh.

Joan Connelly's warning rang in her ears. *Protect the child at all costs.* But how? She had already frightened the crap out of her sister by ringing to warn her of some bogus paedophile in the area. Anything to make her watch him closely, grip his hand a little tighter. Her sister's naivety about the world was a bone of contention between them. The problem with being

in the police was that you knew just how many depraved
people there were out there, and the lengths they would go to
in order to get[p- what they want.

CHAPTER TWENTY-FIVE

Will hummed along to the eighties music playing on his iPod. He liked having the office to himself. Steph was usually called away to Westlea on the late shift, and Jennifer and Susie were going to be at least another hour interviewing their burglary suspect. Michael Corbett, the world's slowest solicitor, was defending him. It was just as well Susie was leading the interview. He had known Jennifer long enough to realise that she was in trouble. She was as bristly as a hedgehog when it came to her personal life and her heated meeting with the DI had not gone unnoticed. Will bound together the completed file and smiled in satisfaction. One down, nine more to go. He stretched, surveying Jennifer's spotless desk. The photo of her nephew Josh was perfectly symmetrical with the penholder, stapler, and paperclips tidily displayed. He pulled open her unlocked drawer, noticing with amusement that her array of pens and pencils were not only perfectly aligned, but colour coordinated too. He was about to shut the drawer when a blue spiral journal caught his eye. It was the same one she had been carrying when she returned from the DI's office. Will glanced at the door and back to the journal.

Jennifer wouldn't appreciate him touching her things. Then again, he didn't have any intention of telling her.

Sliding it out of the drawer, he opened it on his lap and flicked through the pages. The notes were new and nothing that he recognised from work. He frowned as he speed-read the entries. Jennifer was going over her mother's old cold cases, concerned about a modern day copycat killer. Will was plunged into a world full of supernatural theories; spontaneous combustion, possession, dissociated voices and hauntings. But some of her reasoning seemed valid. The links between each past and current death were strong, even if you put the superstitious stuff aside. Yet there was nothing on the police briefing site about any investigation. He pulled a page from his notepad and scribbled down some of the details before returning the journal to her desk. Straightening up the pens and pencils, he slowly closed the drawer before returning to his files.

CHAPTER TWENTY-SIX

Jennifer was relieved to see Ethan return to the office. Two hours of listening to Susie's voice had driven her to the edge of her sanity. Christ, that woman could talk! Between her and that boring old fart Corbett, whose only interest was Susie's cleavage, it was turning out to be a pig of a late shift. At least she had managed to swerve the paperwork which firmly belonged to Susie. Even Will was giving his puppy dog eyes a rest as he got on with his work rather than pleading with her to do it for him.

She was happy to volunteer to accompany Ethan in what was termed as the 'burglary car' for an hour. If resources allowed, they took turns driving the unmarked police car around Haven to stop check any known criminals in burglary hotspots. Ethan had only been attached to the department a short while, but Jennifer was impressed with his local knowledge.

Jennifer took her flats from the back seat and slipped them on her feet. The last time she chased a prisoner in high heels, she'd ended up sprawled over an oversized teenager who'd decided it was a good day to skateboard downhill drunk.

Ethan drove through their local McDonalds and ordered two cappuccinos to help with their night-time stake out. The smell of coffee filled the car as they parked outside a well-known burglary hotspots, a narrow alleyway leading to the back of a housing estate. Jennifer swirled the frothy coffee with the wooden stirrer as they sat in the dark.

'Steph has been keeping you busy,' she said, as the wind whistled through the car.

'Everyone's been great,' Ethan replied. 'It's different from Westlea, where people don't have time to talk.'

'I didn't realise you'd worked at Westlea.'

'I started not long after you left. You're a bit of an enigma there.'

Jennifer groaned. 'Oh God, what did you hear?'

'I heard you were … *are* a very good detective. And that you joined Haven after being on restricted duties.'

Jennifer's face dropped. 'Just because I've been for counselling doesn't make me weird.'

Ethan gave a short laugh. 'My therapist thinks that joining the police was my way of gaining my father's approval.'

'You have a therapist?'

Ethan nodded. 'Yes. After my bout of stalking and axe-murdering, they thought it would be a good idea.'

Jennifer snorted. 'Funny.'

'Mother gives me am allowance as long as I fulfil certain terms. Speaking to a stranger once a month is one of them,' Ethan said.

'I appreciate your honesty. Men aren't usually very good at talking about their emotions.'

'There's one more thing I've heard. Something about you being psychic?'

Jennifer baulked. 'I've moved on from all that now Ethan.

I'm not psychic, no mysticism, end of story.' Jennifer didn't mention that she had been moved for arresting the son of an MP. Her only evidence had been the instincts that told her he was responsible for a series of rapes in the area. Outraged, the councillor had demanded she be fired. Instead, she was put on restricted duties and transferred to Haven. The investigation cleared her of any wrongdoing, partially because her detailed forecasts of further victims came true. The MP's son was eventually charged, but Jennifer was never invited back to her old team.

'Sorry, I didn't mean to upset you,' Ethan said, looking at her lap.

Jennifer realised she had broken her coffee stirrer into little pieces. She shrugged, gathering them up to put in her empty coffee cup. 'Shit happens.'

'So, on a lighter note, are you going to the fundraising party?' Ethan smiled.

'Susie bullied me into buying a ticket so I'll show my face. You?'

'Can't disappoint these desperate women you keep telling me about.'

'That's the spirit.'

CHAPTER TWENTY-SEVEN

Ethan held the smoke in his lungs for a few seconds before releasing it through the crack in the tinted car window. Disguising his smoking habit at work was something he had begun to regret, but the image of a clean-cut probationer was something he thought would appeal to Jennifer. After all, she had taken her sister under her motherly wing, why not a naïve young officer, new to the area? He had thought long and hard about what kind of image to present, and his frustration grew as he realised that gaining her trust was more difficult than he'd imagined. He shrank back in his seat as Jennifer peered out through her bedroom curtains before pulling them shut. Even if she noticed his car parked on her residential street, she would not be able to make him out through the tinted windows of his mother's Saab. Ethan took one last drag of the cigarette and threw it out the window. He tapped his fingers on the steering wheel as he craned his neck upwards. The bedroom light flicked off and the house lay in darkness. Watching Jennifer's house was futile. It was not as if she went to the pub, where a chance of an encounter could lead to something more. The woman was a virtual recluse. He turned the key in the ignition and pulled off the kerb. Time was not on his side and he would have to work harder at gaining her trust.

CHAPTER TWENTY-EIGHT

FRANK – 1992

'You're not going to chicken out on me now, are you?' Frank's eyebrow inched upward as Sam returned from his third visit to the bathroom.

'No man, I told you, I'm cool.' But Sam's hands trembled as he lit a cigarette.

Frank folded his arms, his face stern. 'Because I've already said, you're either with me or against me, and if you're against me ...'

'I'm with you,' Sam said, trying to suppress the sick feeling in his stomach. 'You must have been nervous the first time you did it.'

'Killed someone? Nah. I enjoyed it.' Frank smiled at the memory.

'Weren't you scared?'

'Why would I be scared?'

'In case it goes wrong. In case they fight back, or you get caught.'

Frank clamped a hand to Sam's shoulder. 'They're gonna

fight back. Nobody gives up their life easily. That's why you prepare. Or at least have the know how to deal with things when they happen. That's half the fun. It's a ride, enjoy it.'

Sam took a deep drag of his cigarette, flaring puffs of smoke through his nostrils.

'You'd better get going. It doesn't matter if you're nervous, just tell her it's the first time you've had a lady like her. Be charming, they like that, it relaxes them. And I won't come out until you've done it, so you may as well get a shag before we finish her off.'

Sam nodded and loped towards the door, his shoulders slumped. Frank shook his head, thinking that Sam looked as if he was heading for the gallows rather than the thrill of his life. 'Just remember everything I told you. And for Christ's sake use a rubber johnny or you'll be itchy for a month.'

Shadows fell and the streetlights cast an orange glow on the single bed in Sam's room. The kid didn't have much in the poky box room; a wardrobe, a lava lamp on his bedside table, and a couple of heavy metal posters drooping off the walls. At least he was graced with an en suite bathroom, which would provide a useful hiding place. Frank cracked his knuckles through his leather gloves as he ran through the scenario in his mind. Pity he couldn't fit into the wardrobe, he would have liked to have watched. He lay on the bed and closed his eyes, enacting the scene in his head.

Frank jumped as the key turned in the door. How the hell had he fallen asleep? He jerked forward, softly placing his feet on the floor as he crept to the adjoining bathroom, grateful the hinges didn't creak just this once. Tina's voice cawed through the next room, hoarse from years of smoking. It grated on his senses as he listened in.

Frank's heart pounded as a rush of adrenaline coursed

through his veins. Licking the dryness from his lips, he was barely able to contain his excitement as he stood in the bath and pulled the makeshift shower curtain across.

Sam shuffled into the bedroom, dragging his feet behind him. A streak of light sliced through the bathroom door and Frank strained to hear. Shoes being removed and hitting the floor. Good. Frank wanted her stilettos well out of the way when she entered the bathroom. And she would. The bedsprings bounced.

'Nice place ya got here, for someone your age.'

Sam mumbled in response.

'Not the talkative type, are you? Suits me. Money up front then, twenty quid like we agreed.'

Frank stifled a snicker. Twenty quid! Who did she think she was? She was taking the kid for a ride in more ways than one.

'What are ya staring at? Are you gonna take off your pants or do you want me to do it for you?'

Frank listened as Sam sat on the bed. He was hesitating too much. She would guess something was up.

'Oh for Christ's sake, give me regulars any day of the week. You kids just waste my time. Come here, let me get that tracksuit down.'

'Get off me,' Sam said as the bedsprings bounced.

'C'mon now don't be shy, let the dog see the ...' A rasp of laughter tore through the room. 'Ha! What am I meant to do with that?'

'I said get off me, you stupid bitch,' Sam said.

Tina seemed oblivious to the menacing tone in Sam's voice as she laughed and hacked up a cough at the same time. 'What are ya, queer?'

Fist cracked on skin and Tina howled. 'What did you do that for? I'm pissing blood you little bastard!'

'You shouldn't have laughed,' Sam said, a touch of hysteria

in his voice.

Tina's voice drew closer as she stumbled to the bathroom. 'You'd better sort me out with some more money or my fella will be paying you a visit.'

Tina opened the bathroom door and clicked the light switch. 'Can't you afford a light bulb?'

She stared at the dim reflection in the mirror as Frank stemmed his breath. 'Aw, will you look at that? Shit.'

Frank tensed as Sam paced the bedroom. Things weren't going to plan. But that was OK. He could improvise. Tina bent to unravel some toilet roll as Frank made out her form through the shower curtain.

'Such a waste of time you kids, I don't know why I ...'

Frank moved swiftly as he gathered up the cheap hard plastic and pulled it over Tina's head. Shower hooks popped one by one as she garbled a scream. In one swift movement, he twisted the plastic around her head, and held her in a bear hug with his other arm. Lifting her kicking feet off the floor, he carried her into the bedroom. Sam froze.

'C'mon then, this is your gift! What are you waiting for?' Frank shouted in exasperation.

Sam ran a hand through his hair and grabbed the open holdall from the wardrobe. He threw the ropes on the bed.

'Help me tie her up.' Frank said, a lecherous smile spreading across his face. Tina struggled for breath as she fought and splatters of blood hit the inside of the shower curtain with every muffled cry.

'Sorry old girl, the Grim Reaper is knocking on your door.' Frank laughed as he bound her hands together. She bucked and kicked as Sam held down her legs, desperately trying to breathe through the plastic wound tightly around her neck.

'Shut her up! Get that pillow over her head.' Frank said, breathing heavily.

Sam froze. 'I can't.'

'And what's going to happen to you if you let her go now? She knows where you live. That pimp of hers will slice you to pieces.'

Sam squeaked in a whiny voice. 'I don't think I can.'

Frank grabbed the neck of Sam's tracksuit, curling it up in his fist as he brought him nose to nose over Tina's squirming body. A malevolent look spread across Frank's face and he growled, 'Just. Fucking. Do it.'

CHAPTER TWENTY-NINE

Sam took the pillow in both hands. He straddled it over Tina's face, exerting every ounce of energy into silencing her muffled screams. 'Shhhh, shush now, don't fight it,' he whispered, desperately wanting the noise to go away. After a few endless seconds, the screaming resided and her movements slowed. He pushed harder on the pillow, wanting it to be over for Tina, so she didn't have to suffer any more than necessary.

Frank lifted up the bound wrists and they flopped back onto her body. 'About time,' he said, coldly.

Sam sat, hunched over, his face glistening with sweat as his shoulders heaved. He watched as Frank circled the body on the bed, pulling off the pillow to reveal Tina's engorged face under layers of bloodstained plastic. 'That'll teach you, bitch. Hey Sam, you still got that johnny? I fancy giving Tina one last farewell.'

Retching, Sam ran to the bathroom and threw up. His heaves mixed with choking sobs as he leaned over the toilet. 'What have we done?'

Frank reached for the knife from the holdall and stood in

the bathroom doorway. 'The bulb is in the cabinet if you want to put it back in.'

Sam turned as the glint of the knife caught his eye. 'Sure. Whatever you say, Frank.'

Frank tapped on the door three times with the blade of the knife. 'Like I said, I'm the Grim Reaper. Whose door do you think I'll be knocking on next?'

'What ... what do you mean?' Sam wiped his mouth and turned to face Frank, the walls of the bathroom closing in on him.

'I mean are you with me, or against me?'

Sam faked a smile, wishing he'd stop saying those words. 'I'm with you man, all the way. It takes a bit of getting used to, that's all.'

Frank shrugged. 'You need to grow some balls. Now give me five minutes. Tina and I would like a little privacy.'

Sam nodded and screwed the bulb into the bathroom light before closing the door. The thought of what he had done made him want to throw up all over again. He just killed someone. He had brought her there in cold blood and killed her. What the hell had he been thinking? That Frank wouldn't go through with it? That Frank had been bullshitting him all along? He liked Frank. It was more than that. He wanted to impress him. But deep down, he never really thought he'd go through with it. He bit into his fist as sobs wracked through his body. Frank was nuts. Simple as that. He had no remorse, no feelings. A complete psycho.

Sam needed to skip town, and fast. But Frank knew where his family lived. He had him exactly where he wanted him. Thoughts raced in his head. Perhaps if he went to the police and said Frank had forced him into helping ... He wiped the sweat from his brow. Staring into the mirror, he didn't recognise the pasty face looking back at him. The face of a murderer. What had that poor slag ever done to him? And she was lying dead in his bed while Frank ... Sam's stomach heaved.

Frank called for him from the bedroom. 'C'mon Sam, we're done here. Time to make Tina disappear.' Sam lifted his head from the toilet bowl, wishing he could make it all disappear.

CHAPTER THIRTY

The mundane chatter of the TV show failed to dilute Jennifer's unease. It was not a good night to be alone. She glanced at her watch for the tenth time. Tonight, minutes dragged like hours as Shelly's warning invaded her thoughts. Nine pm, not too late to call her sister and invite herself around.

Her sister looked surprised to see her out on such a bad night. After hanging her rain-splattered coat, Jennifer peeped into the living room where Amy's husband David sat with legs crossed, one slipper hanging lazily on his foot. A glass of red wine was nestled in his hand, and he nodded a greeting before returning his attention to the TV drama. Subtitles replaced sound in the unusually quiet room as Lily snoozed.

Amy ushered her into the kitchen, keeping her voice low. 'I'm glad you came. I was going to ask you over but I wasn't sure what shift you were on.'

'What's wrong? Is Josh okay?' Jennifer felt short of breath, and it wasn't just the run from the car to the front door that caused it. An oppressive atmosphere enveloped the usually buoyant household, and she fiddled with the cross around her neck as her apprehension grew.

'He's been having nightmares. I was hoping you could have a little talk with him, he always settles better after he's seen you.'

'Yeah, sure, is he awake?'

'Yes, although I put him to bed ages ago. It's a bit dark on the landing, the bulb's blown.'

Jennifer frowned. Experience told her the extinguished light was not a faulty bulb but a precursor of something else, and she fought the urge to take the stairs two at a time.

She jumped as Amy grabbed her arm. 'Oh, one more thing. Don't make too much noise.' Amy lowered her voice to a whisper. 'We've only just got Lily asleep and David's had a really tough day at work. People from head office descended and had a go at him about his shop floor.'

Jennifer resisted the urge to roll her eyes. David was a good provider but an old fashioned husband who left the bulk of the childcare to Amy. 'And I dare say you've had a pretty tough day yourself. Don't worry, I won't make a sound.'

'Do you want me to make you a coffee?'

Jennifer's eyes flicked up to the dark landing and back to her sister. She didn't want a drink but needed some time alone with Joshua.

'Yes, that would be lovely, I'll go straight up.'

Jennifer padded up the darkened stairs, the gloom relieved only by the slanted shards of light slipping through each banister. Her senses dictated that she take things gradually. Listening intently, she placed her hand on the doorknob, resisting the urge to pull away from the shock of cold metal. Slowly she rotated the handle, her heart beating hard at the thought of what she might find inside the small box room. She peeped through the glow of the caterpillar nightlight to see Joshua sitting in bed bolt upright, his open mouth releasing a thin wisp of frosted breath. Toys were littered across the soft blue carpet, but somehow she reached him without making a sound. Goosebumps prickled her arms as she sensed a cocktail of manifestations in the room. Whispering his name, she waited for a response. His shallow breaths were barely audible, and Jennifer gently touched his arms, willing life into him. 'Josh, it's me, Jenny.'

Like a wind-up toy springing to life, Josh inhaled deeply, blinked twice, and smiled.

'Auntie Jenny, you came to see me.'

She exhaled a sigh of relief and hugged him close to her chest. 'Yes sweetheart, I did. Where were you?'

Joshua stared at his Fireman Sam duvet cover. 'The bad man told me not to say.'

Jennifer's chest tightened as fury ignited in every cell of her being. *The entity ... that evil bastard ... How dare he?* Joshua's blue eyes stared at her for reassurance and she threaded his fingers through his as she nestled onto the side of the bed. 'Sweetie I know you're scared, but I'm stronger than any bad man and you can tell me. I'm the police remember?'

'He was in here,' Joshua pointed to his forehead.

'Can you be a brave boy and keep him out?'

Joshua's bottom lip trembled as his eyes filled with tears. 'He said he'd hurt you if I didn't let him in.'

Jennifer's heart ached for the little boy she so desperately wanted to protect. 'Josh, I need you to be strong, do you hear me? Like a policeman, or Fireman Sam. You remember when we spoke about bullies, don't you? They tell lies to get what they want.'

Josh wiped his eyes and nodded.

Jennifer forced herself back into police mode. She could shout and scream later, but for now she needed to find out as much as she could to keep him safe from the entity threatening its way into their lives. 'Can you tell me what he looked like?'

'He came from the dark. He's scary.'

'Sweetheart, did you see his face?'

Joshua scrunched his face as he tried to find the words. 'No. He hurts people.'

Another flash of anger surfaced. The 'bad man' had wormed his way into the sanctity of Joshua's mind and communicated images to him. She looked deep into her nephew's eyes. 'Do you know how to keep him out?'

'Yes,' Josh said, pointing to the end of the bed. 'The lady showed me. I close my eyes and make a wall. The light keeps him out.'

'What lady is that?' Jennifer asked gently, the answer creeping into her mind along with the faint smell of apple blossom floating in the air.

'The kind lady.'

'Is she here now?'

'Yes.' A secret smile came to Joshua's lips as his eyes followed the invisible figure at the end of the bed.

'What does she look like?' Jennifer stared into the empty space, trying to pick up the energy. Something soft at the edge of her consciousness was blocked as she probed further.

'She looks like you. But she's not you.'

The words conveyed what Jennifer already knew and her lips moved in silent thanks.

The sound of Amy's feet creaking on the stairs signalled that her time with Joshua was over.

'You're safe now. If you ever need anything, tell Mummy and I will come straight around.'

Joshua yawned and rubbed his eyes. 'Will you drive the police car?'

Jenny chuckled. 'Maybe. Now give me a kiss and get to

sleep.' Jennifer felt the room warm, as any residue of evil dissipated. Joshua was safe for now.

Amy stood at the doorway, rubbing her arms. Jennifer smiled at her sister and tucked Joshua into bed. Leaning over, she whispered in his ear, 'Remember we love you, and we'll keep you safe. Just don't let the bad man in again.'

'Jenny?' Joshua said, his voice drowsy.

'Yes sweetie?'

'Did you bring me any chocolate?'

Jennifer ruffled his hair, 'Next time, I promise.'

Amy walked over. 'I'll leave on the night light, and the monitor is on next door so I'll hear you, OK?'

Joshua did not answer. He was already falling into a light sleep.

Amy sniffed the air as she turned to leave the room. 'I like your perfume.'

'Perfume?' Jennifer said. The only scent she wore was the vanilla body wash that had long since evaporated.

'Yeah. Apple blossom. It's what mum used to wear.'

'Oh, right. It's a tester from Boots.' Jennifer hated lying to her sister, but she had only just been allowed back in the fold.

Amy put her finger to her lips as she pointed to Lily, still dozing peacefully in her Moses basket. Her cherry lips made a soft sucking movement as she snoozed in contentment. Jennifer glanced at the empty sofa, guessing David had gone upstairs.

'Did Josh say anything to you?' Amy shoved across a plate of chocolate digestives to complement the coffees she had just made.

Jennifer sighed. 'He mentioned bad dreams. I managed to make him feel better.'

A frown burrowed into Amy's features. 'I think it's more than just nightmares.'

Jennifer held her breath, wondering if her sister understood what was going on.

'I'm going to have him tested for autism,' Amy said.

Jennifer stared at her sister. 'I don't think that's it.' She paused. 'There was this programme once on the telly about children who had a similar insight as Josh.'

'Oh yeah, what was that?'

'They called them psychic children. They tested them and everything. It seemed quite conclusive.'

Amy laughed. 'I don't believe in that rubbish.'

Jennifer tried another tactic. 'Remember when we were children and we used to play Ring O' Roses?'

'I remember hating that bloody game, you kept grabbing my hand, making me play.'

'That's right. Do you remember *why* you hated it?'

'It's so long ago ...'

'You said that when you held my hands you used to see other children playing with us. It frightened you, so you stopped. Maybe it's like that for Joshua.'

'Imaginary friends that frighten him? I doubt it.'

Jennifer faked a smile. 'You're right, it was just a thought. Anyway, I've got to go. Promise me you won't do anything rash with Josh, you don't want him to pick up on it.'

Amy folded her arms, a hint of annoyance in her voice. 'Knowing him, he probably knows already. But thank you for the parenting advice, Sis, I'll seek your approval before doing anything.'

Jennifer grabbed her bag from the side and fumbled with her car keys. Her emotions began to rise like a tidal wave; frustration at not being able to care for Josh, mixed with anger at being kept at such a distance. All she had ever done was protect her sister. She'd never imagined they would end up like this. She mumbled goodbye and turned to leave. Amy grabbed her shoulder, regret etched on her face.

'Sorry, Sis, I shouldn't have said that. I'm actually really proud of you. Come and see Josh any time you like.'

'Does David agree with that? He seems to disappear every time I come around.'

'It's me he's avoiding, not you. I've been a bit hormonal since Lily was born, but we'll be OK. Christmas is coming and I don't want any bad feelings.'

'Well, if you ever need to talk, you know where I am.'

Amy opened her arms for a hug, and she fell into her sister's embrace. It was the first time Amy had hugged her since she fell ill. She had never understood why her sister punished her for falling apart.

The rain cleared on the journey home and Jennifer's mobile phone buzzed. Joshua came to mind, and she pulled her mud splashed red Vauxhall Astra over to respond. The country lane was a shortcut she used frequently, but the absence of streetlights left it dark and murky, with nothing but the glow of the moon overhead. She hastily pressed the 'accept' button while turning off the engine in her car. The raspy voice on the other end shot a chill down her spine.

'Hello Jen-ni-fer, it's Shelly. I heard you were concerned about me.'

Jennifer frowned. The voice sounded like Shelly's, but the vocabulary was off. She peered through the car windscreen, pressing the central locking button.

'Shelly, yes I was worried. Where are you?'

Manic giggling. 'I'm somewhere very cold. But you already know that don't you Jenny?' Shelly tutted down the phone. 'You shouldn't have stopped him talking to the boy. He was just being friendly.'

Jennifer's heart accelerated at the mention of Josh, and her fingers reached for the small silver cross nestled on her collarbone. 'I don't know what you're talking about Shelly, but if you tell me what you want, perhaps I can help.'

'It's too late for that and you know it. But don't worry, he'll be in touch when the time is right. You won't need to look very far.' The voice gave off a deep throaty laugh and the call ended. Jennifer shivered. It was an unknown number, just like the previous silent calls that had tormented her. She drove home at speed, skidding into puddles and hitting potholes as she fought to keep calm.

CHAPTER THIRTY-ONE

SAM – 1992

Sam stared at the static of the television screen, seeing Tina's face in the visual snow. He lay on the sofa, pulling the blanket over his shoulders as desolation swept over him. For weeks after Tina's death, he had expected the police to come knocking at his door. As much as he tried to dodge the responsibility, he knew he was to blame. Sam replayed it in his head so many times with an alternate ending. Returning alone, telling Frank that Tina wasn't around, even warning her off. Maybe if he hadn't hit her, she wouldn't have gone into the bathroom to mop up the blood. Maybe if he hadn't straddled the pillow over her head, and leaned with all his might ...

As he dragged out the heavy suitcase, Frank said he'd call. That was the last he had seen of him. He'd mentioned taking Tina for a swim but Sam didn't want to know. He just wanted her gone.

The sleeping tablets in the top shelf of the bathroom cabinet called to him. That's what he needed, a very long sleep. Sam dragged his feet to the dingy room, replaying past events with each step. He glanced at the row of empty hooks where the shower curtain used to be. A new plastic curtain would bring the nightmare of Frank's shadow, hiding and waiting for his prey. Sam shook the bottle of pills as he returned to the living room. There were enough to send him to sleep for good. His mother would be horrified.

It pained him to think about her. She had always tried to do her best by him, but her religious views were stifling. That was why he had dyed his hair, packed his bags, and left without saying goodbye. Armed with a handful of newspaper clippings of someone else's crimes, he had smoked dope with his friends as he bragged about how he had evaded the police yet again. But it was all lies. Sure, he had been arrested, but only for pick pocketing; a compulsion born out of necessity to feed his cannabis habit. It had been cruel of him to abandon his mother, but it was too late to go back to her now. He didn't deserve her forgiveness. He was totally alone.

A sob caught in the back of his throat and he curled up in a ball on the sofa. He had the guts to kill someone else, but not himself. Well, if he didn't do it, Frank would do it for him. He cried himself into a stupor and woke to find himself naked in a prison cell. Hunched into a ball, he listened as high-heeled footsteps echoed down the corridor, approaching the cell door. The latch dropped and Tina's bloodshot eyes bulged through the hatch, the remnants of a shower curtain masking her bloated face. 'Lemmie in, let the dog see the bone ...'

'Sorry, I didn't mean to do it,' Sam whimpered, hiding his head in his knees.

An odious smell lingered as Tina hammered on the prison door, *bang bang bang*. 'Sam, let me in.' On and on the voice thundered from the other side, 'I know you're in there, open the door, it's twelve o clock.'

Sam woke with a start, his heart pounding wildly. Impatient fists hammered at his front door. 'C'mon kid, answer the door, we need to talk.'

Sam rubbed his clammy face with his hands. 'OK, OK, I'm coming.' Frank was back. That part of the nightmare was real.

As he expected, Frank was standing with a broad smile on his face, wearing a new suit, and no doubt a pocket full of cash.

Sam faked a smile for the sake of self-preservation. 'Frank, when did you get back? You look great. Come inside.'

Frank's face fell as he looked Sam up and down. 'I'm afraid I can't say the same for you buddy, you look terrible. What's all this?' he pointed to the blanket-covered sofa.

'I've been sick, the flu. I couldn't move,' Sam lied.

'Anything I can get you?'

'No thanks, I'll be OK. Where have you been?'

'Oh, here and there. I've been thinking of investing in some properties abroad and I went to view them. I met a very nice lady out there. Let's just say she took good care of me.'

Sam smiled. 'Nice one,' he said, wondering how the rich old bag would feel if she knew that the last person Frank had shagged was a corpse.

'You sure I can't get you anything? You've gone very pale.'

'I just need some sleep. Sorry I didn't hear you banging at first. I took some pills. You said you wanted to talk to me?'

Frank smiled, but it didn't reach his eyes, which were burrowing their way into Sam's brain, trying to pick out the truth behind the veneer. 'Nothing that can't wait. I just wanted to see if you were OK. I'll call back tomorrow.'

Sam's emotions ran riot as Frank patted his shoulder. His very presence was hypnotic. If only things had been different. But it was all fake. His dark looks drew people in, and his charm ensnared them.

Sam was a rat in a trap and he didn't stand a chance. 'Frank, before you go, can I ask ... Tina, did you ...' Sam swallowed hard. 'Did you have any problems getting rid of her?'

Frank rested his hand on Sam's arm. It was warm and Sam could smell his aftershave as he whispered, 'I told you I'd make her disappear and I have, so don't you worry about it. The cops haven't been sniffing around, have they?'

'No, not at all.'

'There you go, my friend. I told you nobody would miss her. Now clean this place up, it stinks. And have a shave while you're at it. I'll be round tomorrow to tell you about my plans. There's a certain lady I need to even the score with, and it's been a long time coming.'

CHAPTER THIRTY-TWO

Jennifer sat on the plush living room rug and leaned against the sofa with her mug. The hot chocolate reminded her of a ritual she had enjoyed with her mother when she was alive. It was a nice memory; sneaking out of bed when her mum came home late from work, both sitting nursing hot chocolates as they swapped whispered stories of their day. With the house asleep, it had felt like they were the only people awake in the world.

Jennifer's eyes rested on the tape recorder in front of her. She examined the tape, rolling her finger over the smooth edges. To think, her mother had touched it before her. Jennifer had thought long and hard about how Elizabeth had gotten hold of such vital evidence. The station's ancient machine held three cassette tapes. It had been known to break down, and a few years ago if one tape jammed, they would save the other two for court and bin the third. Things had tightened up a lot since then, and now everything had to be accounted for. Jennifer would not have put it past her mother to save the mangled tape and fix it at home. She wound the spool back and sure enough, she saw the tell tale sign of indentations in the narrow brown plastic tape.

She pushed the tape into the Walkman and closed the lid. Her finger hovered over the 'play' button, praying she would find some answers. Was she ready to hear her mother's voice? Taking a deep breath, she pressed 'play'.

PS Knight: The time is 13.47 and my name is Sergeant Elizabeth Knight. I am interviewing. For the purposes of the tape can you give me your name and date of birth?

Sam Beswick: Um, Sam Beswick 14th February 1973.

Jennifer paused the tape. Her mother's voice sounded just like hers. Authoritative and professional, it made her want to sit up and take notice. The quality was not brilliant, but enough to make out the break in the boy's voice. At least that's what he sounded like, a frightened boy. She forwarded the tape past the intros. Sam had chosen not to have a solicitor present, despite her mother's advice. Jennifer opened her journal and began to transcribe the interview.

PS Knight: Sam, tell me what you know about the death of Martina Jackson, known to you as Tina. Start from the first contact you had with her, right up to present day.

Sam Beswick: Oh God, this is awful. I feel sick.

PS Knight: Take some deep breaths.

. . .

Sam Beswick: Deep breaths. Yeah. Okay. It's okay. I didn't mean to do it yeah? It's all Frank's fault, it was his idea.

PS Knight: Please go on.

Sam Beswick: I killed her. There. I've said it. I killed Tina.

PS Knight: OK Sam, can I stop you there? We can refer to Martina Jackson as Tina from now on. Who is Frank and what is his involvement in this?

Sam Beswick: Frank Foster. He calls himself the 'Grim Reaper'. He lives in my block of flats. He put me up to this.

PS Knight: Do you have a date of birth for Frank? Approximate age?

Sam Beswick: He ... he said his birthday was Christmas day, but Frank lies. That's why I didn't believe him at first. I guess ... thirties, maybe forty, I dunno.

PS Knight: Usually there would be another officer making notes, but upon your insistence, I am solo. In order to make sense of what you're telling me, we need to start from the beginning and work our way to the present day. That way we won't need to keep going back and forward. Do you understand?

. . .

PS Knight: Sam look at me. I need you to speak your responses instead of nodding your head. For the purposes of the tape, do you understand?

Sam Beswick: Yeah, I get it.

PS Knight: Thank you. Now to go back to my original question. Tell me what you know about Tina's death starting from the beginning up to the present day.

Sam Beswick: It was all Frank's idea. I thought he was bluffing. I guess I should have known, because his face used to light up when he'd talk about killing. I can't believe I'm here. I can't believe I'm sitting here talking about a murder.

PS Knight: You were telling me about Frank.

Sam Beswick: He ... he told me to offer Tina some money to come back to my place. He said he'd hide and when we had ... well, Tina was a whore. I think they went back a long way. Anyway, Frank brought in this massive suitcase and said he was gonna bump her off. I didn't think he'd go through with it. You've got to believe me, (inaudible) I didn't know.

PS Knight: What happened next?

. . .

Sam Beswick: I brought her back and Frank hid in the bathroom. But I knew he was listening and I couldn't, you know, do it. Tina got real mean, pulling at my pants, telling me to hurry up. I didn't want her touching me so I hit her, you know, to get her off me. She went into the bathroom to clean up. Frank was waiting. I thought maybe that he'd let her go, say it was a wind up. The next thing I know, she's screaming ...

PS Knight: Go on.

Sam Beswick: (Sigh) Oh man, this is hard. If I say all this now, I don't have to keep talking about it, do I?

PS Knight: I can't promise that, but if you give us a clear account now, then it's less likely you'll need to go over it as often.

Sam Beswick: Frank came out of the bathroom holding Tina up off the ground. She was kicking like crazy. He had her in a kind of bear hug, with the shower curtain wrapped around her head. There was blood on the inside of the curtain, but I guess that's from where she split her lip. I almost shit my pants when I saw her, I couldn't believe he was going through with it. He threw her on the bed and made me tie her up. When I saw how strong he was, I ... I couldn't leave. It was awful, I've never hurt anyone before, you've got to believe me. Oh God! (Sobbing).

. . .

PS Knight: Sam?

Sam Beswick: (Sniffled) Everything was going so fast, I couldn't stop it. You know like when you're on a fairground ride with your friends and you're meant to enjoy it? They're all smiling, but it's frightening the crap out of you, and you don't want to start screaming because you might not stop? ... No, I don't suppose you know how that feels at all.

PS Knight: You were saying she was on the bed?

Sam Beswick: Um, yes. Frank gave me a pillow and told me to put it on her face and sit on it. He told me he'd killed someone like that before. I didn't want to, but he said if we let Tina go, her pimp would slice me up. But he kept saying it with a smile on his face. It was really creepy, like he'd lost his mind.

PS Knight: What happened next?

Sam Beswick: I did as he said. After a couple of minutes, I stood up. Frank ... he pulled back the pillow and said she was dead. That's when I threw up. I wanted to call the cops but Frank started flashing his knife about. I thought he was going to kill me too.

PS Knight: And what did you do then?

· · ·

Sam Beswick: Nothing. Frank, um, he cleaned up the flat and got rid of the body.

PS Knight: Sam, I sense you're hesitating there. Did anything else happen that you're not telling me about?

Sam Beswick: No. He ... he just got rid of her. I stayed in the bathroom the whole time. After that, he just took off. In one way I was relieved, but in another way, I needed him around to tell me it would be all right. I didn't know what to do. I'm not a bad person. I wish I never met Frank Foster.

PS Knight: I'm not judging you Sam. My job right now to get an accurate account of what happened.

Sam Beswick: Uh huh. After it happened, I couldn't sleep in that bed anymore. I couldn't sleep at all. I got stoned a lot, to block it out. I couldn't understand how he could be so happy about it. He draws pictures of dead people. He's really fucked up.

PS Knight: Why didn't you call if you knew what he was planning?

Sam Beswick: I already said, I didn't think he'd do it. Tina would leave, we'd have a laugh, and that would be the end of it.

. . .

PS Knight: And afterwards?

Sam Beswick: For the first few weeks I was numb. I kept seeing Tina everywhere. It was really messing with my head. I even thought about topping myself. Then Frank came back. He seemed like his old self. I thought maybe things would get better. But then he started planning on doing it again. That's when I came to you.

PS Knight: OK, I'll need to talk to you about that, but I need to ask you a question first. Was there anything more than friendship between you and Frank?

Sam Beswick: What sort of a question is that?

PS Knight: I wouldn't ask you anything that wasn't relevant.

Sam Beswick: (Chair screeching) Oh man, oh man, when he finds out I've come to you ...

PS Knight: Sit down Sam. I can't talk to you when you're standing up.

Sam Beswick: I don't want to be anywhere near him when he finds out. Are you listening to me? He's a psycho! A complete psycho!

. . .

PS Knight: Either you sit down now or I'm terminating this interview.

... thank you. Now, you were about to tell me about your relationship with Frank.

Sam Beswick: (inaudible)

PS Knight: Speak up please, I can't hear you.

Sam Beswick: When I first met him, he acted as if he liked me, but now I think he'll kill me. Nothing happened between us though. I think he's been playing games with me all along.

PS Knight: Sam, why did you ask to speak to me?

Sam Beswick: I found your card in his jacket pocket. I figured he must have been carrying it around for ages, it was so worn. It felt like a sign, finding your name like that. I knew what I had to do.

PS Knight: You said Frank has killed people in the past and he's planning another murder. What do you know about it?

Sam Beswick: He's planning another one and wants me with him. I don't know who it is, but it's something big. I ... I guessed if I could stop him, I could somehow make up for killing Tina. But it's all his fault, now I'm gonna end up going to prison, aren't I? (Sobbing.)

PS Knight: Sam, I can see you're upset, but I need as much information as I can so we can begin to put things in place.

Sam Beswick: (Sniffles loudly) I don't know much more. He's pissed off with some woman, wants to teach her a lesson. I told him to go it alone, but he said if I even thought about going to the cops he'd kill me. I told him I'd rather die than grass on him, but he's on to me, I know it.

PS Knight: I need more than that. In order to arrest Frank we need evidence, and so far all you've given me is hearsay.

Sam Beswick: I've put my balls on the line coming to you, so don't sit there and say you're gonna do nothing about it! Don't you see? He's a murderer! Oh God, what if he finds me?

PS Knight: Sam, calm down. We'll act on your information, but I need to know more. Start by telling me about his past murders, and we can work from there.

Sam Beswick: He's got a sketchbook. He keeps it hidden. He showed me a couple of drawings. One was of this old guy, tied in a chair. He had a rag in his mouth and there were flames coming from the chair.

· · ·

PS Knight: Give me as much detail as you can remember from that picture.

Sam Beswick: It wasn't like it was a photo or anything, it was just a sketch. He was sitting in a wide chair with arm rests. There wasn't any detail of the clothes he was wearing, just his face. Frank said the guy was a paedo and deserved to die.

PS Knight: Did he say where he was from?

Sam Beswick: Frank travels all around. He was a delivery driver for a while and it took him all over. The guy in the chair looked old, and I'd say he had white or grey hair. I don't know when it happened, but I would say it's been in the last few years.

PS Knight: Would you recognise the man if we showed you a picture?

Sam Beswick: Maybe. I only looked at the picture a couple of times, but his face stood out. I think I'd remember him.

PS Knight: You said that Frank tells tall tales, makes up stories. Why do you believe he's killed before?

Sam Beswick: It's the look in his face when he talks about it, and – I remember now – he said his mum was reading about it in the local paper when she was alive. He used to live somewhere else with her before she died. It can't be too far away.

PS Knight: Can you remember anything else about that sketch? Even the smallest detail?

Sam Beswick: No. Nothing. There was one other picture he showed me. It was a woman, she looked dead too. She was lying back on a sofa, her hand was outstretched like she was reaching for something. I mentioned it to Frank and he laughed and said he had killed her by leaning on a cushion over her face. He thought it was really funny. He said she was an old bitch and had been rude to him. When he talked about stuff like that, he would smile and hold his head to one side like he was talking about going to a wedding, or a good night out. I had to try to smile along with him, like it was the most normal thing in the world to kill someone for being rude to you.

Jennifer paused the tape as she gathered her thoughts. The interview was intense, yet her mother was doing everything she could to keep it calm and controlled. She must have been under pressure knowing her superiors were listening in. She stood and stretched her legs. Her hand ached from transcribing, but she needed notes she could refer back to, particularly if she was following the lines of enquiry from home rather than the police station where it should be progressed. DI Allison claimed he was her friend, yet he showed a complete lack of faith when she came for help. She rubbed her face. She wanted to take a break and process the interview. But she had to keep going, to bring herself back into the interview room with Sam and Elizabeth. She sat back and pressed 'play'.

PS Knight: Thank you Sam, I know this isn't easy. Can you remember what the woman looked like in the picture? Again, any indicator of time, location, anything like that?

Sam Beswick: She was big, well, fat really. She had short curly hair. Frank was good at drawing. He puts a lot of detail into facial expressions. She was wearing some kind of dress. I remember him joking that she didn't give him a tip. Yeah, that's it, it was around Christmas, when he did some volunteer work for the Salvation Army. What a joke. Can I have a break now? I need a whizz.

PS Knight: If I get you a pencil and paper do you think you could draw what you saw?

Sam Beswick: I could try.

PS Knight: In that case, I'm going to stop the interview to get you some drawing materials. Would you object to me bringing in another officer when I continue the interview?

Sam Beswick: I don't want anyone else.

. . .

PS Knight: Sam, it's up to you if you speak with them or not. I'm happy to come in alone with some drawing materials but bear in mind that this is what we call a 'first account' interview. We're making background enquiries, but we will need to conduct a further interview in greater detail. Is there anything further you want to add before I switch off the tapes?

Sam Beswick: Can I go to the toilet now?

PS Knight: The time is 14.10 hours, first interview concluded.

The tape revealed nothing more as it squeaked to the end, and Jennifer ejected it from the machine. It was difficult to associate the authoritative voice on tape with the one who had cared for her as a child. Maybe it was easier that way. Sergeant Knight was, by the sounds of it, a very good detective. She looked after her interviewee without bowing to them, and although officers would have grilled Sam in greater detail, Elizabeth had a good way of extracting the important points. Sam was not what she had expected at all. His emotions were all over the place, and there was no doubt Frank had groomed the young loner for his own use. Jennifer wished she could jump back in time and speak to her mother about the case. She tried to imagine what Elizabeth would be doing if she was still alive. Her mouth rose in a half smile. She would probably be running the station by now. It was time for Jennifer to do her bit too. She may need to defend herself from a killer more dead than alive.

CHAPTER THIRTY-THREE

Jennifer tapped her steering wheel as the car in front of her came to a halt. The brake lights of the Nissan Micra had been flashing on and off for the last ten minutes as the traffic in front of her slowed. She was going to be late again. She slipped her phone from her jacket pocket, her finger hovering over the text button. Her sister was getting suspicious about her texts asking about Josh. Tutting under her breath, she threw her phone on the seat and rested her elbow on the car window ledge. Time was running out. If she didn't come up with something soon ... She flinched as a car horn blared, and she scowled in her rear view mirror in reciprocation. What was the hold up? She craned her neck over the steering wheel to see blue flashing lights in the distance. It was the same car that had sped past her earlier, and the outcome did not look good. *This is all I need – an RTC first thing in the morning*, she thought, as she placed a police business card on her dashboard and parked on the grass verge. Walking towards the bridge, she watched as officers stood, heads together in discussion, while another put scene tape in place. A police car parked diagonally blocked entry to the bridge. Jennifer walked past the rows of cars, feeling the frustration of her fellow drivers on their way to work.

A skinny young police officer approached, waving his hands to prevent entry. 'Hold up, you can't come any further.'

Jennifer slid her warrant card from her back trouser pocket and introduced herself.

The officer dropped his hands. 'Sorry, I didn't realise.'

'That's OK, I was just on my way in to work. What's the problem?' Jennifer asked, noticing that her earlier guess of a road traffic collision was misjudged.

The officer pointed down to the grassy path leading under the bridge. 'Joggers found a body at the edge of the water this morning. Backup's on its way, and we're put up a road diversion in the meantime. Your lot are due here any minute.' His radio beeped as he received a point to point direct call, and he nodded an apology as he turned to answer it.

Jennifer rubbed her arms as visions of Shelly came to the forefront of her mind. A heavy night's sleep had left her feeling disjointed, and she had woken to hear Shelly's name being whispered in her ear. Two more cars arrived on the scene, along with the marine unit, and diversion signs were displayed to offer drivers alternative routes. Jennifer's high heels sank into the grass verge as she strode towards the uniformed sergeant. His fluorescent coat looked the worse for wear as it strained over his portly stomach. 'Hello Sarge, has the body has been identified yet?'

'Jennifer, have they turned you out for this?' His surprise was not lost on her.

Jennifer held his gaze. 'No. I was on my way to work when I got held up in the traffic.'

'We don't know who she is. Middle-aged woman, looks a bit ravaged. Nobody's been reported missing yet.'

Jennifer nodded. 'I'm wondering if it's one of our local prostitutes Shelly Easton. The last time I saw her she wasn't in a great state of mind. Her boyfriend hung himself recently and I'm wondering if she's topped herself too.'

The sergeant sighed. 'We've closed down the scene until the duty DI gets here.' His eyes darted under the bridge as he frowned. 'I suppose it wouldn't do any harm for you to have a quick look, move things along before CSI get here. Check in with the officer holding the scene log over there.'

Jennifer reported her presence to the officer and placed the white overshoes over her heels to prevent forensic contamination. The traffic began to clear as cars were diverted, and police tape now secured both paths of entry underneath the bridge, where the body was still in situ. The path leading down to the scene was usually wet and muddy, and Jennifer was grateful for the hard night of frost that assisted her descent. She scanned every inch of the ground for visual clues as she tried to keep her balance. The familiar feeling of dread overcame her as she approached the edge of the river, and the flash of orange clothing confirmed what she already knew. A lone officer stood a few feet away to prevent onlookers cutting through the tape. She vaguely recognised him as a dog handler by the nickname of Mutley, and guessed he had been in the area when the call came in. He nodded in recognition, his hands tucked under his stab vest as he jigged impatiently in the frosty air. 'Morning. Have they said when I can be released yet? I'm freezing my nuts off here.' Pulling out a ragged tissue, he loudly blew his nose to drive home the point.

'CSI are on their way. I've only come down to identify her,' Jennifer said, her voice sounding detached as she approached the body.

'Fill your boots. The officers on scene were real bright sparks. They dragged her from the reeds onto the bank, then turned her over to make sure she was dead. As if they couldn't tell by the smell, the twats.'

Shelly Easton lay splayed on the banks of the river, her hair clinging damply to her bloated face. Her open eyes were frozen in horror as her expression relayed the final tortured moments of her life. Jennifer covered her mouth and nose as the smell overcame her, making her stomach churn. The decomposition that had had a head start would no doubt baffle the crime scene investigators when the autopsy was underway. She backed away from the body as she tried to regain her composure. 'Who's the duty DI?' she asked, dry washing her hands.

Mutley pulled a strip of chewing gum from a silver wrapper and bent it in half before popping it into his mouth. 'Old frosty bollocks. I wish he'd bloody well hurry up.' Jennifer took him to mean DI Anderson, so called for his cheerless disposition.

'I'll tell them you're asking to be released. I'm sure it won't be much longer.'

She turned to climb up the bank, giving one last glance at Shelly's bloated body. Her premonition had been right but relying on premonitions was like groping in the dark. By the time you tripped over what you wanted, the damage was already done. The killer had racked up four dead bodies for no other reason than that they matched Frank Foster's counterparts. But with the copycat killings complete, where did it leave her? There was no doubt in her mind it was personal; but inviting Joshua into their cat and mouse game was a nightmarish twist. It wasn't as if she could confide in anyone. Being in the police left her as vulnerable as she was useful. If she knew too much about the deaths she would get hauled in for questioning. People would start looking at her funny, as her 'hunches' attracted suspicion. By the time she got to the roadside she had made up her mind. She was no sitting duck. If the killer wanted her, she would face him head on.

DI Anderson stood at the roadside in his navy pinstripe suit, watching her ascend the bank. A tall dour man, his face wore a permanent expression of distaste, and he spoke as if he had just stepped on something nasty. Jennifer pulled off the plastic overshoes, now punctured with two muddy heel marks. Folding them over, she briefed him on the identity of the body.

He looked down the bridge of his bony nose. 'A witness has reported a woman matching her description sitting on the bridge, staring into the water last night. Why they couldn't have called it in as a concern for welfare at the time, I don't know.'

'Well sir, the last time I saw Shelly she was very ill, both mentally and physically. I called an ambulance to her flat, but she had gone AWOL by the time they arrived. She appeared to be self-harming, also.'

DI Anderson sniffed. 'Yes, well, it'll all come out in the post-mortem, I'm sure. Your name is on the scene log if they need to get in touch. Write up a statement covering the iden-tification the body. Her next of kin will be notified.'

'Yes sir, and I'll let social services know when I get to the nick, her children were in care.'

Jennifer expected a buzz of excitement in the station when she got to work, but the atmosphere was flat. The officers in charge of Shelly's death did not spend long at the scene before bagging up the body and sending it to the morgue. Suicide seemed the overall consensus, and given Shelly's chaotic lifestyle, it was not a difficult conclusion to reach. It was not a conclusion Jennifer agreed with, and as she sat at her desk, she put together all the reasons why she should approach DI Allison again. Frank's accomplice, Sam, stated Frank intended to kill again. But Amy needed the DI's approval before she could root around in old investigations involving her mother.

'Sorry I'm late, I got caught up with the sudden death,' she said, taking a seat behind her desk.

Steph tapped her police radio, neatly clipped to the belt buckle on her hip. 'That's OK, I heard the DI's update. You saved time by identifying the body.'

Jennifer paused, her fears and suspicions on the tip of her tongue. 'Yes, I thought it might be her. Any jobs in today?'

'No, it's all Q here so far. Will's doing some enquiries around CCTV. Can you take over and let him get on with his paperwork? I've told him he has to have it done by today, so don't let anyone disturb him.'

Q was code for 'quiet' and every officer knew if they dared say that things were 'quiet' their fellow officers would loudly shush them and make them deal with anything horrible that came in as a result. A silly tradition, but all part of working in the police family that Jennifer enjoyed being part of.

Will smiled in appreciation as she placed a coffee on his desk. 'So poor old Shelly is dead then.'

Jennifer recounted her morning to Will, waiting for him to say it was to be expected.

'I know they're saying it's suicide, but there's something about this that doesn't add up.'

Jennifer raised her eyebrows, 'Will, I'm glad to hear you say that because I've been thinking the same thing. Have you found anything on it?'

Will pointed to the live incident on the computer. 'I've been monitoring it on the box. A witness saw a woman matching Shelly's description sitting on the bridge looking into the water at three this morning. They were dropping a friend home after a party and crossed the bridge fifteen minutes later and she was gone. She wasn't anywhere to be seen. They didn't report it until they saw the police cars at the bridge this morning.' Will shook his head in disbelief. 'I reckon they'd been drink driving and didn't want to get done. Anyway, that's neither here nor there. The thing is, I've been talking to my mate in scenes of crime and she said that if Shelly jumped off the centre of the bridge last night the body would have been swept away further than it was. Granted, there was a heavy frost but she was found not far from where she is likely to have jumped in. The people that found her said she was face down, clutching handfuls of reeds, as if she was trying to pull herself out when she died. Why would she jump into the river then try to pull herself out again?'

Jennifer felt a weight lift as Will dissected the circumstances surrounding Shelly's death.

'And there's something else. I've been asked to study the CCTV for that area.'

'I didn't know there was CCTV of the bridge.'

'There isn't. Not really. But there is coverage of some of the route Shelly would have taken from her flat in town to the bridge. It's pretty crap though, I can't make out the figures very well.' Will clicked on the software to open the download the council had sent him.

'Figures? As in two people?' Jennifer said, leaning forward for a better view.

'Don't get too excited, realistically they could be anyone. But I think it's Shelly. Watch.'

Jennifer noted the time on the CCTV. It was two twenty, forty minutes before the witness stated that they had seen Shelly on the bridge. It would have easily given her enough time to walk down there. Will clicked 'play' and she held her breath as she waited for the figures to come into view. The hazy black and white image was partially obscured by a cobweb and gave little to reveal the identity of the two people with their backs facing the camera.

'This is shit, you can't make anything out. It's just two grey blobs.'

Will clicked the 'pause' button. 'I said it was bad. The light was out on that street last night. It's typical, the only night of the year the bulb blows is when we need the CCTV. But look at the way they're walking. The one on the left has their head bowed so low they can't see where they're going, while the person beside them is bolt upright. Doesn't it seem odd to you?'

Will pressed the 'play' button. The figure on the left wore a sleeveless top and was smaller than the person beside them, who was dressed entirely in black. Both kept walking until they turned the corner out of view.

Jennifer scowled, disappointed. 'Maybe they're just two drunks.'

Will rewound the tape and pointed to the screen. 'Watch. Drunks sway or cling on to each other. These two are walking an exact straight line. I've asked the local businesses but there's no other CCTV on that stretch of road. I've viewed the next couple of hours on fast forward, but there's no sign of anyone coming back. Pity really, because then they would have been facing the camera. I've updated the DI but he's not impressed. As he said, even if we could prove it was Shelly, she knew lots of people, so she may have been out with someone and parted ways before she jumped off the bridge of her own accord.'

Jennifer frowned. It took an awful lot to impress their DI these days. 'Don't you think it's strange Will? Nothing much happens in Haven, then all of a sudden we have several deaths in a short space of time. Charlie Taylor, Johnny, and now Shelly. What if someone is targeting them and making it look like suicide so they can get away with it? It's very similar to a case my mum dealt with when she was in the police.'

Will reached for the spot where his wedding ring used to be on his left hand. Turning the band was a habit he had conquered long ago, but today his thoughts appeared far away.

'If you've anything on this case you should try again with the DI. Don't bother with Anderson, he thinks his shit's custard. He won't listen to the likes of us. DI Allison's in tomorrow. He might be in a better mood then.'

Jennifer did not share Will's optimism. Firm evidence was needed to find the killer's identity, and if the job wouldn't help her, she'd have to find it herself.

Jennifer risked another visit to check on Joshua. Amy seemed glad of the respite from her energetic four-year-old and banished them both to the tree house in the garden. Joshua's bobble hat bounced as he ran up and down the steps, fighting imaginary dragons to save his fair damsel Princess Jennifer.

She pulled her coat tight as she sat in the cramped wooden box, waiting to reward her prince with chocolate. Joshua had not mentioned anything of concern, and she was happy to leave it at that. She looked through the makeshift window to the small enclosed garden. It was far removed from the treehouse she had frequented after her aunt Laura took her and Amy in.

Joshua clambered up the steps. 'I killed the dragon,' he said with a sniff, his cheeks nipped red from the cold.

'Well, you are the bravest prince I've ever met.' Jennifer said, taking a tissue from her pocket and wiping his nose. 'Here you go, fair prince, and I have for you a reward.' She produced a small bag of white buttons from her pocket. 'Kiss first,' she said, before handing them over.

Joshua kissed her on the cheek before wrapping his gloved hands around her neck. 'You're the best auntie in the world. I love you to the moon and back.'

Jennifer closed her eyes as she hugged him back. 'And I love you more than life itself.'

The figure in the bushes smiled. Soon Jennifer would be given the opportunity to prove the sincerity behind her words. Hollow eyes watched as she returned inside, hand in hand with her precious child. He had them exactly where he wanted them. Soon the bonds of blood would be tested.

CHAPTER THIRTY-FOUR

A fundraiser party was the last thing she wanted to attend, but tonight Jennifer had her reasons. Investigations into Shelly's death had drawn a blank, but she had not forgotten the strange phone call in the car from Shelly, and the silent calls that plagued her throughout. Jennifer was very cagey about who she gave her number to. Apart from her colleagues and immediate family members, nobody else could have known it. Joan's prediction had warned her of someone close betraying her. Was the supernatural entity receiving help from human hands? She had begun looking at her colleagues with suspicion, and a couple of hours at the party would be the perfect backdrop for checking their mobile phones.

She wondered if Ethan would be making an appearance. Their time together had been short-lived because he had been pulled back to Westlea. At least DI Allison was not attending the party. It would be easier to blend in without him keeping tabs on her all night. Jennifer knocked back a glass of wine to settle her nerves.

She gave her hair one last blast of hairspray and stared at

the backless dress in the full-length mirror. She may not have been blessed with Susie's curves, but she looked as if she had been poured into the red silk material. The party dress code was 'glamorous', and she was looking forward to seeing Will in the tuxedo he had promised to wear. It was a big improvement on the fancy dress theme from last year, when most people had saved on a costume and come dressed as police officers.

The taxi beeped outside, and her heart gave a flutter as she fixed her strappy red shoes. No doubt everyone else would be well oiled by the time she turned up. Having the party in the upstairs bar of the station was a cheap option, and the savings on the venue allowed the booze to flow. She made her way down to the taxi, wondering if drinking wine on an empty stomach was such a good idea after all.

She jumped out of the cab at the back of the station and paid the driver. Shivering, she wished she had worn a coat. She attracted wolf whistles from the officers queuing for custody. A suitable hand gesture silenced the catcalls and she entered the building. The music throbbed a beat from upstairs. For one night the prisoner's shouts and moans were drowned out, and custody officers would be treated with the echoes of eighties music instead of the usual backdrop of colourful language.

The police bar was heaving, and smartly dressed bodies were dappled with colourful lights flashing in time with the music. Disco Dave was at the helm, and already half cut by the look of him. The blare of the seventies music seemed incongruous with the glamorous dress code, which was rapidly deteriorating as off duty officers removed their ties to wrap around their sweat-stained foreheads to dance to 'Kung Fu Fighting'. Jennifer rested her elbows on the sticky bar and raised her voice to order a vodka and coke. She looked around the room. It was ten past nine and there was no sign of Will anywhere.

'Hey girl, fancy a dance?'

The smell of stale beer breath made Jennifer wrinkle her nose. She spun around to see Greavsy, her custody sergeant, grinning stupidly at her. His green kipper tie swung around his neck as he gyrated.

'Thanks Sarge, but I need a few drinks down me first. Can I borrow your phone? I've lost mine, I just want to ring it.'

Greavsy slid the phone from his back pocket, too drunk to realise that she would not have heard it over the music. Checking call histories was not a fool proof way of gaining evidence as records could be deleted, but at that moment it was all she had.

She handed back his phone and he made his way to the dance floor with his dripping pint, swinging his hips in tune to the music.

For the next hour Jennifer worked her way through the crowd, checking phones and coming up with excuses to borrow them, each time drawing a blank. At ten o clock she rang Will on her mobile, raising her voice over the music. 'Where are you? You're missing the party.'

'Mum's had a fall and she's been taken to hospital. I'm making my way over there now.'

'Oh God, I'm sorry, is it serious?'

'No, it's more of a precaution than anything else. I'll call you tomorrow, yeah?'

Jennifer's arm was suddenly yanked and she was pulled onto the dance floor as an odour of sickly sweet perfume wafted over her.

It was Susie. She bounced as she danced to the delight of many, as her tight black basque left nothing to the imagination. Her bright pink lipstick was slightly smudged, having pressed against several cheeks already.

To hell with it, Jennifer thought as she followed her lead, immersing herself in the music while the room grew warm and condensation steamed the windows. She danced until her feet ached, then limped back to the bar to see Ethan ordering a drink. Sidling up to him, she ordered a vodka and coke. They chatted for a while, Jennifer's inhibitions lowering with each drink she consumed. All thoughts of checking phones were replaced by a drunken haze as the alcohol made its way through her bloodstream. She eyed Ethan appreciatively in his sharp black suit. He had since discarded his tie and undone the top two buttons of his white shirt.

As the end of the night closed in, Coldplay's 'Magic' played and they wavered onto the dance floor, mottled in a series of lazy blue and gold circles cast by the lights.

'Sometimes I wish I could take a night off from being myself, have some fun,' Jennifer said, shuddering as Ethan slid his hand down her bare back.

Ethan nestled closer to her ear. 'Want to come back to mine?'

She shook her head, knowing that as soon as the fresh air hit her face, she would change her mind. The crowd of party-goers had either paired off or were leaning into the bar ordering one last round of drinks. Grabbing his hand, she pulled him forward. 'I have a better idea.'

Giggling, they scurried down the corridor and ducked into a darkened room, which was so small it could be mistaken for a cupboard. The PIRS room was used to assist witnesses to identify criminals. It had a couple of monitors, a filing cabinet, and a small table wedged against the wall.

Jennifer flicked on the light and locked the door from the inside. She reached for the table as Ethan kissed her, tasting of whiskey and surprisingly, cigarettes.

The national anthem echoed through the corridor as the party came to an end, and Jennifer tried to dismiss thoughts of the outside world. She pulled out Ethan's shirt and ran her fingers up his torso. But as his hands slid the length of her body, her lingering doubts returned. What was she doing here with Ethan when she'd arranged to meet Will? He was her best mate and he needed her. Ethan nibbled her neck before he lifted her onto the table, pushing her dress around her thighs. Jennifer gasped for breath. *This is happening too fast,* she thought, her heart thumping hard. *This is all wrong.*

'No, wait,' Jennifer said, her raspy breath abating. But Ethan didn't appear to hear her, as he pulled her towards him. 'Ethan, stop!' Pressing both hands on his chest, she pushed him back.

Ethan shot her a look of disbelief as his hands fell from her sides. 'Are you serious?'

Jennifer slid off the desk onto her feet, now painfully sober. 'Yes ... sorry.'

'Oh,' Ethan said, slightly panting. 'Seems I got crossed wires.' The muscles in his jaw tightened as he tucked in his shirt.

Jennifer nodded as she fixed her dress. All she wanted was to be alone.

Jennifer opened one eye, her eyelids sticky from the mascara that stained her pillow. She rubbed her mouth in disgust at the bitter taste of alcohol lining her tongue. 'Oh God,' she murmured under her breath. A tangle of memories bloomed. Dancing, drinking too much and ... did she have sex with Ethan?

Clasping her head, she stumbled into the bathroom and washed down two painkillers with some water from the tap. Her reflection in the mirror conveyed that she looked every bit as bad as she felt. Her shower was not hot enough to wash away the searing embarrassment from the night before and the memory of rebuffing Ethan returned. Jennifer leaned against the wall as the water cascaded, relieved she made the right decision. At least she had had the hindsight to change to a late shift.

The water dripped from her hair as she pulled the towelling robe around her. A text beeped to inform her that she had voicemail. Susie's voice came breathy and excited down the line. 'I've been hearing all sorts about you and Ethan last night, you little sexpot. Call me!'

Jennifer's stomach heaved. Susie could spread rumour quicker than any tabloid. The phone lit up as Susie's phone number displayed on the screen and her mobile played a ditzy tune. 'Hello,' Jennifer said, wincing as the cheery voice on the other end pierced her eardrums.

'Morning! Or should I say afternoon? I hope I didn't disturb you, but I couldn't wait for the goss.'

'I don't know what you're on about.'

'Ohhh grumpy! Had a hard night, have you?' Susie chortled. '*Hard* being the operative word, ha! Now c'mon spill the beans, was he any good?'

Jennifer rubbed her forehead with the heel of her hand. She winced from the hammering pain in her temples. 'Ah, you got me, what can I say?'

Susie giggled. 'You lucky bitch, the only person leering over me was Greavsy. Ugh. Can you imagine it? Looming over you with those big sausage fingers? Not to mention anything else!'

'I'd rather not,' Jennifer said, her stomach lurching for a second time.

'So go on then, tell all. Did you really shag in the PIRS room?'

'God no. We only had a snog. To be honest he's a bit immature. Not my type.'

Sue snorted. 'That's not what Ethan's saying, it's all

around the nick! They say it's the quiet ones you have to watch.'

Taking a deep breath, Jennifer spoke with as much composure as she could muster. 'It's bullshit. Honestly Susie, nothing happened.'

'Relax,' Susie said. 'You'll be old news by tomorrow. You know how these parties go, people are always looking for something to gossip about.'

Jennifer resisted the urge to fling her phone out the window.

By the time Jennifer walked in for her late shift she decided she'd had enough. Anger rose when she thought of every condescending remark, patronising look and muffled snigger she had been subjected to in the last year. She had once been the golden girl of Westlea CID, whose detection rate was the highest in the county. How had she been reduced to this? A nervous wreck obsessed with cleaning, while the town of Haven was being bled dry because the people that should care were too busy looking out for themselves.

Jennifer strode into the office, ignoring the raised eyebrows. Sliding the scarf from her neck, she hung it on the coat stand along with her jacket. The air was filled with the smell of stale coffee and body odour. Susie watched her approach the DI's office and shook her head to advise against it.

Jennifer straightened her shoulders, knocking firmly on the door before walking in.

DI Allison glanced up from the paperwork that was spread across his desk among empty sandwich wrappers and drained juice cartons. Overtime sheets balanced on the edge, weighed down by a half empty coffee cup. Mould lilies floated on the surface of the brown liquid within.

'Can you spare me a few moments of your time, sir?' she asked, her feet planted firmly on the ground.

'I'm busy as it happens. Is it important?' DI Allison replied, sighing heavily.

'Extremely,' Jennifer said, tugging the handle of the blinds to block out Susie's gaze from the other side. 'May I close these for privacy?'

By the time he had torn his eyes away from his paperwork they were already closed. He gave another harassed sigh and gestured at her to sit down.

Jennifer eyed the dilapidated chair piled high with folders. 'If you don't mind, I'd rather stand. I've come to talk to you about my place on the team, and I want to know about the case involving Frank Foster and my mother.' Jennifer folded her arms tightly across her chest. 'Sir, would you mind not rolling your eyes when I speak? I find it very disrespectful.'

DI Allison cleared his throat, a flush creeping up his skin. 'I ... I'm sorry, of course.'

'To be honest, sir, I'm used to it. I'm bloody good at my job, but instead I get shafted day after day, and have my mental health questioned when I challenge anything.'

DI Allison frowned. 'With all due respect ...'

'That's what I'm trying to tell you. There is no respect. I was a good copper in Westlea. What did I get for taking that serial rapist off the streets? Shafted, that's what. I've a good mind to leave this department and join a neighbouring force where my intuition is valued.'

'Steady on Jennifer, what's got into you?'

'I'll tell you what's got into me. When I come to you for help, all you do is ask me about my counsellor, who I haven't seen in months, by the way. Look at any team of coppers and you'll see they're all messed up in their own way. It goes with the territory. So why do I get singled out as some sort of crazy woman?'

'I'm sorry if you feel that way but ...'

Jennifer silenced her DI with her hand. 'I know you think I'm out of order speaking to you like this, but how would you feel if it was you? You got my dad the sack, and I'm guessing it's because you held a torch for my mum. I don't hold it against you because I respect you as my boss. Why can't you give me the same courtesy? If I was a bloke, would you treat me the same way?'

DI Allison leaned forward in his chair as he intertwined his fingers. 'Just exactly what do you want from me, Jennifer?'

'Either you start using me effectively or I'm putting in for a transfer to another force.'

A ghost of a smile crossed DI Allison's lips. 'Seeing you like this, with fire in your belly; you remind me of your mother.'

Jennifer took a seat. 'It's been a long time coming.'

'In that case, yes. I think I owe you an apology ...'

Jennifer exhaled in relief, 'Sir, after the way I've just lunged at you I'd say we're even.'

'No, it's only fair you know why I've been so off. It's my son, he's come back into my life.'

Jennifer had known for some time of DI Allison's estranged son, the one his wife had not yet discovered. 'Oh. Have you told your wife?'

'No, not yet. The thing is, you know him ... it's Ethan.'

Jennifer's mouth fell open. Why hadn't she seen it before? The same confident stride, the same strong jawline. Was that why he was so fascinated with her? Because she got more attention from his father than he did? 'Oh. I see.'

'Anyway, it's all sorted out now.'

Jennifer nodded, wondering if he had heard the rumours about them. If he had, she didn't want to talk about it.

'I know I've been a jack the lad in the past, but your

mother ... I genuinely cared about her. I promised her I'd look out for you, but I've taken that too far.' He glanced out the window before bringing his attention back to her.

'Anyway, no more excuses. I'll tell you everything you need to know about Frank Foster.'

CHAPTER THIRTY-FIVE

ELIZABETH KNIGHT – 1992

Sergeant Elizabeth Knight nodded to her colleagues as she stood outside the interview room. The mention of Frank Foster brought the chilling memory of her visit to his flat. She wished she had been allowed to bring a colleague to make up the numbers.

Detective Sergeant Scott stroked his greying moustache as he briefed Elizabeth prior to the interview. It was a mannerism she recognised, one that meant he had a slippery fish in his grip. His cockney accent came in soft tones in the narrow hall leading to the pokey interview room. 'The 'softly softly' approach won't work with this geezer. There's no point in stroking his ego either. He thinks he's too good for the like of us. Go in there and act like you don't give a toss, then get under his skin. I'll be sitting out here, so any problems just shout, OK girl?'

Elizabeth nodded. It was not as if they had much choice, given that Frank had insisted he would only speak to her. She peered through the open doorway. He was dressed more like a solicitor than a suspect. His blue shirt stretched over his broad shoulders as he sat with a face set in grim determination. Elizabeth took in the silver cufflinks, the polished black shoes. Even his thick black hair looked as if it had recently been cut. Frank was ready for this day. Taking a deep breath, she entered the room.

'Mr Foster, I'm going to launch straight into interview so we can record everything on tape, OK?'

Frank's eyes lit up in recognition, and he cocked his head to one side. 'Ah El-iza-beth, so good to meet you again. Please, call me Frank.'

'As you wish.' Elizabeth dragged the chair against the cigarette-cratered carpet, resting her notebook on the desk across from him. Frank's presence filled the room. Elizabeth cleared her throat and mentally worked out her exit strategy should things turn nasty. From the things Sam Beswick had said in interview, Frank Foster was not to be trifled with.

Elizabeth unwrapped a fresh set of tapes from their clear plastic packaging and activated the tape machine. She would get Frank to sign them at the end of interview and they would be sealed and exhibited for court. But only if there was a successful case to attach them to.

Introductions out of the way, Elizabeth spoke, her heart-beat racing in her chest.

'Tell me everything you know about the death of Martina Jackson, also known as Tina Jackson.'

Frank cracked his knuckles as his face creased in a macabre smile. 'She's a whore and she's dead. Is that enough?'

Elizabeth locked eyes, refusing to be stared down. 'No, it's not. Start from the first encounter you had with Tina, right up until the last.'

'The first time I met her I was a kid. She had a real

mouth. I remember her saying to me once, "come back when you know what to do with it." I guess I did because the next time I met her I fucked her good.' He paused, taking in Elizabeth's nonplussed expression. 'I didn't see her again until recently, when Sam brought her back to his place. I had a key to his flat and I let myself in, thinking he'd be coming back with some beers. I was surprised when I heard Tina's voice when he got back. I didn't want to spoil his fun so I hid in the bathroom. You know what it's like when you're that age, horny all the time.' His face broke into a salacious smile.

'And what happened next?' Elizabeth said, dropping her gaze to the notepad.

'They went to the bedroom, but Tina started saying he wasn't up to the job. Like I said, she had a big mouth. Next thing I know she comes into the bathroom effing and blinding about having a split lip. That's when she saw me. Well, the old girl went crazy, screaming the house down. Sam grabbed her, there was a scuffle and somehow we got caught up in the shower curtain. Sam dragged her onto the bed, wrapping the curtain around her head. I told him to stop, but he wasn't listening. He stuffed a pillow over her head and suffocated her. I didn't think he had the balls.'

'And what were you doing during all of this?'

Frank shrugged. 'I left him to it. He pulled a suitcase from the top of his wardrobe and said he was going to hide the body. That's about the time the enormity of his actions hit him because he started throwing up. I felt sorry for the kid, so I helped him get rid of her.'

'How?' Elizabeth said, inwardly thrilled with the admission.

'We put her in the suitcase and I dragged it to my car. I drove to the Blakewater River and threw her over the bridge. It means Black Water. Apparently, it's a popular suicide spot.'

Elizabeth leaned forward to clarify the point. 'So, you're

telling me you weren't responsible for Tina's murder, but you did help dispose of the body?'

Frank nodded. 'That is correct.'

'Were you under any duress?' Elizabeth said, in order to negate any defences he might come up with later on.

Frank snickered. 'From Sam? Don't be stupid, he's just a kid.'

Elizabeth frantically scribbled notes to help her keep track. She needed to get through as much as she could with him before examining his story for more detail. 'What can you tell me about a Mr Michael Osborne?'

'What do you want to know?' Frank said.

'What do you know about his death?'

Frank leaned onto the table and unconsciously Elizabeth leaned in to listen. Like a spider drawing in his prey, his eyes rolled upwards to greet hers, the corners of his mouth set in a ghoulish smile. 'I killed the bastard,' he whispered, drawing out his tongue and licking his lips.

Elizabeth's felt the adrenalin rush as she sped through the caution. 'You ... you seem very calm about your admission, Frank. Why don't you start by telling me everything you know?'

'I knew this day would come. I just didn't expect it so soon.' Frank said, now rocking slightly in the chair. Pent up energy radiated from every pore and he seemed unable to keep still. Hardly the type of person that could cope in the confines of prison.

'Why did you kill Michael Osborne?'

'He had it coming. Lots of people do. But you know that, don't you?' Frank said.

Elizabeth remembered DC Scott's words and she reminded herself to play it cool. 'I don't know any such thing.'

'Oh, I think you do. You deal with the dirty leeches every day. Rapists, robbers, people that prey on the weak and vulnerable. It must grind in your gut when you see them get off. And let's face it, most of them do. What if you had the power to give them a little restorative justice? I'm only doing what the rest of you fantasise about.'

'And what are you?' Elizabeth said.

Frank narrowed his eyes. 'What do you mean?'

'You mentioned the criminals I deal with. The rapists, the muggers and the murderers. What are you?' Elizabeth's words dripped with sarcasm.

Frank smiled. 'I'm the Grim Reaper. I tap these people on the shoulder when their time is up. I could have done so much more if Sam hadn't chickened out. Still, his time will come and one day the old Grim Reaper will be tapping on your shoulder too.'

Elizabeth's guard dropped as her face fell.

A smile played on Frank's lips. 'Don't look so alarmed. I'm only stating the obvious. You planning on living forever, darling?'

Elizabeth took a slow cool breath. 'Who else have you killed?'

'You're the detective. You tell me.' Frank cracked his knuckles.

'Why don't we talk about how you killed Mr Osborne and move on from there.'

Frank leaned forward in his chair. 'Ah, look at your face. Have I rattled you? Sorry, it was not my intention. You know, if you took your hair down and dressed a bit more feminine, you'd be a knock out.'

Elizabeth glared at her suspect, hating that her voice had risen an octave. 'It's Sergeant Knight to you. I asked you a question, how did you kill Michael Osborne?'

Frank tutted. 'There you go again, spoiling the party. Let me tell you something. I run this interview, not you. You want to know why that is? Because all the cards are in my hands.'

Elizabeth opened her mouth to speak, and Frank waved a finger to stop her.

'Ah ah ah, now don't interrupt. I'm going to make you famous. This interview will be played all over the country. You'll be able to write a book about it. So, you listen while I talk.'

'Focus on the criminal offences and it's a deal.'

Frank nodded. 'I like that. You remind me of someone. She had a smart mouth too. Unfortunately, she's not with us anymore.'

Elizabeth bit her lip as she thought of the police officers searching Frank's flat. She still needed physical evidence, as he could easily backtrack on his confession later. 'I need specifics; dates, times. When did this all start?'

Frank leaned into the tape recorder. 'I have harboured my feelings for some time. It's the natural order, the way things should be. I expect one day the rest of the world will catch up with my thinking. It's not just criminals that deserve to die. People that abuse their position of power are villains in disguise and the truth is closing in. How is your truth Eli-za-beth? Is your conscience clear?'

Elizabeth was painfully aware of the ticking clock on the wall. She needed a reaction, and purposely stifled a yawn in response to Frank's grand speech. 'Let's say we start from the beginning and work your way through the people you *claim* to have killed.'

A flicker of annoyance crossed Frank's face. 'Claimed! You've no idea who you're talking to, do you? I killed them all right. Mr Michael Osborne – a drug-dealing pimp. I smashed his face in before kicking the chair out from his legs as he whimpered for mercy. He couldn't even die with dignity. Your pathetic investigation failed to recognise the fact that he was murdered.' Spittle gathered in the corners of Frank's lips as the words poured out. 'Then there was Stanley, the kiddie fiddler and retired schoolteacher. Everyone knew he was a child molester, but nobody had the guts to do anything – until I came along and smoked him to hell. Somebody had to take a stand, and it certainly wasn't going to be you.'

Elizabeth nodded, not wanting to break the momentum.

Frank shifted in his chair. 'Yes, I can see I've got your attention. I got Mrs Harris's attention too. What a waste of life that was, flapping around on her back for her inhaler, those big pudgy jaws opening and closing like a fish out of water. Quite funny really.' Frank paused and wiped his mouth with the back of his hand. 'I think that's enough for you to go on.'

Concealing her shaking hands under the table, Elizabeth sighed, as if she was talking to a naughty school child. 'Frank. Everything you've told me so far is hearsay. You've not given me any times or dates, nothing definitive. I'm beginning to wonder if you've made the whole thing up.'

Frank response came in a low grumble. 'That's what Sam thought until Tina.'

Elizabeth stared coldly. 'Are you talking about Tina Jackson? Because we've never found a body.'

Frank clenched his jaw. 'I don't like your tone. You want me to give it to you on a plate? Well hard luck. You're not competent enough to investigate it.'

'Then why did you ask for me?

Frank wiped his mouth again in disgust. 'Because I had plans for you. You were my pièce de résistance.'

Elizabeth responded with a blank look.

'Don't you remember our little meeting?' Frank said, 'I believe we have some unfinished business.'

Elizabeth's fingers bit into her palms as she spun another lie, reassuring herself that DS Scott was sitting outside.

Goading suspects was not a tactic she used often, but it occasionally yielded results. 'I have no recollection of meeting you, Mr Foster. Are you sure it was me?'

Frank cracked his knuckles again, 'You think you're so smart, don't you, playing games. I know you remember that day, so don't try to pretend.'

'I don't, but please explain if it's relevant.'

Frank banged the table with his fists, his face twisted in a scowl. 'You must remember! You came so close that day, snooping uninvited in my room. The sketchpad on my bed, you must remember.'

'So where is this sketchpad?' Elizabeth asked, her thoughts returning to the search team at the flat, hunting for evidence.

'Wouldn't you like to know? Shame you're not going to see it,' Frank said.

Elizabeth gave a condescending smirk. 'Frank, I think it's time you step into the real world and be honest with me.'

'Honest! You're a fine one to talk about being honest. When you interviewed me about Mrs Harris, you lied to try to catch me out, saying she was found right away, and then you lied about not being alone. You deserved to be taught a lesson that day. But I was ready to play the long game. I had it all planned out.'

'Perhaps you would like to enlighten me.'

Frank gave a low growl. 'Believe me, there's nothing I'd like better.'

Elizabeth felt every sense sharpen. She was about to light the keg and she prayed she would come away unscathed. 'You know what I think, Frank? I think you're a fantasist. You met this vulnerable young boy named Sam and compared stories to impress each other. But both were a pack of lies. You lied about your family, your background, and your father being the Chief Constable. He's a downtrodden used car salesman who left you to start another family halfway across the world. Is your real life so terrible Frank, that you would make up this persona of being a serial killer to escape it?'

Beads of sweat glistened on Frank's face as his eyes narrowed. 'You're wrong. You don't know who you're dealing with!'

Elizabeth's eyes flicked to his clenched fists. But she wasn't ready to back off yet. 'Yeah sure, you've already said that. Who's the next victim, Frank? Or are you waiting for some old dear to die of old age so you can lay claim to being responsible?'

'You stupid girl, why would I do that?'

Elizabeth leaned forward, spitting her words. 'Because you are a latent homosexual, and you developed feelings for Sam. But you didn't feel confident approaching him as who you really were; a man in his forties who had sacrificed his life to care for his prostitute mother. You created this persona of a serial killer because you wanted his respect and his fear. But it all went wrong when he killed Tina, and he came to the police to report you for the murders you didn't have the guts to commit.'

Frank drew a sharp breath, pushing back his shoulders as he enhanced his bulk. 'How dare you speak to me like that? I'll show you what I have the guts to commit.'

'Will you, Frank? How are you going to do that, then?' Elizabeth said.

'Go to my house and you'll find the key to a lock-up under the floorboards beneath my bed. The garage at the back of the Grove housing estate, number seven. You'll find your proof that everything I told you is real. While you're there, take a good look at my notebook and see what I've planned for you. Because let me tell you, you are a day away from death. And don't think just because I'm in a police station that you're safe, because you're not. It'll take more than a police cell to stop the Grim Reaper.'

'Thank you, Frank, I'm sure my colleagues will be interested in seeing any evidence you can provide us with.'

Frank stared at Elizabeth in amazement. 'I've just told you I'm going to kill you, and you didn't even blink. What's wrong with you? Didn't you hear me?'

'Nothing you can say can hurt me, Mr Foster. But if you have hurt others then you will get all the respect you deserve in prison. Now if we can get back to the interview, I'd like to discuss the specifics.'

'Fuck you and fuck your specifics! It doesn't matter where they put me, you won't be safe. You or your kid. I'm coming after you both and I'll finish what I started. Everybody will know the Grim Reaper's name.'

'Back up there a minute, what did you say?'

Frank's eyes glittered as he spoke. 'Oh, I know all about you, and I'm going to hit you where it hurts. They say a mother's love for their child is an unbreakable bond. Let's see how far you'll go for your little girl. Jennifer, isn't it?'

'How do you know her name?'

'The Grim Reaper knows everything and everyone. You think you can stop me? This is only the beginning. Soon everyone will know my name.'

'Not if I have anything to do with it.' Elizabeth's features tightened. 'Because nobody will be writing books or giving interviews, and I'll be recommending that your real name be used in the media, not your pathetic pseudonym. And when you go to jail, and believe me you will, I'll be recommending that you're not supplied with any writing materials, or anything that could potentially feed your fantasies. Because that's all you are, a sick fantasist.'

Frank hammered his fists against the table and jumped up, sending his chair skidding behind him. 'You fucking bitch, I killed them, and you're next. Do you hear me? You and your kid!' His screams of rage filled the room as he threw over the table and lunged towards her. Elizabeth jumped out of the way, picking up the chair in defence, jabbing the chair legs towards his chest. The emergency buzzer sounded as officers piled in and grappled Frank to the ground. His screams rang in Elizabeth's ears as she made her exit, fighting to calm her shaking body.

CHAPTER THIRTY-SIX

ELIZABETH KNIGHT – 1992

'Are you OK, girlie?' DC Scott asked, his face flushed with excitement. 'He made some pretty serious threats there.'

'I'm fine,' Elizabeth said, as she grabbed a bunch of car keys from the hook on the wall and scribbled her name on the logbook. 'Can you keep an eye on things here for a bit? I need to speak to the search team.'

'Woah, I'm not sure that's such a good idea. You've just interviewed Foster, I don't think you should be going on scene stamping your size fives all over the place.'

Elizabeth gave him a pleading look. 'He threatened my daughter. I need to know what's in there.'

'If you go to the scene, you're compromising the evidence for court. If you want to keep your daughter safe then the best thing you can do is make sure the bastard gets locked up. All right?'

'I just feel so helpless ...'

DS Scott clamped a hand on her shoulder. 'They'll be back later with the evidence. You can see it then, when it's all bagged up. I'll keep you updated every step of the way, I promise.'

Elizabeth nodded. It would mean another late night at work but there was no way she'd be able to sit at home without being fully briefed of the threat.

'And girlie?'

'Yes?' Elizabeth said, returning the car key to the hook.

'Good work,' DS Scott winked.

The atmosphere was subdued as the search team returned with a big enough haul of evidence to put Frank Foster away for a very long time. Usually such an occasion would have been accompanied by raucous cheers, but the fact that the next intended victim was hours from such a grisly death left them dumbfounded. A small town like Haven had its usual problems, but they had never come across a serial killer before, least of all one who took such relish in taking innocent life.

Elizabeth was waiting for their return. Her shift had long since ended, and she took a deep breath as officers recounted the evidence, laying it on the large wide table before booking it into property. She scanned the haul, which consisted of eleven large bags and numerous small ones. They were all cause for concern. She shuddered at the sight of the spade bagged up along with other weapons; an axe, several different types of hunting knives, and – for more refined work – a set of scalpels. Rolls of masking tape inhabited another bag. Then there were ropes in varying forms, gloves, cable ties, bloodied rags, air freshener, bleach, accelerant and a set of clothes. The garage had been meticulously organised from within.

'It's like a DIY kidnapping kit,' DS Scott said behind her. Another officer hauled in bags of crime books and placed them on the already heaving table. But there was far worse to come. The handheld recorder they seized was still usable under the thick plastic evidence bag, and as DS Scott rewound it, he issued a warning. 'I don't know what's on this folks, but we're dealing with a right sicko. If you don't want to hear it, I suggest you vacate now.'

The room fell silent. Elizabeth clasped her hands behind her back and stood firm. She knew the warning was issued for her benefit but she had no intention of leaving now. She nodded in acknowledgement as he pressed 'play'. What followed would stay in the minds of the five police officers for the rest of their careers. The tape quality was poor, but it did not drown out the tortured screams of the man pleading for his life. DC Scott rubbed his chin, his finger hovering over the 'stop' button as he tried to decipher the cause of the man's excruciating pain. The words were muffled as if the victim had been gagged, and it was then, when the man was in too much pain to beg, that they heard the flames crackle and hiss on his skin. Elizabeth closed her eyes at the inhumanity of it all. Seconds before DS Scott turned off the tape, she heard another sound much closer to the microphone. The hairs crept up on the back of Elizabeth's neck at the sound of a man lightly chortling as he cracked his knuckles.

The officer behind them broke the silence. 'You think that's grim. You want to see what he had planned next, the sick bastard.'

Elizabeth's eyes turned to DS Scott.

'It's up to you love, the way word spreads in this nick you're bound to hear it anyway.'

She nodded slowly, swallowing the bile rising up her throat. Would she have goaded Foster in interview had she known what he was truly capable of?

'We found loads of books, sketch books and journals. He refers to himself as the Grim Reaper in all of them. We think a lot of the items in the smaller bags are mementos. We even found a tooth in a bloodied cloth. Somehow I don't think he's keeping it for the tooth fairy.' He looked at them with a grin that was dropped when they failed to find the humour. 'Anyway, he has a diary about somebody he's been watching. He doesn't name her as such. He starts off talking about a visit he had, a lot of it is rambling, sometimes you can't even read the words. There's a picture of this woman tied up while he's ... well, it looks like he fantasised about rape. Anyway, he seems to have scrapped this idea as he then says it's too good for her.' The officer looked at his notes and followed the words with his finger. 'Here it is, he writes about testing a mother's love to see how far she'd go for her child. He spends a page justifying it because she's corrupt and needs to be taught a lesson. He then goes on for another page planning the kidnapping of her daughter and bringing them somewhere secluded. It gets pretty gruesome from therein. I haven't copied all the details but he talks about tying up both of them and torturing the mother to see how much she can withstand before killing them both. He goes on to make a list of tools he needs, such as scalpels and ropes. The thing is, they're all here. There's no reason to believe this wasn't going to happen. He said he had recruited someone to help abduct the child, and it was planned to go ahead tomorrow. Just think ... if we were a day later ...'

Elizabeth excused herself from the room, scrambling to the bathroom just in time to throw up. *Just what am I still doing here?* she thought. She knelt on the cold tiled floor, her stomach cramping in the aftermath. She had been diagnosed with cancer weeks ago. Choosing to keep the news to herself was a form of denial she had welcomed at the time. It was easier than coping with the devastation that lay before her. The irony was that she had been notified of her promotion to Inspector the same day she had received the news of her illness. But interviewing Frank Foster was what she needed to finally realise what really mattered in her life. The images of her daughters' faces came to mind. Jennifer was only seven, already so obstinate and strong willed, yet desperate for her attention. And Amy, just three years old but a daddy's girl already. A pang of guilt stabbed her as the warmth of her tears salted her lips. She had put her job before them all. Her only comfort was that there was enough evidence found in the lock-up to put Frank away for good. Evidence they would not have found had it not been for her style of interviewing. She could keep some clippings. It would be something for her daughters to read about one day.

CHAPTER THIRTY-SEVEN

The local park was a place where Jennifer was never alone. The large wooden playground attracted Haven's network of children, and the pathways and trails that wound through the woodlands were perfect for walkers and joggers alike. She often brought Josh there, and it held nothing but happy memories. She did not see the elderly priest as she bumped into him, sending his paperwork scattering in the breeze. Father Kelly was a short, portly man. Pink and fresh faced, he looked years younger than his age.

'Sorry,' she said, happy to see a kindly face from the past.

'Why, little Jenny Knight, is that you?' he said, in his soft Irish lilt.

'Father Kelly, do you want me to chase after them for you?' She pointed to the sheets of paper taking flight in the wind.

'Oh no, child, don't worry. It was just a sermon. I can print off another one. The joys of modern technology, you know.' He winked. 'Perhaps some lost soul will find hope in it. Now, let me look at you.' The priest stood back, playfully wagging his finger. 'I haven't seen your face at mass for a very long time.'

Jennifer shrugged uncomfortably. 'Sorry Father, I've been busy with work and everything.'

Would you walk with me? You look like you could do with a friendly ear.'

'That's very perceptive of you, Father. Yes, I could do with some advice.'

She fell into the priest's steady stride, and her shoulders dropped as she unburdened herself. 'This is going to sound strange. I don't know if you'll be able to help.'

The lines on Father Kelly's face fell into a smile. It seemed to be his default setting. 'We won't know until we try. What seems to be the problem?'

'Remember how you helped me deal with ... uninvited visitors as a child? Well, it's all started up again and I don't know what to do.'

Father Kelly pointed to a bench. The silence was agonising as doubts crept in. Perhaps he had only been placating her as a child, and the stories of exorcisms and ghosts were invented to make a traumatised child feel better. It wasn't as if they had ever told anyone else. Every second that passed affirmed her concerns that he believed she was either mentally ill or making it up.

They sat staring out at the green, watching children chase their football as the breeze took it. Finally, he spoke. 'Why don't you start from the beginning?'

She exhaled in relief and relayed her concerns of para-normal activity, the voices in her head, the feeling of being watched and the suspicious deaths in the area. The more she spoke, the crazier it sounded. Intertwining her fingers, she lowered her gaze to the ground.

Father Kelly patted her fidgeting hands. 'I've been a priest for several decades and seen things I'll never be able to explain.'

Jennifer leaned in closer to hear as the wind took his voice away.

'Perhaps there is a rational explanation in your case, or perhaps it's something trying to get your attention.'

Father Kelly looked to the sky, searching for answers. 'The problem is, you can't block it because you're curious. That curiosity is opening a door that's hard to close. Come back when you're ready to return to the church.'

Jennifer disguised her disappointment with his lacklustre response. 'Thanks, Father, for hearing me out. I feel better now.'

The priest gave a gentle chuckle. 'I'm glad to hear it, although I think for now, we should keep it between ourselves. Talk of contact with the dead tends to unsettle people.'

Jennifer kept it in mind as she answered her front door to a sheepish looking Will that afternoon.

His hands were stuffed in his jacket pockets, and his chin tucked into the grey woollen scarf she had bought him for Christmas the year before. He shuffled on her doorstep. 'Bloody freezing cats and dogs out here, are you going to let me in?'

Jennifer waved him inside as he wiped his boots on her doormat. 'It's *raining* cats and dogs, not freezing. Come into the living room, I've got the fire on.'

Will unwound his scarf, groaning at having to remove his shoes. His new clothes budget did not stretch very far and Jennifer laughed to see his right toe poking through a small hole in his black sock.

'This Christmas I'm buying you some new grey socks to match your scarf. How's your mum?'

Will followed, rubbing his hands as he took a seat beside the fire. 'Mum? Oh yeah, she's fine.'

Jennifer frowned as she caught sight of the grazed knuckles of his left hand.

'What happened to your hand?'

'How about a coffee? One of your fancy ones, from the machine,' Will asked, furtively.

Jennifer shook her head. 'Not until you tell me what's going on.'

'You're not going to like it.' He picked up the poker and began digging at the flames. The Victorian cast iron fireplace added charm to the sterile room.

'Never mind the fire, just get to the point,' Jennifer said, impatient for answers.

Returning the poker to the fireplace, Will took a breath and met her gaze. 'I punched Ethan.'

'You what?' Jennifer's voice rose an octave. This was not what she had been expecting at all. Solid, reliable Will had hit someone? Not just anyone, but their boss's son.

Will rubbed his stubbled chin. 'Calm down, let me explain.'

Jennifer clamped a hand to her forehead as she stood. 'Why the hell would you do that? You could lose your job.'

'He was stalking you.' The words hung in the air. 'You mentioned being followed so I thought I'd keep an eye out for you. I wasn't expecting to see anything, but when you left work, Ethan drove behind. I jumped in my car and followed him. He parked up the road from your house and sat there, watching your window.'

'Right. And you just decided to punch him?' Jennifer groaned. It sounded ludicrous when she said it out loud.

'Well, that was kind of it. I walked up and tapped on his

car window. He got out and I asked him what he was playing at. He made up some cock and bull story about how you were seeing each other. We got into an argument and ... well, I punched him in the mouth. Don't give me that look – he deserved it. I think he's the one who's been putting the frighteners on you. I just haven't figured out why yet.'

Jennifer sat and rested her head in her hands. She didn't have the energy to cope with this crap on top of everything else. 'I take it you haven't spoken to Susie since you got back.'

'No, why?'

'You owe Ethan an apology. He was kind of telling the truth.'

The colour drained from Will's face. 'What? You're shagging Ethan?'

Jennifer cringed 'No. We had a fumble at the party, nothing more. It could have gone further but I knocked him back.' Silence passed between them as her words sank in. 'But that's not all. Ethan is DI Allison's son.'

Will turned a pasty shade of white. 'You're kidding me. Why didn't you say?'

'I didn't know you were going to smack him one, did I? I take it he hasn't called it in.'

'I don't think so. I would have been nicked by now.'

'In that case I'll call him, try to smooth things over.'

Will stared vacantly into the open fire, shaking his head. 'I never would have guessed it, you and Ethan.'

'There is no me and Ethan, it was a drunken snog, nothing more. I've enough going on in my life without a bloke complicating things.'

Will groaned. 'If it was a one off, why was he following?'

'I don't know Will, but we can't go around making accusations, we might have this all wrong. I need to speak to Ethan.'

'You can't blame me for getting the wrong end of the stick. I mean, look at all that's happened. As you said yourself, there are four dead bodies, and nobody's doing anything about it.'

Will stayed and chatted over coffee, but a nagging feeling distracted Jennifer. It was not until he left that the reason for her discomfort became apparent. Will's words replayed as soon as she closed the door behind him. 'There are four dead bodies, and nobody is doing anything about it.' Four. Not three, like she had told him, but four. The death of Joan Connelly was not common knowledge and there was no way he could have known of the link. The admission fell like a stone, casting ripples of mistrust. How did he know about the fourth victim?

She dialled Ethan's number, praying for answers. 'What the hell is going on?'

'I take it you've heard about the assault.' Ethan spoke in clipped tones.

'Will's just called around. Have you reported it?'

'Not yet. And I'm fine, thank you.'

Jennifer ignored his churlish behaviour. 'Don't start acting all peeved with me. There are rumours going around the nick about us, and from what I've heard, you've done nothing to set them right. And what were you doing outside my house?'

'I was about to knock on your door to apologise. If Will gave me a chance I would have told him as much. It was a lucky punch you know, he caught me off guard.'

Men and their bruised egos, Jennifer thought, trying to placate him. 'It's my fault. I told Will I was being stalked and he got carried away. You're not going to make a complaint, are you?'

'I'm thinking about it.'

'I see. What does your father, DI Allison, think about it?' Jennifer said, unable to resist the dig.

'Who told you?'

'It doesn't matter who, why are you keeping it a secret?' Jennifer's opinion of Ethan was rapidly nose diving. She was getting answers, but not the ones she wanted.

'We thought it best to keep it to ourselves. I wanted to be accepted by my colleagues on my own merit.'

'What are you going to do now? Things will get messy if you launch a complaint, you know that don't you?'

'Oh, for God's sake, I'm not going to report him, I was just making him stew.' Ethan's voice softened. 'I'm sorry things didn't work out between us. But if you have concerns for your personal safety, you need to ask him what he was doing there, not me.'

The conversation left a bitter taste in Jennifer's mouth. She went to the park for the second time that day. She needed fresh air and sober thoughts to get her head around everything. The shadowed streets fell victim to the evening chill, and there were rumours of heavy snow ahead. She chose her footsteps carefully on the frost-glistened path as she walked from her car, her mind working hard to decipher everything that had occurred.

Why the hell had she messed things up by snogging Ethan? she thought, seeking out a bench. It grated that she had made herself a subject of gossip once more. She was no nearer to finding the murderer now than ever. The street-lit bench chilled her legs, but the isolation was welcome. She took a deep breath, exhaling a foggy breath as she profiled the killer in her mind.

Quite often murder victims knew their attacker. Intelligence suggested that somebody was hanging around with Johnny before he died, promising him alcohol. The ouija board muddied the waters, but whatever was going on wasn't solely supernatural. A physical being had to be involved too, mimicking the deaths of Frank Foster. The person spending time with Johnny, the dark figure on CCTV with Shelly before she died – even Charlie had mentioned being taken in by someone. Then there was Josh. The thought of her nephew being involved made her shiver. It *had* to be someone Jennifer knew.

CHAPTER THIRTY-EIGHT

Sam Beswick glanced around the prison visiting room for the final time, glad to see the last of the familiar faces. Couples sat head to head, their fingers tentatively touching across tables. Inmates sat with clenched fists as their criminal counterparts kept them abreast of the dealers muscling in on their territory. And in the furthest corner, contraband was passing hands, the precious currency that was the lifeblood of the prison. Sam extended his hand as he greeted his visitor. 'I was surprised to hear from you again so soon.'

The man shook his hand briskly before pulling up a chair and sitting across from him. 'I decided to make a special visit. How's it going? Not long left now.'

Roman letters spelt out a recent tattoo on Sam's forearm as he stretched in his chair. 'To thine own self be true.' Life had dealt him a strange hand, but he was learning to live with himself, and make plans for the future. 'I've been in and out of this place so often, every time I go, I say it's my last.'

The man leaned forward, clasping his hands together as he rested his elbows on the table. 'And will it be? Your last, that is.'

Sam nodded thoughtfully, rubbing the back of his shaven head. 'I think it's different this time, now I've made my peace with the world.'

The man's eyes narrowed as he cocked his head to one side. 'Does that include old friends too?'

'I'm sorry? I'm not with you.'

'Have you made peace with old friends, Sammy boy?' His lip curled in a sneer as his voice changed in tone.

The shock of recognition drew Sam's words in a stutter. 'I ... I don't have any friends.'

The menace in the visitor's voice demanded attention. 'Oh, I think you have. In fact, I'm delighted to announce that one of your best friends has paid you a visit today. I told you I'd be back, didn't I?'

'I don't know what you mean,' Sam said, his Adam's apple bobbing as he swallowed.

'I appear different, but you recognise me all right. I can see it in your eyes.'

Sam frowned. 'What sort of sick joke is this?'

The man gave a fiendish grin as he spoke in a low whisper. 'It must be dreadful to discover that you're still in that nightmare you thought you had woken up from. Mr Double Standards, squealing to that little bitch in the station. Remember what you said the last time we were together, over twenty years ago? That you wouldn't grass on me if it killed you. Remember? Right before you spilled your guts.'

Sam almost forgot to breathe.

The man gave a kindly nod to the guard as he cast an eye in their direction. 'Don't look so scared. I'm prepared to forgive your misdemeanours. You were young back then, and the time inside has given you an edge. I have plans for you, kid, and I've come such a long way. Now wouldn't you like to live forever?'

Sam was lost for words. The thought of resuming contact with the killer struck him with terror.

'Frank, is it really you? I'm not a kid anymore. I won't go back to that life.'

The man tutted. 'I'm not Frank, I'm the Grim Reaper. You're either with me or against me, remember?' he said, staring with dead eyes.

Sam shifted in his chair, disorientated as he tried to accept the situation that was nothing but surreal. Frank was dead. But something evil had detached and been left behind. Something had taken form, a living breathing person. How?

The man's voice broke into his thoughts. 'How is your poor mother these days? Still visiting?'

Sam grabbed the man's wrist in a warning, then recoiled at the coldness. He hissed under his breath as he leaned forward, 'You leave my mother out of this.'

'Why? She's having a wonderful time, telling all her prayer group friends how she's reconciled with you after all these years.' The man took on a woman's tone as he rasped, 'He's turned to Jesus, praise the lord!' He sniggered as he raised jazz hands to the air, an act utterly out of place with the persona he presented. 'It's a shame I've never been properly introduced. If you like, I could show her what she's been missing. Remember my farewell to Tina?'

The man winked, and Sam drew back in horror. All at once, he was a teenager again, throwing up in his toilet while the room closed in on him. The vision of Tina's bloated face and the smell of her blood was more than he could bear.

'You leave my mother alone, you sick bastard. Just stay away from her, you hear me?' Sam's voice grew louder, and the guard approached their table.

'Everything all right here?'

'I want to go back to my cell,' Sam said, stumbling back, his chair crashing to the ground.

The man shrugged innocently. 'We can speak another time.'

CHAPTER THIRTY-NINE

FRANK – 1993 TO 1995

The jury echoed a unanimous verdict of guilty in the packed courtroom, and the disgust on their faces was evident. The admission in interview, his threatening behaviour, and the evidence that linked him to each of the murders ensured Frank Foster was going to jail. Frank's barrister wished for the tenth time that he had never taken on the case. Against his advice, Frank had changed his plea to not guilty. Without the evidence he had stupidly handed over to the police, Frank may have had a fighting chance with his excuse of police oppression in interview.

Standing in the mahogany panelled pew, Frank remained deadpan as he was sentenced to serve several life sentences, but his insides felt like the inner workings of a faulty clock, wound tightly by anger and terror in equal measures. Standing tall against the backdrop of the sniffles and cries of 'how could you?' from the public gallery, he wiped a trickle of sweat from his brow. He gripped the lip of the bench before him. One day he would speak to the reporters in the gallery and they would get it all straight. After all, the police were allowed to kill people, so why couldn't he? He should be getting a medal for cleaning up the streets, not being locked away. If it weren't for him, the drug dealers, pimps and prostitutes would still be roaming the streets. Not to mention the kiddie fiddler he had sent to kingdom come. Killing them had sent a message, and the others had curbed their activities while he was in charge. It was a shame he couldn't have included crooked police officers in that line up.

His work was part of the natural order, and it was only fitting he take satisfaction from it. If only he had more time to recruit others to carry it on. Now things would go back to the way they had always been, and it was all the fault of the bitch that had put him here. There was one positive aspect that gave him hope. Meeting others just like him. Best of all, he would be serving time with the notorious 'Demon.'

Frank had first discovered the 'Demon' as a starring feature one of his detective magazines. The man, originally known as Percival Smith, was a legend in his eyes. An unassuming bank clerk, Percival was happily married up until the day of his forty-fifth birthday when he was arrested for the murder of over a dozen people. Impressive, given that his killing spree had begun just six months earlier. Investigations revealed that he was heavily involved in the occult. His wife Cheryl stated in her interview with *Crime* magazine that Percival's personality had undergone a complete transformation in recent months. Instead of the kind caring man she married, he had become cruel, rough and demanding in the bedroom. Upon entry to prison, he became as much of a recluse as he could in such circumstances. His padded flesh disappeared as he ate only enough food to sustain life. With his balding skin and hollowed eyes, he was a walking skeleton.

Percival killed the only man that befriended him by slitting his throat in his sleep. Ten years later, and he was still housed in a solitary cell.

Frank seized every opportunity to be near the Demon when he was forced to exit his cell for food and exercise. Months passed before the Demon crooked a bony finger and invited him inside. The small space seemed colder than Frank's cell as he sat on the hard chair next to the metal-framed bed. The Demon regarded him with curiosity and Frank felt his heart pound as his soulless eyes bored into his mind.

'What brings you to my door?' His tainted breath was hot on Frank's face as he leaned over him, his back bent in a bell-shaped curve.

Frank cleared his throat, unprepared for the moment he had waited for. 'I wanted to meet you.'

The man tapped a heavy finger on Frank's shoulder, which he felt all the way down to his toes. 'You name yourself the Grim Reaper. You are a mere mortal, are you not?'

Frank choked on his words as the Demon stood over him, smelling of corpse and looking no better. Feeling like a trapped animal, he stuttered his words. 'I ... I do what I believe is right. You killed those people for the same reason I did; they were of no value to the world.'

A rasping sound followed which resembled a laugh. 'Pay no heed to those scurrilous tales. I killed for no other reason than that it was my enjoyment to do so. But it is only a matter of time until mortality catches up with you, is it not?'

'I don't understand,' Frank's mouth was dry and he swallowed back the lump in his throat. His feet felt glued to the floor, and he could not have left, even if he had wanted to.

'Would it please you to carry on your work without fear of

reprisal? Such is within my power. But leave me now. You will return tomorrow.'

Frank twisted restlessly in his narrow bunk bed that night. The Demon scared him, but freedom of any kind was tantalising bait. He returned the next day, and every day he was able. The Demon stated that he had been in existence for hundreds of years. He had overcome death and could show Frank how to do the same. The claims were outlandish. Surely it could not be true? A roaming entity, using human bodies upon will? Frank asked the only question he could think of.

'Why do you choose to spend time rotting away in prison? Why not inhabit the body of someone who is free?'

The Demon stood behind Frank as he faced the window, his words whispering in his ear. 'I am free to leave whenever I wish. But there is no better place to observe the darker side of human nature, is there?'

Frank shrugged, unsure of the question. He did not always understand the Demon's use of language, but he had no doubt of the conviction in the words.

Frank's visits to the Demon became a regular occurrence as he taught him the ways of the occult. The prison guards seemed happy to leave them to it, although Frank would not have wanted to share a cell with the man. He was not someone you turned your back on at night.

A blood moon hung in the sky as Frank entered his cell one night, and there was an energy he had not felt before. His perception of the supernatural had grown, and with it a sense of dark adventure ahead. Even the Demon seemed different, rubbing a hand over his marble-white skull as he inhaled. 'Can't you smell it? Feast on the misery. It's a veritable banquet.'

'Yes,' Frank said, staring at the newly drawn occult symbols chalked on the cement floor. He knew better than to question them. He avoided all eye contact with his mentor. The dark hollow wells revealed a glimpse of the Demon's soul. The memory of what lay behind those eyes would haunt him forever.

The Demon's tendons stood out on his neck as he spoke, a visible pulse throbbing with life from his pallid flesh. 'We must make haste. But heed my words before departing from this earthly plane.' His words grew hypnotic, and Frank felt as if he was being enveloped in a thick web. Talk of departure from life should have sent warning bells to his brain but they had been strangely numbed.

'You cannot harbour all your memories if you are to inhabit another. Take your most valuable possessions; anger, hate, and lust. When you depart your body and feel your existence carry you, you must first find a host. Houses and buildings are ripe for habitation, but not as satisfying a haunt as people. But taking a human as your steed carries its own risk. To hurt your host is to hurt yourself. You are but a parasite in that state.'

'Is Percival your host?' Frank asked, his words feeling like they were coming from another room.

'Yes. I am one with him. He gave himself freely and I will stay until his body withers and dies. Percival was not the meek husband his wife thought him to be. He developed an interest in the occult through a dark young lady. She introduced him to the world of ouija boards and that was how he summoned me. I gradually took over every aspect of his life. His wife was quite delicious you know, our time together was most enjoyable.'

Frank felt a flutter of excitement. He had had his doubts at first, but now he could feel the truth of his words from the chill in the air to the probing that reached every cell in his body. It called him in teasing whispers. 'I think I understand. I can come back after death, but I need a host to sustain me.

I can briefly use others and feed off their pain. But if I am to experience true existence, to live again on the earthly plane in flesh and blood as you do, I need to conjoin with someone who accepts me.'

'Yes, but if you merge and they deny your existence, they will expel you from this world. You must give your host a reason for letting you in.'

'I understand.' Frank said, the thought of freedom tantalising.

'Then I believe it's time,' the Demon said, clamping his cold clammy hand over Frank's mouth.

In the cold dark cell with the smell of rotting flesh lingering in his nostrils, Frank did not want to die. He should have expected it, but the slash of the razor across his throat still came as a shock. Trying to stem the sudden flow of blood, Frank clawed at his killer for mercy.

The Demon's grey-blue face smiled down upon him, cradling his body as the warm blood soaked his clothing. 'Shhh,' he whispered. 'Don't fight it. Control your fear. Focus your power. You are the Grim Reaper, are you not?'

As Frank's life drained away, the heaviness lifted as he left his physical body behind. Writhing, he recognised Gloria's soft voice whispering his name from far away. Frank fought the pull, resisting the urge to go towards the light. His hatred rose to the surface, breaking away in brittle black splinters from his soul. Birthing a new existence, he grew in strength. His formless shape had all the senses, and the freedom of flight. He rose to the prison ceiling and beyond, free from the confines of bars, free to live again. Leaving his killer behind, he fled the prison walls as the dull ring of the alarm alerted prison guards to the death scene. The Demon, now naked in his cell, was bathed in the blood of Franks' lifeless body. But he was no longer Frank. He was the Grim Reaper, and he sped through the night searching for his host.

CHAPTER FORTY

The station car park had been turned into an ice rink by the overnight freeze, and the elderly caretaker walked with a stoop as he threw handfuls of rock salt from his black plastic bucket. He waved at Jennifer, hastily throwing some in her direction for fear she might slip and fall in the snow.

Jennifer slung the loose strap of her handbag over her shoulder before thanking the caretaker. Her choice of footwear was not the most sensible given the weather, but she loved the feeling of power a good pair of heels gave her. Judging by his steel toe capped footwear, he neither understood nor worried about such things.

She pressed her tag against the back door scanner and a soft buzzing vibration came from the bottom of her bag. 'Who's ringing at this hour of the morning? It's not even eight o clock yet,' she muttered as she searched for her phone. Her heart gave a flutter as she glanced at the unknown number lighting up her display. 'Hello,' she said, steeling herself for the reply.

'Hi Jennifer, it's David.'

Jennifer exhaled in relief at hearing a familiar voice. Her sister's husband did not call very often, but when he did it was normally for something boring, such as borrowing her lawnmower or asking for advice on shoplifters. 'Oh hello, is everything all right? Your number came up as unknown.'

'Yeah, I'm ringing from work. Listen, I booked Amy and myself a weekend in Paris as a surprise. I'd arranged with Laura to take Joshua, but she's broken down on the motorway with her horse box and doesn't think she'll be back on time. Could you do me a favour and pick him up this afternoon? I know you're probably working, but if we can't get someone to collect him from nursery, I'll have to cancel the whole thing.'

'I'll be happy to get him. It's the nursery beside the church, isn't it? Two o'clock?'

David exhaled in relief on the other end of the line. 'Thanks, you're a life saver. If you can drop him over to Laura later that would be great.'

Jennifer rolled her eyes. Heaven forbid she be entrusted with Joshua for a whole day. She swallowed her pride, happy to have him at all.

'I'm sure Amy will be thrilled with the surprise. What about Lily?'

'I didn't think Amy would want to leave her behind so she's coming with us. She's starting to sleep through the night, whereas Josh ...'

'You don't need to explain. You wouldn't have much of a romantic night with him creeping between the covers, would you?'

David laughed. 'Yes, you could say that. Anyway, Laura has the details of where we're going. I'm sure Josh will enjoy seeing you.'

Jennifer responded with a smile in her voice. 'I'm looking forward to it.'

She expected to have to plead with her sergeant for the time off, but as it turned out, there were enough probationers that day to cover her shift, and she agreed to work until twelve.

Jennifer grimaced as she checked through her emails. Her application to visit Sam Beswick in prison had been turned down. Without a valid case to investigate, he had to agree to her visit. She wasn't ready to give up yet. She would write to him and explain.

The clock ticked by slowly and she briefed Will on any outstanding jobs before she left. She was not expecting the call from the nursery while she was out shopping for pizza, DVDs and popcorn.

'Hello, is that Jennifer Knight? This is Little Ducklings nursery, we've been given your contact details.' A shaky young woman's voice spoke on the other end of the phone.

'Yes, have I got the time wrong? Joshua's due to be picked up in an hour, isn't he?'

'Yes, he is. I don't suppose any member of your family collected him early without telling anyone?'

Jennifer's heart began to thrum in her chest. 'No. His parents are away and the only other person is my aunt, who's been delayed. Please don't tell me he's gone.'

The sound of a hand over the receiver gave cause for alarm as muffled whispers gave instructions to keep looking. 'Hello?' Jennifer said, dropping her shopping basket and hastily returning to her car.

The woman returned to the phone. 'I'm sorry but he seems to be missing. The children were out in the garden playing in the snow and when they came in he was nowhere to be found. I'll have to call the police.'

Jennifer felt like screaming that she *was* the police and how could these idiots be so stupid as to lose a four-year-old child? But it was imperative they moved quickly. There would be time for recriminations later. 'You do that. I'll look everywhere I know and if you find him, call me.'

Breathless from searching the local playground, she expanded her search to her home. Her mind ran wild with different scenarios and none of them ended well. With shaking hands, she reached for her mobile phone to call Will. It rang before she dialled the number.

'Hello?' she whispered, praying for good news.

'Jennifer, is that you?' Father Kelly's voice echoed down the phone line.

'Father, I can't speak right now. Joshua's missing and I need to keep the line free.'

'That's why I'm calling; he's with me. I was at the nursery when he disappeared. I remember him saying his aunty Laura promised to bring him to the boathouse this weekend, so I drove over, and there he was, sitting on the doorstep, the little tyke.'

She sighed loudly, tears threatening to brim over. How on earth had he got to the boathouse by himself? The question was replaced by relief. 'Thank God, I was so scared. I'll come and get him now.'

'I've told the nursery and I've found a spare key under a rock so we've let ourselves in.'

Jennifer nodded as she grabbed her coat from the hook in the hall. 'I'll be with you in a few minutes.'

As she was slamming the door behind her, the phone buzzed again. She ran her hand through the sleeve of her coat and accepted the call.

Will's cheery voice rang down the phone. 'Hi Jen, everything OK?'

'No, as it happens. Josh went missing and it frightened the bloody life out of me. Father Kelly's just called to say he's found him at the boathouse. Can you find the incident and update control that he's safe?'

'Sure. Want me to pop over? I'm not far from there.'

'No mate, I'm fine. I'll call you when I get there.'

Will hesitated. 'Jennifer wait, something doesn't feel right. Are you sure everything's OK?'

'I'm fine, but I really have to go.'

Will hesitated. 'OK but call me when you can.'

Jennifer drove in a trance, clipping the footpath when she took a corner, and crossing traffic lights blindly as she followed the drivers ahead. How could a four-year-old boy make the two mile journey to the boathouse in half an hour? Turning right, she took the road marked 'Shady Pines' and parked at the entrance to walk to the cabin. Looming pine trees flanked the path to the river, their branches bowed with snow. She blinked against the glare as she followed the double set of footprints to the boathouse. The only noise was the snow being crushed underfoot.

She stomped her feet, scattering crumbs of snow across the front decking of the cabin. Father Kelly's voice rose from inside.

'We're in here.'

She entered the cabin, her shadow falling ahead of her. The gloomy wooden walls seemed to carry a vibration of negativity, and there was an audible hum in the air. It was as if the boathouse was alive. 'Hello?' Jennifer called, waiting to hear Josh's footsteps running across the wooden floorboards.

Father Kelly stood by the stone fireplace, his arms folded. 'Close the door,' he said stiffly. Jennifer glanced at the grandfather clock in the corner, the hands frozen at exactly one thirty.

'Where's Joshua?' Jennifer asked, her eyes darting around the room.

'They did a good job rebuilding this place after the fire. You'd never imagine it had been burnt to the ground,' Father Kelly said, as he turned and cracked his knuckles.

CHAPTER FORTY-ONE

'Joshua didn't come here by himself, did he, Father?' Jennifer said, the joint set of snowy footprints outside having told her as much. 'Now, are you going to tell me where my nephew is, or do I have to find him myself?'

'Why, he's right here.' Father Kelly walked to the adjoining bedroom door and opened it slightly, allowing Jennifer to peep inside at the blond-haired boy reading a book. Entranced, his lips moved as he read the words, but he did not appear to hear her.

Jennifer opened her mouth to speak, and the door closed before her. 'We've got some business to take care of first,' Father Kelly said, taking her by the elbow.

She stared into the empty hollowness in his eyes, wondering if any part of the gentle priest had been left inside. Calling for Joshua, she was greeted with silence.

'He can't hear you. Now sit down before I hurt someone.' The slick voice confirmed what Jennifer already knew.

'I know who you are,' Jennifer hissed, as she was backed towards the chair.

The priest's clerical attire contrasted strangely with his twisted features. 'So, tell me, who am I?'

'You're a pathetic coward who used Father Kelly to kill people just to get to me. If you even think of harming Josh I'll finish you off, do you hear me?'

'Fighting talk, given that you are a mortal and I am immortal.'

'I am more than you think and I can end you,' Jennifer spat, prodding the cold air with her finger. She wanted to stand to deliver the words but Father Kelly loomed over her, his frame married to a graveyard darkness.

He jabbed his thumb back at the bedroom door, delivering his words in a fit of rage. 'And I can end your brat in there so shut the fuck up before I kill you both.' Jennifer slumped in the armchair, hope dissipating like sand.

'That's better. What's a man got to do to get a little respect around here?' He tugged on his clerical collar as the room grew dim.

Crippled with the fear of losing Joshua, Jennifer tried to invoke guidance from the other side. She transmitted a tendril of thought, but a bolt of pain ripped through her skull as the entity intervened. She clasped her throbbing forehead. 'Ahh! How can you stand there mimicking a good man? At least show yourself, Grim Reaper, Frank, or whoever you are.' She sensed something outside her periphery but could not tune back in.

Father Kelly gripped her hand, infiltrating her thoughts with images of a terror-stricken Joshua being dragged from the room. A knife glinted against his throat. 'Enough!' she shouted, pulling her hand away. 'You can have what you want, but only if you release Josh.'

'All in good time.'

Jennifer felt another tug of her consciousness. Someone was coming. But they were not strong enough to protect her from what lay ahead. The best she could hope for was to save the child whom she loved more than her own life. The humming grew louder and she flinched as the priest touched her hair.

'It was quite a surprise to discover we're both the same. Spawned from loveless parents and rejected by our peers, we never had a chance to be accepted in their world. You're not one of them. But you've never failed to disappoint *me*. When your body grows old, I can make you immortal. We are destined to be gods. Can't you feel it?'

'I am not you, I'm nothing like you,' Jennifer said, with a tremor in her voice.

'But you have a touch of death about you, wouldn't you say? Who do you think is responsible for the demise of all those people?'

Jennifer whispered the words, 'Father Kelly.'

The priest threw back his head and laughed. 'It's been a long time since I had such a good chuckle. I'd forgotten what it's like.' He wiped the corner of his eye. 'You disappoint me, Jennifer, I thought you would have worked it out by now. Father Kelly was not my host. I met him when he tried to exorcise me from another of my steeds. Well, you can see how that worked out, can't you? He proved useful when I visited Sam in prison, but he is a temporary home. Far too much godliness in this body, it makes me sick. No, someone far darker led the executions.'

Jennifer searched her mind for answers. 'I don't understand. If Father Kelly isn't responsible then who is?'

The priest opened his arms, his smile wide as he delivered the news. 'Why you are, my dear.'

Jennifer recoiled in horror. 'No, you're lying. It's not true!'

Father Kelly leaned over her, gripping the armrests on

each side. She shrank back in the chair to avoid his rancid breath, the same rotting smell that accompanied every encounter.

'Don't deny the darkness in you. It's beautiful. Remember when you prayed for the death of your father? That's when I found your soul. I came here looking for revenge against your mother, but when I heard your sweet prayer, my disappointment at her death vanished. At first, I wanted to kill you, but then I discovered you were more of a prize than I could ever imagine.'

Jennifer thought back over the recent weeks. The back door left open, the scratches on the back of her neck, how she'd felt that Joan and Shelley were dead long before she got there. She clasped a hand over her mouth and retched.

'Don't worry, I've helped you cover them up. After all, you're no good to me in prison. No good at all.' Father Kelly locked his fingers as he stretched. 'Your manipulation of Johnny was a joy to behold. You even brought the rope from your shed, all knotted in preparation. It's a shame you couldn't have stayed to watch the floor show.'

Jennifer shook her head in disbelief. 'But you spoke to me in custody through him.'

'You weren't going to listen to me any other way. All the others were puppets, but you were destined to be my true host.'

'Charlie?' Jennifer wiped her tears with the back of her hand, as her voice broke into a sob.

'Of course. By the time Charlie drank the whiskey you bought, he didn't feel a thing. Spontaneous combustion is a trick I learned from a prison friend and you took to it beautifully.'

'Lies, it's all lies.' Jennifer watched the half man, half entity as his eyes gleamed fiendishly.

'Don't deny what you've seen for yourself. Remember

walking Shelly to the bridge? It was quite amusing watching you pointing to your image on the CCTV, wondering who it was,' he cackled, savouring every moment. 'As for Joan, she got such a fright when she saw you again, she had a heart attack on the spot. Levitation is an excellent way of breaking the ice, don't you think?'

Jennifer threaded her fingers through her hair, wishing she could wake up from the nightmare she found herself in. But when she raised her head, the priest was still there, she was still in this godforsaken room, and she was still accountable. 'I can't … remember.'

'Now you know you the truth, perhaps that puts a different slant on things. Do you deserve to live a so-called normal life after killing all those people?'

Jennifer shook her head in response. Her hands were tainted with the blood of the innocent. No amount of scrubbing would wash her guilt away. She jumped as fists pounded at the door from outside and Will called her name.

'It's time. Surrender yourself wholly to me or I'll kill the boy and take you in your grief.' The priest's words came quick fire.

Jennifer had little choice, and she needed to be sure that her nephew would be spared. She wanted to see Josh one last time, but she was frozen to the spot. The pounding grew louder and Will shouted at her to open the door. What would he think of her when he found out what she was?

The priest gave Jennifer a wintry smile. 'You think he can help you? The more people you involve, the more people will die. Is that what you want?' He raised his hand and Will fell through the door, frozen in shock as he stared at the half man, half entity before him. A thick mass swelled from its body. The stench was overpowering, and Jennifer screamed, breaking the spell.

'Get Josh out, now!' As the entity turned to Will, Jennifer

screamed her nephew's name. Joshua burst through the bedroom door and ran into Will's open arms. 'Get him out, I'm behind you,' Jennifer shouted as Will scooped up the frightened child and ran through the open door. But Jennifer knew escape was futile, and locked the door firmly shut behind him.

Weakened, she dropped to the floor, her knees hitting the wood as she emitted a cry of despair. From the moment she'd walked in, she'd been under the entity's control.

The floorboards creaked as Father Kelly stood over her, nudging her body with his black leather shoe. 'I was going to spare you the pain, but after that little trick, you can have it all.'

'No,' Jennifer said, her hair falling limply around her face. 'Take me. At least if I know there's something of me inside, then you won't hurt Josh.'

The priest chortled. 'I will go as far to say there could be some truth in that. Yes, I will have you, whole and intact. Your body will live a long and well-screwed life. Sound like a deal?'

Jennifer nodded numbly, picking herself up from the floor. Sobs wracked her body as she stood before him, awaiting his instruction.

'Now my sweet, give me your hands and lower your guard. Soon we will be taking the same breath.'

Jennifer nodded numbly, lowering the wall of protection from her mind. Will was calling from outside and her last tear fell with relief as she sensed Josh was safe. The grasp on her hands tightened as the entity invaded her fingertips. For a moment she lost her sight, falling into darkness. Tendrils of hatred found her blood, now under his ownership.

With rapture, he discarded his old steed, finding her organs and mingling his presence with hers. He was no longer a puppet master, but alive inside her body, grounding himself to the earth and savouring every moment.

Jennifer fought the urge to claw her throat as his presence slid upwards. Gasping for breath, black spots appeared in her vision as the darkness filtered through her brain. She saw his childhood, his upbringing. His first fumbled sexual encounter and the murders that followed. His life was her life and her heart pounded against her rib cage as her nightmares took flight. Her hands grew numb and moved without her instruction.

As the last of the entity left the priest, Father Kelly fell to the floor; a marionette whose strings had been cut. Jennifer fought to keep her eyes open. It would have been easier to retreat inside her body and hide. Her natural instinct fought her acceptance and rewarded her with agonising pain.

Blue-lipped and ashen-faced, Father Kelly dragged himself upwards as he gripped the chair. Pulling a small bible from his inside pocket, he began to recite an exorcism. Jennifer's eyes rolled back into her head. Numb, she forced her hands to clutch the silver cross around her neck. Between gasping breaths, she whispered the words, 'I do not accept you,' because she knew the only way to rid herself of the entity was to reject him when he was naked to her world.

The whispers hidden at the back of her mind grew louder as many voices spoke in Latin, casting the entity out. She sank to her knees as light splintered through her being, and she was lifted to the other place. 'No!' The entity screamed a torturous cry. 'You are mine, I will not let you go!'

Jennifer opened her eyes. Father Kelly, her mother and Charlie stood with their palms outward, commanding the being to leave. Jennifer did not care if she was alive or dead, she just wanted the infection eliminated. Maggots of hatred squirmed from inside her as evil fought the expanding light.

Caught in two worlds at once, her earthly life hung by a

wisp. A warm hand touched her hair and caressed her face. 'Jennifer, stay with me.' Will's voice seeped through her mind. She tried to speak, but her words were foul and contemptuous. She groaned in relief as the pain eased, and Father Kelly's voice brought her back to the other place. 'Expel him my child. He is spent now.' Jennifer retched and a dark ball of smoke dissipated in the light. The muffled sounds of an ambulance rang in the background and Will's hand squeezed hers tightly. Jennifer closed her eyes and exhaled, releasing herself to what would be.

CHAPTER FORTY-TWO

The IV line tugged on Jennifer's arm as she tried to move. She turned to see Will in the chair next to her bed, his chin touching his crumpled tie as he snored gently.

'Will?' She croaked through dry lips as she peered around the solitary hospital room.

Will snorted as he woke with a start. 'You're awake. How are you feeling?'

'Awful,' she said, glancing at the flowers crammed on a small table at the side of her bed.

'They're from the office, Amy, your aunt. Everyone's asking after you. Will I get the nurse?' Will gestured towards the door.

Jennifer leaned back onto her pillows, the sheets rubbing against the plastic mattress cover. 'Not yet. Tell me what happened first.'

Will rubbed his eyes. 'You don't remember?'

Jennifer shook her head, wondering who had dressed her for bed. 'All I remember is getting to the boathouse and finding Father Kelly there with Joshua. I know Josh got out safe, but the rest is a blur.'

'Josh is fine, don't worry. After we spoke on the phone, I had a nagging feeling that something was wrong. I drove to the boathouse to check you were OK, but everything was really still. I looked in through the window, I could see you were in some kind of trouble. It all sounds crazy now ... ' Will shook his head. Jennifer gave him an encouraging nod to continue.

'I thought maybe Father Kelly abducted Joshua and you were trying to stop him. But when the door opened and I saw ... I don't know what I saw, it was like a black shadow coming out of the priest. I was rooted to the floor.' He paused, still absorbing it all. 'I thought you were behind me when I brought Josh to the car. By the time I got the door open, you were both in a heap on the ground. The paramedics were couldn't figure out what was wrong. Doctors had to keep you hydrated, because you couldn't keep anything down. You spoke a lot in your sleep.' Will blushed.

Jennifer guessed she had mentioned his name a few times. She hoped she hadn't spoilt things by calling out to Ethan.

Jennifer wriggled her fingers and toes, relieved to feel life, but not knowing why. She guessed by Will's stubble that he had stayed in the hospital overnight. She could not fault his loyalty. She thought of Haven and wondered what Steph and DI Allison were making of it all.

'What have you told work?' Jennifer said.

'As far as everyone else is concerned, Josh went missing, the priest found him, and you drove there to get him. Something went on between you and Father Kelly, then I turned up and called an ambulance for you both. Joshua said he doesn't remember, but I've got a feeling he knows more than he's letting on. He's a very special kid, that one.'

Jennifer nodded quietly. Her arms ached to hold her nephew. He had been placed in danger that day, and Amy would not have taken the news well. But now was not the time for recriminations. All she wanted to do was to move on.

Will found her hand and entwined his fingers between hers. 'I'm afraid the priest didn't make it. Heart attack.'

Jennifer vaguely remembered him praying over her from a place of peace. 'He's in a good place,' she said, shifting in the bed. A nurse walked into the room, smiling at the sight of her recovering patient. 'We can remove your drip now. Can I get you a cup of tea? A slice of toast perhaps?'

'No thanks,' Jennifer said, holding out her arm as the nurse gently removed the needle.

Will leaned forward. 'It's not like you to turn down food. Why don't you have something to eat?'

Jennifer touched Will's face, and he tenderly placed his hand over hers. 'I'm fine. Go home and get some sleep. And Will, thank you.'

He leaned in and kissed her forehead. Jennifer closed her eyes as she blocked out the physical world. She needed to rest, heal and decipher all that had occurred in the last few days.

Jennifer stretched her stiff limbs and covered her yawn with the back of her hand. She opened her eyes to see a familiar face enter the room.

'Ethan? What are you doing here?'

'I would've come earlier but Will's been standing guard.'

Jennifer pushed herself up into sitting position. The thought of being alone with Ethan made her uneasy, although she was yet to understand why.

Ethan dragged his chair over to the side of the bed. It was the first time she had seen him in casual dress. Even in chinos and a sweater, he was immaculately groomed.

'Are you OK to talk?'

Jennifer nodded and Ethan got up and closed the door. He turned to see her eyeing him suspiciously. 'Don't look so worried, it's fine.'

Jennifer prickled with impatience. What was so important that he had to come see her in the hospital? 'Just cut to the chase Ethan, what do you want?'

'It's tricky. I can't disclose everything until you come on board.'

'I'm with Will now so you're wasting your time,' Jennifer winced as she blurted the words, wishing that for once she would engage her brain before her mouth.

'What I'm offering has nothing to do with ...' Ethan cleared his throat, '... personal feelings. I'm here to discuss to my unit. I want you to work for me.'

Jennifer raised an eyebrow. 'Work for you? I've no plans on leaving the police.'

Ethan sighed. 'You wouldn't have to. I manage a specialist unit *within* the police investigating preternatural events. I've been watching you, Jennifer. We need people with your abilities.'

Jennifer blinked. She wasn't hallucinating as Ethan was still there. The radiator beside her bed pumped out heat and she felt her armpits dampen. Such detail wasn't normally afforded to her in dreams, so perhaps concussion was to blame. She took a sip of water as she digested Ethan's words. 'You're not making any sense.'

Ethan slid his warrant card from the back pocket of his black chinos.

Jennifer's mouth dropped as she read the rank. 'How the hell did you become a DI at your age?'

Ethan's eyes lit up as he spoke about his vocation. 'I earned it. And you can too if you're willing to join my team. I'm talking about working *with* your powers instead of against them, and I'm not going to be sending you to occupational health because you have a different way of thinking.'

'Are you sure? Because I'm half expecting the men in white coats to come knocking any minute now.'

A hint of a smile crossed Ethan's lips as he picked up his briefcase and pushed open the double buttons. 'I don't normally recruit from hospital beds, but time is of the essence. In the last couple of decades, paranormal events have been occurring at an overwhelming rate. The government have done all they can to suppress it in the media, but it's come to the point where it's getting out of control. We need people with a link to the other side.'

'One foot in this world and one foot in the other. It's hindered me all my life.'

'It doesn't need to. You joined the job to make a difference, didn't you? Take a look at these.' He opened the briefcase and spread thin cardboard folders across the bed. Jennifer gasped as she flicked through the confidential paperwork. These were no ordinary crimes. Witness evidence from beyond the grave, doppelgängers, shape shifters, possessions, there were so many to choose from, and Jennifer wanted to investigate them all. Reluctantly she allowed Ethan to reclaim the paperwork and place it back in the suitcase.

'It's restricted. I'm going against protocol showing it to you. But I figure if you go to the papers, I can pull the crazy card.'

Jennifer laughed. 'Thanks for the vote of confidence.'

Ethan's face was a picture of sincerity. 'This is serious. This type of work, it becomes your life. You can't just walk away from it. It can also be dangerous. But the extra responsibility is reflected in your pay scale.'

'Where are you based?' Jennifer said, the pay scale the least of her concerns.

'Our main office is in London but we have branches in

historic towns dotted throughout the UK where activity is most prevalent. We're opening a branch in Haven. Think about it Jennifer, this job is made for you.'

Jennifer took a deep breath. 'I can't believe this is real. I've so many questions.'

'Plenty of time for that later. I'm under a lot of pressure to set this unit up and return to base. I know I'm rushing you, but are you on board?' Ethan held out his hand, waiting for her to shake it.

Jennifer stared into space, deep in thought. Of course she was on board. But the desperation in Ethan's eyes gave her a bargaining tool, and she wasn't going alone.

'Would I be working alone or partnered up?'

'Partnered.'

'In that case I'll join you, but under one condition.' She wriggled her toes under the starchy blankets as she tried to hide her excitement.

'Name it,' Ethan said, biting down on his smile.

Jennifer wondered if he was as keen with all his new recruits.

'I want Will as my partner.'

Ethan threw Jennifer an incredulous look. 'You're kidding. Have you not listened to what I've just said? We need people with abilities, not officers who are friendly with their fists.'

'He has abilities. If it wasn't for him, I'd be dead now.'

'Well, you've more faith in him than me.' He shook his head as an internal argument seemed to take place. Finally, he continued. 'The best I can offer is a six month trial for Will, and that's only if he acts professionally. If he picks a fight, there are no second chances.'

A wide grin spread across Jennifer's face. 'Deal.' She held out her hand and Ethan grasped it.

'Good. I'll send the paperwork over when you're discharged. I want you to start right away,' Ethan said.

'Won't I have to give notice?'

Ethan pushed his chair back against the wall. 'Your colleagues will be told you've seconded to another team. But this is highly confidential. We have to keep a tight ship to prevent the media getting a hold of our remit.'

'Did I breathe a word when you asked me about my experiences?'

'To be fair, no you didn't. You passed all my tests with flying colours.'

Jennifer blushed. It was unlikely their snog at the Christmas party was part of his test.

Ethan cleared his throat. 'Get some rest. You're going to need it.'

Ethan left the door ajar as he left, and Jennifer settled back into bed to the tune of the hustle and bustle of the nurses in the hall.

As much as she tried, she was unable to recover the full memory of what took place in the boathouse. Instead, she seen her mother's face, warm and approving, telling her all was well. The worse of the experience had been lost, but Frank Foster lived on somewhere in the ether. Not as the cold blooded murderer, but the little boy who had lost so much faith in the world. His death experience returned his childhood innocence from the depths of his soul. At last, he joined the woman waiting on his periphery. 'Gloria,' Jennifer whispered. She recognised the name because somehow, she had been shown his life. Jennifer smiled at the vision of the woman gently taking the little boy's hand. Perhaps now he could start again.

Elizabeth's face came into view, delivering a gentle smile. Jennifer blinked. The shadows creeping into the room told her time had passed. Had she been dreaming?

She closed her eyes, trying to hold onto the fading image of her mother. Joshua had been right. They did look alike. It was comforting to know they were both protecting him. But she would have to be strong for what lay ahead. Charlie, Joan, and now Father Kelly. Each of them had given up their lives. She slid from between the sheets and tip toed to the window, grateful for the cool tiled floor. *I must be in a private room,* she thought, peering through the blinds at the busy car park. A flock of sharp eyed crows clung to the telephone wire; a black beaded necklace. *A murder of crows,* Jennifer thought. Her newly found strengths would shine like a beacon for dark souls. In a place like Haven, entrenched in history and myth, it was only a matter of time before they found her. But next time would be different. She was not going to hide. Next time she would be ready.

The nurse returned to her room. 'You're looking brighter,' she said, 'can I get you anything?'

'Yes, please,' Jennifer said with a smile. 'I'll have that cup of tea now.'

A LETTER FROM CAROLINE

Dear Reader

I would like to express my heartfelt thanks to you for choosing to read Don't Turn Around. With DC Jennifer Knight, anything can happen and nothing is as it seems. I hope you continue her story with the remaining books in the series, Time To Die and The Silent Twin.

If you've enjoyed this book, I would be truly grateful if you could write me an Amazon review. Even a single one line review can make a huge difference to my books. I love to hear from readers and each one feels like a warm virtual hug.

I've enjoyed fusing my personal experiences of the paranormal and the police to create this series. If you'd like to hear more about my true story, then check out my book, Paranormal Intruder, on Amazon. It is not for the faint hearted. If the paranormal is not your thing, then I have many other published works from psychological thrillers to crime thriller series that I'm sure will suit.

To download a free short story and be kept updated of new releases, join my newsletter here.

Once again, thank you for your support. It is hugely appreciated.

Caroline Mitchell

ABOUT THE AUTHOR

Caroline Mitchell is a NYT, USA Today and International #1 Bestselling Author. Shortlisted by the International Thriller Awards for best ebook 2017 and the Killer Nashville Best Police Procedural 2018. Over 1.5 million books sold.

Originating from Ireland, Caroline now lives with her family on the coast of Essex. A former police detective, she has worked in CID and specialised in roles dealing with vulnerable victims, high-risk victims of domestic abuse, stalking and serious sexual offences. She draws inspiration from the courageous survivors she safeguarded, combining it with her knowledge of police procedure to write crime thrillers full time.

Her stand alone thriller Silent Victim reached No.1 in the Amazon charts in the UK, USA and Australia and was the winner of the Reader's Favourite Awards in the psychological thriller category.

The first in her Amy Winter series, Truth And Lies, has been optioned for TV.

Download a free short story and be kept updated by joining her free reader's club at www.caroline-writes.com.

Follow her social media accounts below.

facebook.com/CMitchellAuthor
twitter.com/Caroline_writes
instagram.com/caroline_writes